Cathie Dunsford is the author of five novels including *Cowrie* and *Manawa Toa*. She has edited numerous anthologies and is director of Dunsford Publishing Consultants (www.dunsfordpublishing.com), which has brought more than 150 new and award-winning Pacific writers into print. A former Fulbright scholar, she has taught writing, literature and publishing at Auckland University since 1975 and now teaches workshops through Global Dialogues, Frankfurt. Her series of novels about Cowrie has been published in English, German and Turkish. Her non-fiction guide, *Getting Published: The Inside Story* was launched at the 2003 Frankfurt Book Fair. Cathie Dunsford has received arts council funding for her novels and was awarded the Landshoff Literary Grant (Germany) in 2001. In 2003 she toured Germany and Turkey speaking about her books and has been a guest at several international writers' festivals in the UK and Europe.

OTHER BOOKS BY CATHIE DUNSFORD

Fiction
Cowrie
The Journey Home: Te Haerenga Kainga
Manawa Toa: Heart Warrior
Song of the Selkies

Poetry
Survivors: Überlebende

Non-fiction
Getting Published: The Inside Story

Anthologies
New Women's Fiction
The Exploding Frangipani [co-editor]
Subversive Acts
Me and Marilyn Monroe
Car Maintenance, Explosives and Love [co-editor]

Ao Toa
EARTH WARRIORS

Cathie Dunsford

SPINIFEX

Spinifex Press Pty Ltd
504 Queensberry Street
North Melbourne, Vic. 3051
Australia

women@spinifexpress.com.au
http://www.spinifexpress.com.au

First published by Spinifex Press, 2004
Copyright © Text: Cathie Dunsford, 2004
Copyright © Typesetting and layout: Spinifex Press Pty Ltd, 2004
Copyright © Woodcut designs: Cathie Dunsford, Artist, Starfish Enterprise
Art, New Zealand 2004
Thanks to the Landshoff Literary Foundation, Hamburg, for awarding a
literary grant that provided for the research and writing of *Ao Toa*.

Edited by Janet Mackenzie
Typeset by Claire Warren
Cover design by Deb Snibson, Modern Art Production Group,
based on woodcut design by Cathie Dunsford

Made and printed in Australia by McPherson's Printing Group.

National Library of Australia
Cataloguing-in-Publication data:
Dunsford Cathie, 1953-.
  Ao Toa : Earth warriors
  ISBN 1 876756 43 8.
  I. Genetic engineering - Fiction. I. Title.
  NZ823.2

Ao Toa is dedicated to all those
working towards a GE-free world.

Acknowledgements

Mahalo, thanks, to:

Dr Karin Meissenburg: critical feedback at all stages of the writing and research and her total belief in my work and the need for a GE-free world.

Dr Susan Hawthorne: critical feedback and sharp editorial skills that improved the text.

Dr Renate Klein and Dr Susan Hawthorne: supporting alternative South Pacific, indigenous and academic writers into print through Spinifex Press.

Dr Laurel Guymer, Export Manager, Spinifex Press: instrumental in getting Cowrie novel series into translations in Europe, for her affirmation of the novels and her energy and humour while working to get Pacific authors into foreign translations.

Silke Weniger, German literary agent: her belief in my work and selling German rights.

Janet Mackenzie: acutely perceptive copy editing skills and making the process enjoyable.

Beryl Fletcher: Literary support, aroha and humour at all times during the writing.

Dr Monika Treut: Touring Tai Tokerau with me and filming Maori alternative political activists, visionaries and those working towards a GE-free future.

Keri Hulme, Witi Ihimaera, Powhiri Rika-Heke, Carolyn Gammon, Katharina Oguntoye, Lili Neuheus: being mentors and always supporting my work.

Professor Ahimsa Bodhran: for teaching the Cowrie novel series at Brooklyn College, New York alongside Patricia Grace and Kiana Davenport.

Rogner & Bernhard, Hamburg, and Okuyanus Publishers, Istanbul: publishing the Cowrie novel series in translation in Germany and Turkey and supporting literary tours and performances in Europe.

Tamaki Makarau and Tawharanui Whanau, who support me daily in my life and work.

Dunsford Publishing Consultants: allowing me time off editing manuscripts to write.

Addenda: NZ distribution and marketing of Cowrie novel series.

PERMISSIONS

Mahalo to all those who gave permission for their work to be included in this text:

Barbara Kingsolver: "No Glory in an Unjust War on the Weak", *Los Angeles Times*, 14 October 2001. Kia ora, Barbara, for your courageous books and for fighting for a better world and speaking the truth. You have been a stunning mentor. Mahalo.

New Zealand Green Party: Co-leader Jeanette Fitzsimons and Sue Bradford, MP: for permission to use their parliamentary speeches in this novel.

Thanks also to: Greenpeace; GE-Free Register; *North Shore Times* (Pat Booth); and all others who willingly gave permission to use their work towards a GE-Free Aotearoa.

Na rangi taua, na Tu-a-nuku e takoto nei: You and I [all of us] are both from the sky father and earth mother. Mahalo – thanks.

She surfs the jade wave on the shell of a turtle, then strokes ashore to banana leaves mounded up with papaya, coconuts, pineapples and mangoes. Persimmons are sliced so that their bright orange flesh and black seeds flow onto the fruits below like Pele erupting over Kiluaea. The turtle swims into the belly of the wave while Maata dances up the hot sand towards the feasting fruit. Her mouth waters in anticipation. A pink smoked salmon reveals fresh cream cheese oozing from her insides and bright green fennel billowing from her wake like waves. The aroma of mussels cooked in garlic and feijoa champagne greets her. Fresh rock oysters lie seductively in their shells, swimming in lemon juice and basil pesto. Haunting flutesong echoes over the waters. A powhiri is called from the dunes as the wahine emerge, each bearing fresh fruit and salads and taro leaves which embrace purple and yellow kumara dripping in butter. They welcome Maata in celebration. It is her sixteenth birthday.

Maata prepares a waiata in reply, but suddenly she notices the ground beneath her moving. The salmon twitches to reveal it has three heads, its tail flapping wildly on the mat. Black blood drips from the wounded persimmon and green sludge oozes out of the mussels.

1

Swelling cream cheese releases pus, and boily protrusions burst from the sweltering fruit. She tries to run but her feet slide deeper into the black sand until it reaches her neck. She screams.

"Maata, sweet Maata. Calm down," Mere croons, holding Maata's head in her lap. "It's just a nightmare. You're safe, here in the Hokianga, in clean green Aotearoa." Clean and green – that's what they say when fighting against nuclear power plants and now for any cause imaginable. It reinforces the sense that to live in paradise, you have to protect that paradise.

Maata is still shaking, horrified by what she saw. She tries to describe it to Mere.

"You've been spending too much time with Irihapeti and Cowrie doing all that work against genetic engineering. It's put weird ideas into your brain. Now think of the beauty of nature, imagine Tane Mahuta nurturing you as a part of the forest and all wildlife within." Mere caresses Maata's hair and soothes her nerves. "Or Tangaroa protecting you in the ocean."

"Or Turtle Woman rescuing me from the sea, like that day when I nearly drowned," adds Maata.

"Ka pae. Laukiamanuikahiki is always there for you. Never forget that." Mere grins and reaches for Maata's cherished furry friend, Willemina Wombat. Maata clasps the grinning creature in her arms, as if a child again, and lets the tears fall to the flax mat.

Irihapeti and Cowrie show the tamariki of Te Kotuku
how to cut the flax leaves to preserve the plant. Iri
begins at the edges. "These outer leaves either side are
the grandparents and you work inwards towards the
parents and then the children. This way you always
make sure the plant has a heart from which the source
of new life can spring."

"Ya mean you cut off the oldies to preserve the kids?"
Kiri looks up gleefully.

"Another way to look at it is that you take the best
leaves to make your flax kete and leave the rest for
regeneration," replies Iri, with a grin.

"And a bit more respect for your whanau wouldn't go
amiss, Kiri." Cowrie hands her the cut flax leaf.

"Ka pae." Kiri holds it up for all to see.

Once giving thanks and harvesting of the spiky leaves
has taken place, Cowrie gathers the tamariki around to
show them how to prepare the flax strands for weaving
by shearing them with the shell of a green-lip mussel.
"You hold the flax like this and then strip the leaf by
firmly moving the shell down the flax until you have a
much more flexible strand to use for weaving." The
tamariki are keen to try, and in the course of the
morning they end up with a mound of broken mussel

shells. Cowrie returns to see how they are progressing.

"What's this, Tama? You're s'posed to be weaving, not preparing a midden!" Everyone laughs, looking at the mound of broken shells next to Tama, as if he has feasted on them all.

Tama looks up, surprised, then grins when he sees the midden of shells from all the others too. "No worries, Cowrie. I could eat that lot in one go! Beats McDonald's any day!" The kids snigger. There is no McDonald's in the entire Hokianga area, much to the delight of their parents. But when the kids finally got to Kaitaia to try this mythical food, they barfed on it, declaring it tasteless and the bread like cardboard. "Give me rewana any day!" shouted Kiri with glee, taking a piece of the Maori potato bread from her backpack and exchanging it for the sad-looking cheeseburger. Not all the boys agreed, of course. Some liked the wrapping and image and were not to be put off.

Cowrie retreats to the nursery café to catch up with Irihapeti. "How's that lover of yours, Iri? Haven't seen her in a while."

Iri pours spirulina into both their glasses. "I dunno what's up with Koa. She's been real sick. Constant sore throat, vomiting, diarrhoea, nausea. You name it, she's got it."

"Poor thing. Sounds like she's got the bot, girl."

"Yeah, but she's had these symptoms for years now. It's not just a few weeks or a few months. It began long before I met her and she's been to heaps of doctors and they all just say it's some form of ME cos she's exhausted all the time too."

4

"Koa's got such a great energy and spirit. I'm amazed. She hides it well."

"She's used to it. She seldom goes out after dark and gets heaps of rest. Only those really close to her get to see the real Koa." Iri slurps down her last sip of HOGS – Hokianga Organic Green Stuff, as spirulina is locally known.

"What'd she do before coming here, Iri?"

"Worked at Moana Botanical Gardens for twelve years. She discovered a new breed of flax by crossing the red with the green, and it's great for weaving."

"She's not into genetic engineering is she?"

"*No* way! She specialises in grafting so that's why she's been a taonga from Pele for Te Kotuku Organic Nursery. But she's as anti GE and GM as we are."

"Glad to hear it, too!" Cowrie tucks into a roasted kumara with grilled Puhoi blue cheese on top and sea-green basil pesto running down the purple sides of the sweet potato. "Ahhhh. Bliss. Beats a lover any day!"

"That's just cos you left Sasha in Orkney. Bet if she was to turn up here tomorrow you'd swap a roasted kumara for her in a second."

Cowrie grins. "Well, no, I'd insist on both. And clap-shot to boot!"

"What the hell's clapshot? Sounds like some very nasty genital herpes."

"Bugger off, Iri. It's the most delicious vegetarian dish you'll ever eat. Orkney potatoes mashed up with swedes and turnips and butter and onion – whatever you like – and served as hot as sweet chilli sauce on the tongue. Yum!"

"Yeah, I think I read about that in your letters to Mere. She laughed and said 'Bloody typical. My daughter likes the Orkney food a lot better than the weather.'"

"I sure as hell did, too. But clapshot was nuthin' next to Orkney scallops from Seafayre and spoots from Waulkmill Bay and lobster dripping with Swanney cheese and home-grown garlic . . . yum . . ." Cowrie licks her lips at the memory.

"Stop it, girl. You know I am a hundred per cent vegan now. I can't do all that kai moana any more."

"Wish I could say the same, Iri. But I live for the fruits of the sea. It's in my bones. While cousin Keo is still fishing at Punalu'u, it's the least I can do to support the family heritage."

Irihapeti grabs a bowl of marinated barbecued mussels and places them before Cowrie. "Okay, girl. Go for it. I'm off to see how the tamariki are enjoying their weaving."

"I'll follow soon." Cowrie plunges into the mussels, savouring every mouthful. Some still have beards poking out deliciously from their orange and brown vulva lips. Perfectly hermaphroditic, notes Cowrie, as she dips them into the garlic sauce and wishes Sasha were here with her now.

The Pratt family sit down to a roast dinner after a hard day's work on their farm. Moana insists on karakia to give thanks for their meal. Tony insists on carving the roast, as it's a bloke's task. "Now Matthew, James, Robert, watch how I do this because you will be carving meat for your wives and children before long. You don't want to make dicks of yerselves." He jabs the long fork his grandfather gave him into the rump of the pig until blood oozes from its thighs. "Bloody hell, woman, a pig's not s'posed to bleed. How long've ya cooked it?"

"Long enough. It'll be fine, Tony. And I'd rather you called the boys by their real names: Mattiu, Hemi and Rapata. That's what we agreed and they'll get mocked at kohanga reo and kura kaupapa schools for using those Christian Pakeha names. We named them so at birth and nothing's changed."

Tony looks up from the bleeding leg and raises his knife toward Moana. "Heaps has changed, Moana. I bought this land and got the kids away from Te Kotuku marae so we wouldn't be lectured to by those brown bastards. They're *my* kids and they can go by proper Christian names. It's the twenty-first century and we ain't livin' in the Stone Age no more. Right boys?" The three brothers nod their heads quietly. They know better than to contradict their father. But they also know to use their Maori names at school for fear of being ostracised. One of the struggles of their bicultural parentage is to learn the knack of trying to combine the two cultures to please everyone. It's not easy.

Tony launches an attack on the pig, slicing thick, juicy steaks from its loins and making a show of plonking them onto the plates so they see how clever he is at getting precisely the same serving each time. Precision is important to Tony when it comes to portions and fairness in sharing out food. His family never had much, and he is determined his kids will fare better. Slice by slice, the once happy, grunting beast foraging in the fields near their house is whittled away until its bones gleam from its carcass. As the last slice lands on Mattiu's plate, he bursts into tears. Tony glares at him. "Pull it together, boy, or I'll have to use my belt." He loosens his belt in preparation and slides it from his waistband. Mattiu shrinks further into his seat.

"Go easy, Tony. He's still upset that you killed Babe," whispers Moana.

"Babe? *Babe*! This ain't no bloody Hollywood film about pigs that babble like bloody women! This is a working farm and this" – he rips a hunk of Babe from her bones – "this is bloody pork, not some bloody cartoon character from a Disney film. I farm this pork and I bring home the bacon and without this work, you buggers'd all starve. Get real, Matthew. Be a man! You eat bacon and this is pork! Pull yerself together, boy. You look like a bloody fruit-cake whimpering there low down in ya seat." Tony picks up his belt and cracks it against the back of Mattiu's chair, making the boy cringe even further into his seat. "I'm warning you, boy. One more whimper like that and you'll get this belt across your bloody arse!" Mattiu shoves his chair away from the table and runs to his room. Tony grabs his belt and follows. Moana pulls his arm, trying to get him to drop the belt, but he throws her aside and enters the room. The house is eerily silent as they listen to Tony whipping Matthew hard. One, two, three, four, five . . .

Moana rushes to the door. "That's enough, Tony. Once more and I'll take the kids back to the marae." Tony's arm stops in mid-air as he is about to crack the belt down on Matthew a sixth time. He doesn't want her to leave, or the boys. He needs them all to make the farm work. He'd have to hire outside help if they left, and he knows Moana realises this and uses it against him deliberately.

"Okay, Matthew. If you want to be a baby and have your mother keep rescuing you, then be a wimp. See if I care. But one day, you'll thank me for teaching you to be a man. You can stay in your room until tomorrow. And that means no dinner either." Tony slams the door against Mattiu's whimpering and strides back to the table. He knows that Moana will sneak Mattiu some food later. It does not matter, so long as the boy realises who's the real boss.

The rest of the dinner is in silence and polite but safe conversation. They know better than to rattle Tony when he is already mad. It'd mean beatings for them all, including Moana. Hemi and Rapata were angry that their Pakeha mates at school thought all Maori men were like violent Jake the Muss in the film *Once Were Warriors*. Their father is Pakeha and is just like Jake when he gets angry. They know not to challenge him at such times. Survival means being cunning. And Moana has taught them survival. But Mattiu is the youngest. He still has to learn.

"So, what're you boys up to tomorrow?" asks Moana, wanting to distract Tony from his argument with Mattiu.

"Whad'ya reckon, boys? I reckon we'll dose the farm with Roundup and zap on a bit of Santa's DDT, eh?"

"Can we use the sprayers, Dad?"

"Sure thing, Hemi. You and Rapata can have a spray pack each. And Mattiu if he behaves himself." He sniggers. He knows he has one up on Moana for using their bloody brownie names. That always gets her on board, thinking he is coming round.

Moana smiles at him. "Thanks, Tony." She tucks into her peas. But she is not happy. Finally she gets the courage to say what is bothering her.

"Tony, I dunno about Roundup or DDT after what Irihapeti has been telling me. Didn't the government ban DDT in the late eighties? If it's illegal, I don't want our boys using it. For health reasons as much as anything else."

Tony glares at her, then laughs. He splatters gravy all over the table cloth, but he is laughing so hard he does not even notice. "Bloody hell, woman. Money doesn't grow on the manuka trees around here, y'know. Jacques at the garage handed me some waste DDT they were trying to get rid of it. Santa's Helpers, he said. That means we got it for free. Ya don't look a gift horse like that in the bloody teeth now, do ya?"

Moana is careful. "I see your point, Tony. But you know the boys have had gastric problems. Diarrhoea, vomiting, nausea. And that happened after the last DDT spraying you all did. I'm not sure I want them around that poison again. Surely the government would not have banned the stuff if it was safe, now would they?"

This sends Tony into paroxysms of laughter and guffawing, getting the boys onside as he speaks. "Now, look here, boys. You reckon that gut-ache was DDT or Roundup? Bloody hell, it was more likely your mother's bloody raw pig. Or those bloody rabbit-food salads. Rabbit calici virus. That's what ya get if ya eat too many of them salads!" He bursts into laughter and gets the boys laughing with him.

"Or maybe it was Cowrie's oyster pasta? I reckon she vomited it up and served it raw! Remember that green pesto stuff? Looked like kikuyu grass barfed up for the occasion," adds Hemi, looking to his father for approval for his story. He is not disappointed.

Tony reaches for the Watties' tomato sauce and sprays it over the remains of Babe on his plate. "I wouldn't wanna eat anything barfed up by that Cowrie chick. Ya could catch AIDS or something far worse than the DDTs, boys!" He laughs at his own joke.

"Don't be foolish, Tony. Just because a person is gay it does not mean they have AIDS, for God's sake. Half the population of Botswana and the rest of Africa have AIDS and not all of them are gay."

"Serves them bloody right. They are all activist troublemakers. The Bible warns us against them all.

Sodom and that Gomorrah fella and Nelson Mandela – they all come from the same bloody melting pot. All criminals, all diseased. They should stick them on Robbin Island, Waiheke Island, Tasmania, and any other bloody island you like. Let George Speight be their dictator from his own bloody Fijian island prison. I don't care, so long as they stay there and do not infect my boys here." He pours more sweetened tomato sauce over his pork, and apple sauce over that, then burps loudly in appreciation of the kai.

Moana winces, knowing tonight is not the time to challenge him again. Enough for one night. She waits until he takes the boys into the lounge to "watch the Warriors lick the arse off the Ozzie Cowboys", does the dishes and sneaks some food to Mattiu, who is still crying beneath the covers.

"Don't worry, Mattiu. Dad wants to take you boys spraying tomorrow." Moana caresses his brow with her hand.

"I don't wanna go, Mum. Let him take the others. I'd rather stay at home and learn to cook that banana and spice cake for the nursery workers. I was real sick the last time I went spraying. For weeks after. Please let me stay and cook, Mum?" Moana holds his hand.

"Ka pae, Mattiu. You stay with me and we'll let the others go poison themselves. But I want to talk to Irihapeti about this. I'm worried about using Roundup, let alone that DDT."

"Me too, Mum. I love you." Mattiu cuddles into her arms as Moana croons waiata into his ear. She knows Tony will be chipper tomorrow. He'll rise as if there had

12

been no argument at all and get the boys out into the fields spraying by 6 am. And they'll love it once they start. They just adore being with their father and getting his approval, no matter about the dangers involved. And he likes to keep it that way. If he witholds his love, he knows they are always hanging out for more of it. Tony knows he is cleverer than the missus or anyone else realises. He has worked it all out. He needs them, and so long as they need him, all will be well.

"Caught anything yet?" asks Cowrie as Mattiu baits his hook with raw mussel and throws it out over the end of the Opononi wharf.

"Just a few sprats." Mattiu nudges the bucket at his feet to reveal half a dozen live sprats swimming in salt water. "For Pele."

"Your cat?"

"Yeah."

"Where's your bros today? Thought Hemi and Rapata were keen on fishing?"

Matthew looks down at the sprats. "They are. But Dad's taken them spraying. They like using the back-packs."

Cowrie stiffens. "How come you didn't go?"

"Don't like it. One time Dad used up the end of the spray on a sparrow, showering it with DDT till it couldn't breathe any more. The others laughed. I didn't. From that day on he always called me a wimp."

"You're not a wimp just because you don't believe in killing for the sake of it, Mattiu. Never forget that." Cowrie ruffles his hair affectionately. Inside, she's fuming and resolves to try to educate that Pratt bastard if it's the last thing she does. DDT has been banned for years, but he clearly has a stockpile.

14

Moana emerges from the Opononi store along with Maata, Kuini, Irihapeti and other wahine from Te Kotuku marae. They walk down the wharf, laughing and pointing into the distance. A giant hummingbird hangs in the sky then plunges down in front of them, skimming the surface of the sea and swooping up again.

"That's bloody Flyworks." Kuini gestures rudely towards the helicopter.

"Taihoa, Kuini. I'm thinking of going for a job with them when I leave school. They're expanding their tourism operation and Uncle Piripi says it will be good for the local economy." Maata munches on a muesli bar from the store.

"I'm all for supporting more jobs, but not when they continue spraying poisons on our land," mutters Kuini.

"Yeah, most of their work is chemical spraying and that risks all the hard work we've all put into making the Far North a viable organic area," adds Irihapeti.

"Give it a break, Iri. We're s'posed to be having a day on the sea. Can't we give politics a break for a few hours?" Maata complains, ripping into another munchie.

"Activists don't get to have days off. If we do not live and breathe our work, then we do not remain vigilant. That's when the polluters do their worst – when we are off guard." Iri checks her watch. "Where's that damn' boat?"

"Yeah – but we can still enjoy the day, or I'm not going." Maata lays a stake in the sand.

"Fair enough. It's pure pleasure as we surf the waves. The revolution can wait until tomorrow," offers Cowrie, grinning. "Besides, I have the backpack with the kai.

15

You have to agree with me or starve. Simple really."

Maata grins, loving her aunty for her ability to always get food into the conversation. "Ka pae, Cowrie! Hope there's some treats for me there too."

"You bet. But you have to wait until later."

Maata tries to reach into the backpack but Cowrie swings around, nearly losing her balance. Mattiu glares at her. "Sorry, Mattiu. Nearly lost your kai too." She grins.

"It's okay. Pele has enough anyway. The rest go back into the sea."

"Ka pae, Mattiu." Moana looks pleased with her son for not lashing out like his father.

"Sustainable catch, I'd say. That calls for a celebration." Cowrie takes her koauau from her breast pocket and plays a sea waiata on the small bone flute.

Mattiu is entranced. "Will you teach me how to play?" he asks.

"Sure thing. Stay after kura kaupapa next week and you're on. That okay, Moana?"

"So long as he has time for his homework. Tuesday would be best."

"Ka pae. Tuesday it is."

By now the old trawler, Manawa Toa, has docked at the wharf, and they clamber on board to ride out to sea while the water taxi takes tourists over to the Hokianga dunes.

16

Spray rips into their faces as *Manawa Toa* sails over the treacherous Hokianga spit. Sun dances through the spray, splashing a rainbow over the bow. The wahine hold onto the front rails, grinning.

"This brings back a few memories, eh Cowrie?" Kuini nudges her cousin as two dolphins surf the bowspray.

"Sure does." Cowrie turns her back to the waves and looks toward the cabin of *Manawa Toa*, recalling the French officers boarding the ship when they were protesting nuclear bomb testing at Moruroa. "Remember when they were asked to give us the message from the French Government banning us from entering the nuclear test zone waters?"

"Yeah – and you insisted we lower down the sick bucket, empty this time, to receive their instructions," adds Irihapeti. "We had a few good laughs, despite the gravity of the occasion, eh?"

"Yeah. But our protests finally stopped nuclear testing in the Pacific. So it was worth it." Cowrie addresses Maata who was not on board for that trip.

"But we learned at kura kaupapa that people are still sick with leukemia and stuff like that," chips in Maata, forgetting it is she who has banned serious talk for the day!

"All part of the Pacific colonial heritage, Maata. But I thought you wanted a politics-free day?" Cowrie grins as she reaches for one of the backpacks.

"We eating already?" asks Maata, her eyes lighting up.

"Not yet, Maata." Cowrie retrieves her bone koauau from the pack. "We're going to thank the dolphins for guiding *Manawa Toa* so well on that journey and this." She places the bone flute to her lips and blows into the wind, the flute song beginning to wail hauntingly somewhere between her mouth and the bone. The dolphins keep pace with the boat, playing in the wake. But once they hear these ancient sounds, known to them for centuries past when local fishers played to them, they change course, taking *Manawa Toa* with them, heading toward calmer waters further down the coast, running parallel with the shore. After they have negotiated the boat wake, the dolphins begin to play, jumping out from the bow and doing flips over each other. Soon they are joined by more dolphins, until the boat is surrounded.

"Can we stop and swim with them a while, Cowrie? Please?" Maata looks deep into her aunty's eyes, pleading.

"I thought you'd be too afraid. Are you sure?" Cowrie holds Maata's hand.

"Yes. Besides, so long as you come with me, I have Turtle Protection."

"That's Laukiamanuikahiki – Turtle Woman. Not me," asserts Cowrie.

"I wouldn't be too sure about that." Kuini holds up Cowrie's arm. "Check out these fins, Maata. Look – she's webbed from shoulder to wrist. Now if that ain't Turtle Woman, what is?"

Cowrie makes finning motions with her arms and the dolphins seem amused by this action, jumping high over the bow to get a better look.

Once in the water, the women leap and play with the small Hector's dolphins, who nudge close and dive beneath them. Maata is entranced. She forgets she ever had a fear of the sea and fins alongside, trying to catch up with the cheeky leaping one. The dolphin swims past her and then returns, edging close. Maata knows not to catch hold of her fins, as people so often want to do. She floats on the surface, waiting for the spirited one to return. But it has gone. Suddenly she is being carried along, as if sailing. The dolphin has slipped under her and takes her for a ride. It is exhilarating. The others watch in silence. This seldom happens. But the dolphin is heading rapidly out to sea. Maata panics. Then, as if sensing her alarm, the dolphin flicks its tail and propels itself back toward the waiting women, diving deep when it reaches them, releasing Maata back into the arms of her sisters. She shrieks with joy. Cowrie is relieved.

After drying themselves, they sail down the coast with the wind behind them, making the journey a relatively calm one. Portside are miles of rugged West Coast beaches, jagged rocky outcrops and the rusted ghostly skeletons of old sailing ships that never made it to shore. Many of them sank on unknown reefs, taking their colonial sailors and gold booty from the once rich Empire with them. Beyond the breakers, in the far distance, they can see the mighty Waipoua Kauri Forest, presided over by Tane Mahuta, God of all trees, its girth as wide as a pod of whales, its height towering in their wake. The morning mist still hangs eerily over the lush rainforest and it's easy to imagine giant dinosaurs crashing through the forest in times past, foraging for wetas and other rich insect life as well as ferny vegetation, maybe even venturing in for a swim. Waipoua is primeval and remains sacred to Maori. By the time they pass the cream lighthouse at Pouto Point and enter into the calmer sea of the Kaipara Harbour, the dolphins have headed back into the ocean depths, knowing better than to enter and be trapped in the shark-infested waters of the largest harbour in the Southern Hemisphere.

Manawa Toa edges up a small waterway, allowing them to enjoy the bright yellow, beak-shaped leaves of the kowhai trees stretching out over the water. Snow-throated tui hang like skilled aerialists by their claws, digging their beaks deep into the golden flowers, extracting their luscious honey. The rainbow-splashed *Manawa Toa*, with the carved kauri dolphin at her bow, is reflected in the still water like an Impressionist painting, hazy at the edges but exhilarating in its blend of colours and textures. Blue-grey matuku moana glide over them and land in the branches of pohutukawa trees where they are nesting. One of the herons feeds her young by disgorging a small sprat, its tail still waving, into the baby bird's beak. As soon as it has swallowed the fish, it cries out for more, sending the mother soaring back out over their heads to the sea to catch her next feast for her young. The wingspan seems huge as she flies over them looking like a pterodactyl escaping from the dinosaur-infested Waipoua Forest.

Further down the river they glide past the old township of Helensville, resembling a ghost town with its skeletons of old buildings gleaming from the riverbanks, rusted cars and railway tracks, deserted houses and stacks of bins crawling with water rats in the daytime. The city had tried to get rid of the rats and ended up poisoning an old fisherman, it is said – the authorities released poisons into the waterways and left as much damage as the rats had done in their wake. A few more riverbends and they come to a community of tangata whenua who live right on the water's edge. The locals are carrying all their groceries into shared sheds lined with freezers, bursting with fish. Cowrie spots Eruera. "Kia ora, bro. How's tricks?"

"Choice, Cowrie. Good trip down?" Eruera looks up from his work. "Kiri. Cowrie and the girls are here. You got the goodies?"

"Ka pae. Be with ya in a minute." Kiri is hanging out the last of the Warehouse clothes on the line and bends to pin up her knickers. She then strides toward the shed at the end of the pier and calls Eru to help her with the large bucket. Together, they haul it over to *Manawa Toa*, now docked alongside the wharf, and yell for a rope. Cowrie, grinning, lowers the same rope and hook they used to provoke the French military when protesting nuclear testing at Moruroa. Kiri winks back. "There ya go, girl. Haul her up and have a great day!"

"Mahalo, Kiri. You too." Cowrie pulls the heavy bucket on board, releases it from the hook, and then fills it with fresh organic kumara and bright purple urenika yams, Maori potatoes mottled cream and dark blue, topped with fresh orange carrots still sprouting their

21

green dreadlocks. Small golden pawpaws and large yellow and green fleshy babacos, which taste like papaya and lime, mandarins, lemons, oranges and grapefruit from Te Kotuku Nursery are in the last kete.

Kiri receives the fruit with joy. "Ka pae, Cowrie. Kia ora. Where you sisters off to now?"

"To a great feast on the waters," grins Cowrie. "Tell ya about it next trip down. Thanks, Kiri. Your girls doing okay?"

"Not bad. One's nearly finished kohanga reo but Franny's been ill. Vomiting, diarrhoea, nausea, you know all that stuff."

"Food poisoning?"

"The tohunga's not so sure. We even had medical tests done. Gone on far too long. They dunno what it is, really. Just gotta live with it, I reckon. Come to think of it, we've all been ill this winter."

"Maybe it's that rat poison the council dumped on the town which got into the waterways?"

Kiri grimaces. "I wouldn't be surprised. But ya can never prove it, eh? They'd just say it was tank water or food poisoning or something. We'll survive. Anyway, have a choice day. Wish I was coming with you fellas. I could do with a day off."

"Why not? Hop up here." Cowrie points to the rope ladder dangling from the side of *Manawa Toa*.

Kiri hesitates a moment, looks at Eruera, who does not seem to mind what she does, and glances back. "Bugger it, I will. Give me a moment to change." She flies off indoors and Eruera continues fixing his boat.

Half an hour later, they chug into a small estuary,

shaded by gigantic totara, kauri and pohutukawa sprawling over the water, and drop anchor. Cowrie has been down in the galley preparing the kai and not letting anyone near. Soon they discover why the other bucket seemed to be moving when it was sitting idly on the deck. It had been full of live crayfish swimming in salt water and itching to be free or meet their fate. The wahine lay a flax mat on the deck of the boat and from the galley bring platters made from nikau palm bowls decorated with fresh banana leaves. Crayfish with hot butter and garlic dripping from its white belly and down over its red body; purple urenika boiled to perfection, still firm and covered in herbs; a fresh salad with mustard and rocket greens from their garden dotted with sweet red cherry tomatoes; papaya, watermelon and babacos slit open to reveal their juices and pink, yellow and cream insides. Cowrie places one of Maata's home-made honey wax candles in the centre and pours out organic feijoa champagne and spring water for all. "Kia ora, Maata. Happy Surprise Birthday."

Maata is stunned. "But I thought we were just delivering vegetables to Kiri. I had no idea . . ."

The others laugh and after karakia, they feast the rest of the day, sharing wild talkstory. Later they drop Kiri off and then return late in the afternoon to the Hokianga dunes. It is a glorious sunset as they enter the harbour, purple and orange clouds reflected in the water. Mere and tangata whenua from Te Kotuku marae greet them at the Opononi pier with freshly made lei of leaves and flowers, and they feast and sing late into the night. Maata declares it's her best day ever, and even Cowrie

23

and Kuini managed to forget their activist politics for a few hours – well almost, she tells Mere, grinning.

Cowrie pokes her nose around the door of Maata's room in Mere's cottage. Shafts of sun slide across the bamboo blinds and dance over her face as the wind moves the bamboo. Maata stirs, opens one eye. "Do I have to get up yet?" she murmurs.

"Not unless you want whitebait fritters with lemon and Mere's special kumara fries dripping with sour cream, to say nothing of organic orange and mango juice . . ."

Maata rolls off her mat and reaches for her lavalava. "So long as I don't have to do the dishes afterwards."

Cowrie grins. "You can't milk these birthday treats forever, girl! But there is a special treat for you, so hurry. Besides, neither Fisher and Paykel nor AEG have yet come up with a dishwasher suitable for banana leaves, so you may be lucky today."

Maata rubs her eyes and raises the blind to reveal dunes stretching out to the rolling breakers. She's always loved this old cottage and staying here with Mere and Cowrie. She had moved in when Cowrie left to do her PhD in the States and stayed ever since. Mere was like a grandmother to her, and Cowrie an aunty. Her father had abused her as a child, and her mother had returned to Te Kotuku to raise her; she now lives with her new partner in Sydney, glad to be able to leave her daughter in the safe arms of Mere. Since Cowrie came back from Orkney, the three of them have lived here.

By the time Maata reaches the verandah looking out to sea, the table is piled high with delicious whitebait fritters mounded up like Kiluaea, with a crater in the middle to hold herbs from Mere's garden. Sliced lemons and sprigs of green rocket swim around the edges of the plate. Beside Maata's banana leaf platter is a letter propped up against her glass of juice. On the address label, Flyworks Helicopters. Maata picks up the letter eagerly and tears it open. She's dreamed of working for them several weeks now and has got through two interviews. But what if they do not want her? She hardly dares to look at the page.

FLYWORKS HELICOPTERS
We Fly You to Paradise
RD 1, Opononi, Hokianga
www.flyworks.com

Dear Miss Ropata,

Thank you for your application to join our team at Flyworks. We are pleased to offer you a job as our receptionist. We feel a Maori presence will be advantageous to our company since we are expanding into the tourist trade. We expect a high standard of dress code and will supply you with a uniform to ensure this is retained. Further training in computer accounts is needed and we will give you time off to complete a diploma in computer studies at Northland Polytech in Rawene as discussed.

Please read the contract enclosed, sign and return to us within 10 days. Welcome to our team.

Raymond Dixon,
Director,
Flyworks Helicopters.

Maata fights back the tears. She's been wanting this so much, but is also wary of Cowrie's response after her reaction to the chemical spraying so near the organic nursery.

"Well, come on. Tell us the news!" Cowrie nudges her gently.

"I don't think they want me." Maata looks down, trying not to laugh.

Cowrie's arm hugs her warmly. "Maybe it's for the best, Maata. We'll help you find work."

Maata contemplates teasing them further, but fears what Cowrie may say next. She cannot hold it in any longer and throws her arms out like an albatross soaring from a towering cliff. "I got it. I got it! I am the new Flyworks receptionist – *and* they agree to time off for further study. Whoopeeeeeeee!"

Mere glances at Cowrie, warning her not to disappoint Maata, no matter what she thinks of Flyworks. They hug her, genuinely pleased she has found a job that includes an opportunity to study. Any work is good work in the Hokianga region – jobs are scarce, with more layoffs than growth in recent years. Cowrie bites her tongue and supports Maata. There are always compromises to be made in this respect, although Cowrie is not one to cave in under such pressure usually. She loves Maata and wants the best for her. Maybe this will be a stepping stone which will lead to better work in the future. Earlier Mere and Cowrie had discussed how to react whatever the letter had in store, and they knew the special breakfast would cushion the blow, whether for Maata or for Cowrie.

While Maata celebrates, Cowrie reads the letter. She does not like the feeling that Maata's culture is being used for the company's convenience, nor the implication that she might not dress suitably if not put into one of their dinky uniforms. But since when did tourist operations, outside those promoted by Te Puna Kokiri, really care about these issues? Maybe this is a chance to have some positive input, and who better to do this than Maata? Maybe this could be a really important opportunity after all?

"C'mon Cowrie. Bet I can eat more whitebait fritters than you," Maata challenges.

Cowrie hands the letter back with her left hand and forks a fritter with her right. "Wanna bet, kid? Who taught you the art of feasting in the first place?" She drizzles lemon juice over the fritters and digs in.

"Taihoa, you two. Let's just enjoy this kai, eh? I don't think we need a race to prove what gluttons you both can be." Mere pours more of the delicious orange and mango juice into their glasses and proposes a toast. "Here's to Maata, who, on her sixteenth birthday, got her first job and an opportunity for further study all at once. Congratulations, Maata. You've made us feel very proud. Eh, Cowrie?" Mere nudges her daughter with her elbow under the table.

"You bet we're proud of you, Maata. Besides, those choppers could come in handy next time we have a political protest. They would've been very useful at Moruroa on board *Manawa Toa*, or when we protested the Springbok Tour at Eden Park. Maybe we can redeem their spraying chemicals with some useful community work? Or teach them to spray seaweed fertiliser instead of agro-chemicals."

"You just keep your activist nose out of there until I get established in my job." Maata steals the last fritter off Cowrie's leaf. "Or I'll beat you in our bet."

Cowrie grins. "Looks like you've done that already, kid. A woman after my own heart. Go for it." She squeezes lemon juice over the fritter, holds it up for Maata to eat half, then munches into the remaining half before Maata has time to protest. Maata pretends to look shocked, then bursts into laughter. "Bugger! I thought I had you that time."

"Good training to remain sharp and on yer toes when you work for that Raymond Dioxin fella at Flyworks."

"It's Dixon, not Dioxin!"

"We'll see about that."

"Bet you'd rather name him Raymond Kelp?"

"Well, yes. Now you come to mention it. I think that name has a much more poetic ring. Maybe you should suggest it to him?"

"C'mon you two. Stop bickering. This is a time for celebration. What say we invite Kuini and Irihapeti over

29

later and Maata, you should call your mother in Sydney and tell her. She'll be very proud of you." Mere eases the papaya onto fresh banana leaves and hands it to each of them, secretly pleased that the morning has gone so well.

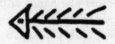

NORTH SHORE TIMES ADVERTISER,
Tuesday, 7 August 2001, page 7
GE debate brings back memories of thalidomide
By Pat Booth

An old, old story may help committed scientists and members of the Genetic Modification Commission to understand why hundreds of thousands of New Zealanders are angry. They reject the decision to "proceed with caution" on genetic modification.

It's a piece of fiction involving an announcement to passengers beginning a long flight. The voice says: "Welcome aboard this historic journey. You are on the world's first fully automatic flight on this computer-controlled aircraft on which nothing can go wrong . . . go wrong . . . go wrong . . . go wrong . . . go wrong . . . go wrong . . ."

If that doesn't strike you as relevant, let me share a few words with you. Words like thalidomide. Like asbestos. Like dioxin. It's not a word, but add in DDT.

Each of these had the seal of scientific acceptance – scientists swore on a stack of Bibles and computer printouts that there were no risks, nothing could go wrong.

It did – in huge and disastrous ways. Thalidomide was one of those wonder pharmaceutical products of the late 1950s, prescribed for pregnant women as a certain and safe sedative and a treatment for morning sickness "with no side effects", scientists said. It produced a worldwide generation of shockingly handicapped children, babies born without arms or legs, with flipper-like hands at their shoulders – the variations were tragic and endless.

Its distributors inexplicably denied a link, repeating that "nothing could go wrong" and fighting a well-documented legal battle with Harold Evans, then editor of the British *Sunday Times*, who risked his career campaigning against thalidomide.

He won. Its use was banned. But thousands of adults live on as the real losers, their lives permanently ruined by a drug which "could not go wrong." Latest reported use is as a treatment for leprosy in the Third World.

For decades, asbestos was a universally accepted building material, particularly as insulation – until its dangers were detected. New experts have named a killing lung disease after it – asbestosis, resulting from inhaling asbestos particles – and they evacuate buildings now, no questions asked, when it's detected.

Then there was DDT – or dichlorodiphenyltrichloroethane, as its "nothing can go wrong" scientist friends knew it. This insecticide, which was going to rid our pastures of creepy crawlies, had an unforeseen ability to concentrate in the bodies of grazing animals and seriously threatened health and markets before it was banned after years of use.

As was "nothing can go wrong" dioxin, which revealed itself as a persistent pollutant linked with cancer, nervous disorders and birth defects. Contamination from it forced the evacuation of places like Seveso in Italy.

The world should have learned by now from these and hundreds of other examples. They are the reason why concerned lay people and some scientists too do not accept well-intentioned assurances. These pledges come from those who honestly but mistakenly believe that terrible variations of Murphy's Law ("if anything can go wrong, it will") somehow do not apply to science.

The evidence is that they have done – and will again.

Cowrie finishes reading and Irihapeti picks up the paper. "It's right, y'know. We've seen all this before. I reckon we should contact the Far North Organic Growers and mobilise all interested groups and plan a hikoi on parliament to show our opposition to genetic engineering and the dangers involved." Kuini reaches out her hand and Iri passes the paper to her.

"Yeah, I agree. But maybe we should wait and see what the Royal Commission Report on Genetic Engineering says first, and save the march on parliament for then, when we can really have impact – especially if they go against us." Kuini looks to Cowrie for support.

"We've learned it is better to bide our time and have a stronger impact. I'm for Kuini's stance. I mean, 92 per cent of New Zealanders making submissions were against genetic engineering – so it has to go in our favour, eh? Surely no thinking person who has ever read the literature and research could ever agree to the risks involved with genetic engineering?"

"If we want a GE-free Aotearoa – where we are organic by 2020, as Organic NZ is pushing for – then we have to oppose GM. It's simply not feasible to support buffer zones between genetically modified crops and our organic crops. We know they do not work and this has been proved overseas. We simply have to convince them we are right." Irihapeti moves toward the fire. "Anyone want a brew of manuka tea and our organic pohutukawa honey?"

"You bet" comes the chorus back as Iri pours rainwater from their filtered tank into a billy and places it over the fire. She then takes a kauri spoon carved by

Piripi, its tail like a whale fluke, and plunges it into the white creamy pohutukawa honey, extracting a large chunk which then goes into the ceramic teapot that Maata made them at her pottery class. When the water has boiled, she pours it over the honey, then adds the sprigs of fresh manuka, picked from the tree beside them. It seeps into the waiting liquid, seducing every ounce of its juices and blending with the swirling honey until the luscious concoction is ready to imbibe. "Cowrie, pass over those cups and I'll pour." Cowrie grabs the strange and wonderful clay creatures, each shaped by her students into vessels with heads and fins and tails and decorated with koru fern and taniwha designs. Iri pours the steaming hot liquid into the cups and they savour the exquisite taste, mulling over the issues in their minds.

Cowrie wakes late and plunges into the lounge of Mere's cottage to find her already hard at work on their shared laptop.

"What's up, Mere? Not like you to be at it this early."

"What would you know, Turtle? You've been a late riser ever since you stayed in Orkney. I reckon they must take about as much notice of clock time as we do." Mere laughs. Maori time is famous in Aotearoa. It means you just go at the pace needed rather than following Greenwich Mean Time, which is totally irrelevant on an island in the Pacific, as much as an island off the coast of Scotland.

"Ya got me there. You want some of Iri's lovely sourdough for brekky?" Cowrie starts slicing into the grainy bread covered with pumpkin seeds.

"Na. Had some of our oranges, thanks." Mere gets back to her screen.

"What's the rush?"

"Come and look, Turtle. This is from my old school-mates, now living in England. Farmers. They say the situation is hysterical there with this foot-and-mouth outbreak. It's as if the British government, caught out earlier by the crisis over mad cow disease, is punishing the farmers now and wanting to destroy everything in sight, no matter what the risks involved. They've gone stark raving mad – and all these farmers are losing their incomes and families."

"Serve them bloody right for treating animals as slaves. Maybe it's time this happened?" Cowrie is plastering her pumpkin bread with Vegemite yeast extract and layers of fresh tomato and basil from their garden.

"Cowrie, you can't be so cruel. These are struggling families who deserve our support as much as those who will become victims of your precious GE."

"I can't see how you could make any comparison. Organic farmers respect the earth and all animals. They work in harmony with nature, not against it." Cowrie bites into her grainy toast.

"Well, come and read these emails, Turtle. See what you say then."

Cowrie moves toward the screen reluctantly, munching her crisp toast as she goes. Mere brings up on the screen a series of emails from the UK farmers she knows.

This next item comes from today's *Western Morning News*, UK.

Blood tests reveal foot-and-mouth case

Another case of foot-and-mouth disease was yesterday confirmed in Devon. Blood samples taken from sheep at Ashley House, Wembworthy, near Chulmleigh, were tested positive with the disease. The total number of cases in the county now stands at 168. The infected livestock had already been slaughtered, on May 28, as part of the contiguous culling policy, when neighbouring East Ashley Farm went down with the disease. But two other premises could now be slaughtered. A spokeswoman for the

Department of the Environment, Food and Rural Affairs (DEFRA) said that 30 out of 49 of the samples taken had proved positive with foot-and-mouth disease. She said they were now in talks with the two contiguous farmers over whether to slaughter their 130 sheep and 150 cattle. The latest case comes in the wake of a new case in Somerset, which has been dubbed a "bolt from the blue". It is not known how the disease found its way to Eames Farm at North Newton, near Bridgwater, an area which up to now had largely remained foot-and-mouth-free. The nearest outbreak had been 15 miles away at Wiveliscombe more than a month ago. The first case in Somerset was at Bidisham, near Axbridge, on March 9. The county has now seen a total of five cases. Anthony Gibson, regional director of the National Farmers' Union, said the Devon case was far less worrying than the outbreak in Somerset not least because it had been dealt with two weeks ago, while in Somerset it was still not known how foot-and-mouth had found its way to Bridgwater. Even so, two neighbouring farms at Wembworthy could now face the culls.

ENDS

And today – in the *Western Morning News*:

It would seem that the culling of Britain's livestock is the key issue here. How it is done and for what reason is irrelevant.

This is not just a cull of animals but of farmers, for many of them have lost their lives. Many, like my parents, have lost their way of life, perhaps for ever. Some cases have actually left them dead, like the poor farmer who hanged himself the other day, not able to stand the pressure any longer.

Where have the animal rights people been? It would be logical to think these vegetarian, farm-hating concerns would be happy to see the end of livestock farming in this country. As long as they make no fuss about the cruelty and devastation of foot-and-mouth, they will be guaranteed their precious ban on hunting from "nice" Mr Blair.

I urge the town dwellers to think about why they like to visit the countryside. Surely, Devon has maintained its tranquil beauty because of its rural traditions. The rolling landscape with its sheep and cattle, the quaint farmhouses and yards full of chickens. The stone walls, the hopeful sighting of a wild animal. Farmers are the guardians of the countryside and generations of them have made this country what it is today . . .

We may have lost the battle for my parents but, as far as I am concerned, and I know many are in agreement, the war is not over!

If FarmCorp get their way, they will cull the last remaining farms in Knowstone. This is mainly due to not one but three separate incidents of bungled culls, which had been carried out by FarmCorp and enabled them to slaughter every animal in the area.

Am I mad? Am I the only one who thinks this whole episode has been just too convenient for the Government?

ENDS

Please note there will be NO MESSAGE tomorrow from us, back on-line again Wednesday.

Cowrie looks up from the screen. "Kia ora, Mere. You're right. There's more to this than the newspapers report. I don't always support the farmers, but here they are being used as pawns just as the organic growers are. We do have to make a stand. Can you print it off so I can show Iri and Organic Growers? I'm sure they will give their support. Except for the assumption that all vegetarians are 'farm-hating'. That's going a bit far. We just prefer organic methods of farming which don't involve chemicals and pesticides."

"Now. That's more like my Turtle. Thanks, Cowrie."
Mere begins printing off the emails. "Can I tell my UK
mates you are all in support?"

"Yeah, why not? We need to join forces against the
bureaucracies who want to destroy small farmers here.
Let me hear back from the Organic Growers group first,
though." Cowrie bites into her last slice of the delicious
pumpkin bread toast.

"Okay, Turtle. You're on." Mere takes great delight in
downloading and printing off all the material. Cowrie
watches, amazed. Just a year ago, the internet and email
were a foreign agency to Mere, but now she has taken
to it like hoki to salt water. In this time, she's developed
a global network of friends and activists from her Peace
Movement and anti-Vietnam War days. It has exploded
her isolation on the marae and given her perspectives
and ways to remain activist in her older years. She has
even been in touch with Elizabeth Green, Sahara's
mother, to find out more information against the French
Government and military when writing about the protest
at Moruroa and its aftermath. Elizabeth and Sahara are
currently working together to lobby large supermarkets
in the UK and Scotland to buy only certified GE-free
foods – and so far, from all accounts, they have been
very successful, with even the major chains Tesco's and
Sainsbury's coming on board. Previously, she'd helped
them in the fight against French Nuclear Testing at
Moruroa.

"Here's some green ginger tea with rewarewa honey."
Cowrie places the brew beside Mere, and she nods in
thanks, keen to get back to her screen.

Cowrie watches Te Kotuku tamariki as they eagerly poke holes into the trays of compost and humus collected from the surrounding bush, then gently place seeds into each of the holes. Pohutukawa, nikau, mamaku, mahoe, manuka and kanuka – all needed to revegetate the nearby coast and forests in order to preserve the bird and animal life that lives under their canopy. Irihapeti wheels over another set of seed trays. The kids place cardboard rolls on end in the trays and then add the compost and humus and plant the seeds of the larger plants inside. That way, they can be replanted without their roots being disturbed.

"I dunno why all nurseries don't used reclaimed bog rolls. They're choice," pipes up Mattiu.

"Yeah, and the worms like them too," adds little Moana. The tamariki have become very excited by the progress of their worm farm after establishing it just a few months ago. They are now supplying other schools with worm farms and helping the kids learn about composting, growing Maori potatoes and the purple urenika yams just months after they lay their first heap. The results have been very satisfying for them.

"Did you get a chance to read Mere's emails from the UK farmers?" Cowrie takes another tray from Iri.

"Ae. I feel for their situation but they also sound like a bunch of redneck farmers who hate Labour and want to see their established plots preserved. I know some of them are organic – but most would not give a stuff about using pesticides on their land and yet still claim to care for it."

"Yeah, I know. And Mere knows that too – but I think she is looking at the humane side of this and feeling for the plight of the farmers." Cowrie reaches for the cardboard rolls to place inside her tray.

"But you can't claim to love the land and the animals and then poison them with pesticides." Iri turns to her. We need to be careful here, Cowrie. We know that once GM is endorsed then we can no longer have true organic farming. There's no second chance once the field trials begin – so we need to be as careful over any causes we support."

"So maybe we should acknowledge their plight but also state where we stand on this. Perhaps they will support us over the GM issues?"

"Fat chance when one of them said that all vegetarians are 'farm-hating'."

"Yeah – I find it hard to get my head around that one too. We just have to explain our position better and seek coalitions where possible."

"Yeah – and you can't call yourself a vegetarian with all that kai moana that passes your sweet lips, Cowrie. Poor wee cockles boiling in their own juices, mussels and scallops roasted alive over the fire, crayfish pulled from their resting caves and encouraged to leap into the cave of your stomach . . ." Iri loves teasing Cowrie like this, watching her spring to her defence. But this time Cowrie is quiet.

"You're right, Iri. But it is our ancestral food."

"So were Pakeha, but I don't see you eating them up like cockles," Iri grins.

"I dunno. Some are pretty sweet if you ask me," teases Cowrie. "I seem to recall you quite liked that Suzy from the Women's Centre a few years back. Haven't seen her in a while. She seemed a very tasty morsel at the time." She grins. Iri bombards her with loo rolls, and the tamariki laugh as the whole pile smashes around them.

"She's back with the boys," whispers Iri, bending down to pick up the rolls.

"Well, definitely too much gristle for you, girl. Let them choke on her. Keep to yer lettuce, I'd say." Cowrie beams, handing over a beautiful frilly lettuce and running her hand along the edges of its skirts, like labia folded over and around each swirl of its luscious greeny-red leaves.

Irihapeti blanches. "Not here, Cowrie." But it's too late. Now the tamariki are all holding up lettuces and feeling around the edges of their leaves, enjoying the sensation without any clue of what preceded the action.

"Plants like to be touched, eh Iri?" says Moana, running her finger over the leaves. "Mum says it makes them grow better."

"It's true. Even some scientists admit this now," adds Iri, returning to her nursery role. "They like the touch of the wind on their leaves and respond to it. They like music and being talked to and they will all grow much better if you talk to them."

42

"Can we sing to them too, Iri?"

"Sure can, Piripi. Why don't you try?"

Piripi looks shy, then begins his favourite waiata. Soon all the class join in. It's a love song so it is perfect for the plants. The tamariki each hold up the plants they like best and sing to them. Later they sing to the entire nursery of plants, and the ferns and tall kauri and kahikatea and rimu at the back of the nursery sway in the wind and mingle with their voices as if dancing in response. The tamariki are fascinated and enthralled, and they decide they will sing every time they work in the nursery to help make the plants grow faster and taller and stronger.

There is a tear in the corner of Irihapeti's eye. "Well, girl. You've really started something here, eh?" Cowrie nudges her and winks.

"Was you with your seductive lettuce, e hoa," mumbles Iri.

"Yeah – well, it makes our work worthwhile and puts all of these debates into perspective if we can raise a new generation of tamariki who feel this way about plants and the soil. So I'm happy to take some credit," grins Cowrie.

One of the tamariki pulls out his koauau and plays haunting melodies on the ancient carved bone flute. The sounds shiver through the spines of the kauri and rimu and down into the leaves of the native sea spinach and spicy mustard plants, shimmer through the waves of jade lettuce and perfect blue borage flowers, drip onto the nectar of the orange and gold nasturtiums. A bee lands on a nasturtium flower, humming into its shell, vibrating with the sounds, then flies out over the singing plants and into the seaspray beyond the nursery, taking with her the ancient bone flute melodies, the sweetness of the plants, the purity of the air, and singing them into each new flower she lands upon, dipping her feelers into new nectar, infecting the land with joy.

"Have you thought any further about support for the UK farmers yet, Turtle?" Mere glances up from her reading. Cowrie relates her discussion with Iri, and Mere seems quite satisfied at the qualified support; she agrees to request help for GE-free issues and a letter to the Royal Commission on GM. In return, she will send their emails to her Pakeha farming friends, especially the rural division of women farmers, and let them provide support. Mere agrees that the GE and peace issues must take prominence for now.

The daughter of a close friend of Mere's is now working as a nurse and relief worker in Afghanistan, and she and Mere are both very concerned after she shared some of the terrible stories of their oppression by various governments over the past decades. Even the United States supported the Taliban there when it served their needs. All this is new to Mere, and she has been emailing Katrina and giving support to her and her family. The Pacific anti-nuclear struggles have prepared her for a deeper understanding of some of these issues, and she knows that Western countries often say they support one cause while undermining it with their multinational companies and secret war strategies. She can see that action on the GE issues is as vital as fighting against nuclear testing in the Pacific or war in Afghanistan. In Mere's mind, they are now inter-linked, so that it is impossible to look at one without considering the others. It worries her that many privileged people still do not make these obvious connexions.

Cowrie squeezes lime juice over her carefully cut slices of fresh papaya and adds some ladyfinger bananas from the plantation surrounding Mere's cottage. She then mixes some organic muesli from Hokianga Wholefoods at Rawene, and pours on delicious Verona Farms acidophilus yoghurt. She hands a bowl to Mere and keeps one for herself.

Mere glances up from her copy of *The Listener*. "Kia ora, Cowrie." She places the bowl on her lap and holds the magazine behind it. "Listen to this, Turtle. It's a letter from Dr Robert Anderson, a member of Physicians and Scientists for Responsible Genetics." She sips the juice from the muesli bowl as if to whet her appetite and then reads: "Labelling of GE foods will be delayed for yet another year . . . Should labelling eventuate, as in Europe or Canada, what 'percentage' of GE do we get? A recent Canadian article said it all. 'It's amazing how a consumer-driven market is extolled when it benefits the sellers, but is blinded by regulation when it does not. To label as 'GM-free' food that contains less than five percent genetically modified constituents reminds me of a Swedish campaign ridiculing the idea of 'designated smoking areas' in restaurants: it's like setting aside a urinating section in a swimming pool.'" Mere laughs. "Well, it's true, Turtle. It will never work. Even I can see this now, after resisting for so long, holding out the hope that genetic modification would help all those with non-curable diseases."

"Yeah, but the release of GE materials and field trials will not be reversible. That's sure like pissing in a pool. It seems so crazy that this same Labour Government devotes a huge budget to supporting our so-called clean, green image, even throwing money at Peter Jackson's film of Tolkien's *Lord of the Rings* because it is set in this clean, green paradise and promotes our country, yet they look as if they might now relent and let anyone come and piss in our pool. This country could be a resource for clean organic food for the world if we refuse GE, and for seeds once other countries have learned how wrong it was to let GE go ahead. But now it looks less hopeful by the day."

"Don't lose hope, Cowrie. I have a lot of faith in our Maori MPs and their ability to lobby the Greens, Alliance and Labour. Maori are against GE and most are for an Organic Aotearoa by 2020. And I am sure that Helen Clark would not sell out on us now, after she has courted our support for so long. We didn't elect a strong woman Prime Minister to let us down on this issue."

"I hope you're right, Mere. I've always voted Labour as you know, then switched to the Greens when I saw what an alliance between Labour and the Greens could achieve, with Jeanette Fitzsimons co-leading the Greens and bringing Labour back into line. But I am getting a strange feeling about this Royal Commission. At first it seemed a great idea, really going out and getting involved and hearing submissions and finding out that 92 per cent of New Zealanders are against GE. But as they sift through this material, I know how persuasive the corporates will be, with all their bloody spin doctors whispering into the ears of politicians and making veiled threats of withdrawing money and support if the government goes GE-free. I don't trust the buggers."

Mere sighs. "You might be right there, Turtle. That lobby formed by federated farmers to sell their dairy produce overseas, MagicMilk, have already said if Aotearoa goes GE-free they will take all their money and research overseas. If they withdraw, that will be a lot of money and support. They are something like the ninth-largest dairy company in the world, and the country relies on this primary produce so much."

"Yeah, but maybe it's time we relied more on the potential for our organic dairy future, which will be inestimable once the rest of the world is polluted." Cowrie digs into her muesli, taking a large spoonful, as if its organic presence might visually reinforce her point.

"Pity they cannot see you now, Turtle. Who'd have thought a keen Kiwi kid who loved the crackling on the pork and freshly fried bacon would now be gorging herself on organic produce, with some kai moana thrown down the hatch in between? Maybe this is the future of our people?"

"Maybe," grins Cowrie. "But not if a power-hungry government has its way. In the end, I wonder any more whether there is much difference between National and Labour. We could always rely on the socialist leanings of a Labour Party to rescue us from the jaws of an elitist National Party – but maybe it's power and not policies that feeds them?"

48

"Remains to be seen, Turtle. Don't judge the tiger by its stripes until you see how well it runs." Mere chews on her bananas, savouring their lemony sweetness.

There is a shuffling on the porch and a tap at the door. "Kia ora. Haere mai," Mere calls out. Moana appears, her face veiled in a lavalava with a pattern of hibiscus flowers swirling yellow around the bright purple cloth. "Tena koe, Moana. Sit down here and Cowrie will fetch you a cuppa." Mere has noticed already that Moana is very quiet and in need of sustenance.

"The kids are with me. Can I send them to play outside?"

"Sure. Cowrie will look after them. Maybe they'd like to visit Te Kotuku nursery and see the new plantings and help out a bit?"

"Ka pae, Mere. Thanks." Tears slide down Moana's face and drip onto the stamens of her hibiscus-flowered lavalava. It is then that Mere notices the bruise on her cheek, turned away and partially covered by cloth.

"Cowrie – after making us tea – can you please take Moana's tamiriki to the nursery and amuse them a while? Don't bring them back until lunchtime. Moana and I have things to talk over."

Cowrie is about to protest as she has work to do, but then she reads the seriousness in Mere's eyes. Something is up. "You want gumboot tea or fresh garden peppermint, Moana?"

"Peppermint will be fine, thanks, Cowrie." Moana drops her head low, as if in apology for interrupting them.

After a few moments, Mere and Moana are alone in the cottage and Mere demands to know what has

49

happened. Moana is reluctant at first but knows she will never pull the wool over the eyes of her kuia. She then asks if she and the tamariki can return to Te Kotuku marae, until things are better with Tony. It's all got too much for her. First the kids getting so many sicknesses this year with vomiting and diarrhoea. Even the doctors could not pinpoint the trouble. Then Tony getting ill too and taking it out on her and the kids. Every day he could not work he would get morose and depressed and then lash out at one or all of them. They are now behind with their payments on the house, and the power has been cut off. Finally, Tony got drunk and hit her hard last night. He left and said he'd be back the next night. Moana decided to get the kids to a safe place first and intended going back. But when riding to the marae on horseback, she decided it would be better for them to return home to Te Kotuku, lick their wounds and have time to think about the future.

Mere holds both her hands. "You did well, Moana. You cannot let our tamariki be raised in such an environment. Kuini is away for a few weeks and she won't mind you staying in her housetruck over that time. The kids will love it. There's a tent pitched alongside for friends who visit and you can use that too. I'll email and let her know. She's down working with whanau in Opotiki on a new Rape Crisis Centre. She'll be pleased that her Tainui waka is of use."

"Ka pae, Mere. Thanks. I need time out to consider what I want. I think Tony is losing it. He is so emotional and extreme these days. Nothing we do seems to be okay for him."

"You take all the time you need, Moana. And know you are free to come here day or night."

"I've been thinking for a while about going back to study. I'd like to do some healing work. Maybe massage, maybe herbal medicines, perhaps learning about those Bach flower remedies."

"You forget about the Bach flowers, Moana. I will teach you the plant remedies of our own people. Maori have long used herbal and medicinal remedies, and Cowrie and Irihapeti have got interested in this also. Maybe we'll work together on it. Perhaps you could produce some remedies for the marae, and even sell some through the nursery to support yourself at a later stage?"

Moana's eyes sparkle as if a fire has been lit behind them. To Mere she looks like Pele with her ashen and bruised cheek but with the fire of Kiluaea in her face, pohutukawa flames flickering from her pupils, black lava running down the ridge of her cheekbone. Her hidden strength simmers in the coals, ready to be released and sent on its path over the lava slopes to the welcoming coolness of the waiting sea.

"Gidday mate. All set for the 1080 drop tomorrow?" The Department of Conservation bloke sets his cap on the counter and wipes his sweaty brow.

"Sure thing," replies Raymond, his head buried deep in the large spray rig, trying to test the sprockets out.

"Got a prob with the sprayer?"

"Yeah. Bloody thing went haywire yesterday when we were doing a dioxin drop over Hal's farm. Four hundred litres of poison meant to land directly on the new pasture went astray when the sprayer jammed and we had to drop it on the way back. Turns out we dusted the town of Kawakawa by mistake."

"Hope it didn't land on Hundertwasser's Creation, eh. That's their main tourist attraction."

"Buggered if I care. Some bloody Euro arty-farty who made friends with all the local niggers. If the best he could do was build a bloody fancy bog for the residents, then he won't mind if it gets a bit of our star dust." Raymond clears the end of the sprayer and runs some water through to test it.

"Wouldn't get caught calling the local Maoris niggers around here if you wanna stay," advises Dominic, placing his cap back on his head.

"Don't worry. I don't do it to their faces. Even got

one working for us. See out there in the office. Martha. Not a bad chick, either. She's good for the tourists who wanna see brown faces when they book their flights. And helps us keep in with the local marae. We wouldn't want any land claims or hassles over environmental issues, now would we?" Raymond winks.

Dominic doesn't much like this fella and does not bother to mention he is Nga Puhi as well as Yugoslav-Pakeha. Not worth the energy. Besides, DOC needs Flyworks for its possum-eradication programme and work in the Waipoua Forest, so he knows better than to get offside with Raymond. If he argued with every racist or sexist Kiwi bloke he met in the course of his work, his time would be soaked up educating them – to little avail. He prefers to let things be. The way God meant them to be.

"Make sure the spray rig is fixed by tomorrow, Ray. We wouldn't want any mistakes in the Waipoua Kauri Forest. After the Cave Creek disaster, we have daily memos to be careful about public perceptions of what we do. There are all sorts of checks and balances. Best to be on the safe side."

Raymond smiles. "Like you wouldn't want us to do an Agent Orange drop over your precious forest instead of 1080 poison, eh?"

Dominic blanches. "Yeah. That'd be a disaster."

"Well, Dommy old boy. There's not much difference between the two. Just a matter of proportion. But don't tell all the Greenies or we'd be out of business in a day." Raymond laughs loudly, enjoying his confession, knowing he's safe with DOC. He goes on. "We had some fella from Hokianga Wholefoods trying to sell us some of his tofu shit the other day. Said he could supply the workers with healthy organic lunches from local gardens and it would support the growers as well as us. We convinced him we were organic Greenies and had a garden at home the size of a footy field. Truth is, once he left, we tucked into a fry-up of bacon and eggs, and little did he know it was Pinky we were eating."

"The same Pinky who won the Best Children's Pig Award at the Rawene Agricultural Show?"

"Yep. And she sure tasted sweet." Raymond licks his lips in memory of Pinky.

"A bit rough on your kids, Ray."

"They gotta get used to it, man. They can't grow up around farms and not know this is the great Kiwi lifestyle. This means learning to be tough and eating your mates sometimes."

And these are the same fellas who arrogantly call Maori cannibals, thinks Dominic, but knows better than to share this thought.

"Besides, if you cared so much you wouldn't be zapping your precious possums with 1080, DOC Man. You know what Agent Orange did to the Vietnamese and Yanks who felt the drop. Some died, some are still ill, some went bananas. With the 1080 drops we have done for you fellas at DOC, just in the Northland region, there's gotta be a few mean and mad and mangly muts floating about the bush, those that have not been zapped by us. And judging from the letters to the papers on this bloody GE issue, I'd say most of those bush-dwelling Greenies and niggers, oops, Maaaareees to

54

you, have had their brains zapped by your precious 1080, so you might as well get off ya high horse now, Dommy." Raymond's lips curl upwards in a cruel smile, knowing he has got the better of Dominic. He's an okay bloke, this DOC Man, but he has no idea about the power of the poisons he is ordering them to drop all over the land. Best to let him stay ignorant, thinks Raymond. But worth it just to see him squirm a bit.

Maata knocks at the door of the workshop. "You fellas want a cuppa?"

"That'd be lovely, thanks." Dominic is relieved to escape from Raymond and relax with the workers a while.

"We'll be there in five," mutters Raymond, adjusting the nozzles of the sprayer.

"Shouldn't you have gloves on for that job?" inquires Dominic.

"Na, man. You'd be putting gloves on and off all bloody day. Besides, I've had two kids and fondled the wife with these strong hands, and none of them have carked it yet." Raymond holds up his right hand and spreads out his fingers. He folds his fingers into his wrist and makes a lewd gesture by poking his middle finger up into the air. "And she likes it too, mate," he smiles.

Dominic looks at his finger, stained with nicotine and carcinogens from his sprays. Despite Raymond's constant washing, he can never remove the cancerous substances he is constantly spraying over the land. They remain like a blight on his scrubbed torso, reminding any keen observer that his own poisonous practices will also remain bleached into the landscape forever despite the rain. Dominic shudders, wondering how long Ray and his wife might be so lucky. It's like playing Russian roulette. "I'll see ya in the lunchroom, Ray. Hanging out for that cuppa."

"Yeah, you go ahead. I'll give it a miss. Too much work here and we need to get your chopper ready for tomorrow's drop."

"Thanks, Ray. Much appreciated." Dominic winces that he is always having to thank this man he dislikes so much.

"No worries, mate. Us poison droppers need to stick together, eh?" Raymond winks at him. Dominic knows this is a veiled threat, but pretends not to notice. He walks up the stairs and down the corridor into the lunchroom, where Raymond's wife Barbara is preparing some food while Maata makes the tea. He cannot help looking at her hands as she butters her muffins, wondering how close she is to Ray during the day and if any of the poisons infect her fingers. She turns around and offers him a plate of goodies. Dominic politely refuses but accepts the steaming gumboot tea that Maata holds.

"Ka pae, Maata. I could kill for a good brew."

Maata passes the cup. "How's Roimata and her tamariki? They over that terrible flu yet?"

"No. Seems like most of us in the Kaipara have had it bad this year. Streaming eyes, running noses, itching, skin rashes. Worst bloody flu I ever saw."

"I heard Kiri and Eruera's kids had it very bad. Had to go to a specialist in Tamaki Makaurau."

"Where's that? Never heard of it." Barbara is a bit miffed that Dominic has refused her muffins.

"Auckland," replies Maata.

"Well, why don't you use the proper name?" Barbara wipes the edge of the plate with her hand, and Dominic cannot help noticing it is also stained yellow like Raymond's fingers. He raises his eyebrows to Maata, who raises hers back. Not worth an argument over this being the correct name for the place before the British took it over. They ignore the question and move on to discuss their shared whanau and friends. Barbara is surprised he knows so much about them. She thought he was 100 per cent Pakeha, albeit with a bit of Dally blood. But nobody could be offended by the Dalmatians. At least they do something worthwhile with their land, like planting it with vineyards and providing New Zealanders with some of the best early wines in the country. Not like the Maoris, who waste the land, letting it grow back into bush and growing their horrid little purple and cream, tasteless potatoes and thinking they are special. Barbara bites into one of her special chocolate muffins, wondering why nobody else seems to want them. Dominic and Maata are thick in conversation by now. Barbara sweeps up the plate of muffins with her left hand and strides down to the workshop. At least Raymond will appreciate her hard work. The others barely notice she has left.

Raymond looks up from his desk. He hates paperwork and is relieved she has come with a steaming plate of muffins. He grabs her and places the muffins onto the work table with a thud, stuffing one into his gob and winding his thick, hairy arms around her waist and sliding his hands over her bottom, pulling her toward him. He shuts the door behind them and raises her skirt

57

above her pants, pulling at his zip. He is pleased to find he is hard already and thrusts himself inside her, pushing up against the door. Barbara hopes they cannot hear the noise from the lunchroom. At least she can always rely on Raymond to appreciate her, no matter what. They need each other, that's what Ray always said, especially when her family accused him of marrying her for her money and her land for his chopper business. But he'd rescued her from her rich, boring family who expected her to marry a doctor or a lawyer or a stockbroker. If only they could see her now, fucking him like a dog on heat. How shocked they'd be.

This thought makes Barbara enjoy the rebellion of fucking even more and she lets Raymond pound her against the wall, wrapping her long legs around his waist, enjoying the smell of his work clothes and the strange mix of chemicals that waft around him like a noxious perfume, one her family would hate and which makes her love it even more.

"There's going to be a hikoi to parliament organised by the Far North Organic Growers. Local iwi, hapu and the Greens are supporting us. We'll leave from the tip of the North Island several weeks before the final government decision in response to the report from the Royal Commission on Genetic Engineering and it will be timed to arrive at parliament the day of the decision. Who can walk with us and who can lend support?" Irihapeti is delighted when a cheer comes from the local organic growers and iwi representatives at the meeting. Everyone is keen to be involved in some way, even though most of the growers exist on very little money and eke out a sustainable existence with their hard labour. Few can afford time away from the land, but all want to lend their support in some shape or form.

"How many do they expect to start the hikoi?"

"They're hoping for a good turnout at the start, and for more to join the march as it progresses. Already, local growers have offered to set up food stands along the main highway south and to provide food and shelter on the journey."

"We'd have whanau in nearly every town if we pooled resources, and we should be able to provide shelter all the way. Let's put a map on the table and I'll place cockle shells on the towns where any of us have family. I'll read them out, and if you have mates or friends or family, yell out and I'll mark the map. Later we can collate the details and then email the results to them tomorrow."

"Choice idea, Hemi. I've got a free camping map in my wagon. I'll get it now."

They pore over the map for the next hour, finding that they have friends and whanau spread all over Te Ika a Maui and they know most of them will support the hikoi. Nobody knows any tangata whenua who are in support of GE, despite the corporates and the government wanking on about this or that Maori here or there where they have managed to twist the arm of some Uncle Tom or bribed him with offers of riches or land to support their cause. The very nature of gene splicing is totally foreign to Maori and especially the mixing of animal and human genes, which interferes with traditional ancestral spiritual beliefs. Only those very alienated from their hapu, iwi or whanau could ever contemplate the idea of GE on spiritual grounds, let alone the fact that none of them wants to eat genetically altered food.

"What are the likely effects if genetically altered fish get into our kai moana?" asks Ramiri.

"Yeah, we saw those Frankenfish the Greens made models of on the telly. Bloody gory too. Fish with two heads and fins coming out of their eye sockets and no tails."

"We've got them already around Moruroa and Faungatuofa and all the Tahitian Islands after decades of French nuclear testing. We were there on the peace flotilla a few years back on board *Manawa Toa*, and we saw all kinds of strange fishy mutations. Not only that, but there were also photos of severely mutated humans – they're known as jellyfish babies – with two or more heads, distorted limbs or none at all, and bodies that looked like blobby jelly. It was devastating." Tears tug the edges of Cowrie's eyes.

"So do the nuclear chemicals have the same reaction as some of these GE experiments?"

"It's a different process, but yes, some of the results are similar. Already, it's been reported that one salmon company in the Marlborough Sounds has been experimenting with GE, trying to grow salmon twice as fast and twice as large. They were forced to pull out of the experiment when it became known that their salmon were being born with two heads and enlarged, distorted bodies as well as twisted tails. Some could not even swim properly, and others drowned with the weight of their own bodies."

"Yuck! Gross! How could anybody even contemplate taking a risk like this and letting field trials go ahead where just one of these monsters could infect our entire food chain?"

"I heard that some wankers are planning a fin fish farm at Peach Cove, Whangarei Heads. Kingi said it'd ruin the local resource and pump tons of chemicals and raw sewage into the harbour."

"I doubt that the Labour Government under Helen Clark, with the Alliance and the Greens against GE, would dare endorse any of this, let alone a GM report that recommended going ahead – so I think we are safe on that score." Irihapeti tries to reassure them.

"But what about the vast amount of pressure and the spin doctors that the big corporates who pay the scientists to do their Nazi experiments will put onto them? You can bet that will be huge." Piripi pauses. "Despite the fact that 92 per cent of Kiwis put in submissions against GE, I'll bet that their 8 per cent of funded puppets will dominate the media debates because they own the media and also have the power to get their opinions known. They'll do the usual discrediting of any alternative opinions as the 'looney left' or the 'wild greens' or eco-activist groups who are never taken seriously by the media or the public."

"Yeah, but Clark has always been pretty socialist. There's no way she'd sell out on this issue. She needs the left-wing vote and also the Maori vote. She knows all feminists, liberals, Maori and most of the educated people in the country are against GE. Only a very small group with a vested interested are for it. And she knows that, despite their money, it's the majority who votes Labour in or out."

"Let's bloody hope so. But we can never trust the main parties. We have learned this in the past. The only party which has not compromised on this issue is the Greens. Jeanette and Nandor and Sue get my vote anytime."

"Kia ora. Hemi's right. Let's all sign up. It's only five dollars, and we can donate some money from the slush fund to make sure every family is committed to Mana Motuhake or the Greens or any group or individual who is categorically against GE. We might not all like the system, but it's the only way we will get our say."

"Until we have our own sovereignty – let's hear it for tino rangatiratanga!" yells out one of the tamariki. But not all the elders agree. They know it is not that easy. Though they want to have their sovereign power returned, they know that it must come with wisdom or it will be open to the same abuses as the systems that already exist. Besides, they are now getting used to the idea of partnership, and many believe it can work if there is trust on both sides, Maori and Pakeha.

After their korero, a feast of freshly dug cockles, pipis and tuatua is laid out on groaning trestle tables and they offer karakia for the safety and protection of their ancestral food supplies. Now, more than ever, they appreciate their guardianship of this sacred kai moana. They cannot let it fall into the hands of people who are so greedy they would grow ika with two heads and bodies so large that they sink. It is against the laws of nature. It is against the spirit of tangata whenua.

Heat surges up her spine like waves caressing the land then swooshing out again. The waves have tiny tendrils which lick her body like a tongue. Its hot wet warmth moistens her skin, touching every fibre of her body. Koa moans with relief as Irihapeti's hands and tongue touch every part of her being, bringing life back into this war-torn frame which has suffered for so long after the poisoning of te whenua.

"Thanks, Iri. Your green fingers are not only healing for the plants. You have healed me too."

Irihapeti grins. "That's what I'm here for, Koa. To bring the joy back into your body, your soul, your life."

"You've done that better than all the others, from local doctors through to alternative healers. Plus the added bonus of living here at Te Kotuku in an organic nursery. That's healed all my past experiences of working with plants for city council parks and being poisoned by the chemicals we used as a part of our daily work."

Iri props up the pillows behind Koa and leans her head on her hands, lying beside her. "You've never told me the full story. Just that you were diagnosed with ME but that it was a long saga before that."

Koa sighs. "I didn't want to bore you with all the details. Are you sure you want to hear it all?"

"I want to know everything about you, Koa. Everything that you want to share with me."

"Okay, then get us a fresh brew of manuka tea, 'cos this may be a long talkstory."

Iri lights the gas stove in their caravan at the side of the nursery and looks into the giant black mamaku ferns towering above them, waving their fronds in the wind. She's so lucky to be here in this beautiful place with Koa beside her. Lucky to have found a soulmate who shares her love of plants and everything organic, and who nourishes her soul as well as her body. How could this strong woman ever have become so ill? What could possibly break this spirit that soars above the trees and surfs so lusciously into her soul? The kettle bubbles and she breaks off twigs of wild flowering manuka and throws them into the large clay pot she made last summer, then pours over the hot water. The twigs float on the water and she stirs them with another twig, then adds a teaspoon of fresh manuka honey. She reaches for the cups and places them carefully on the tray beside the teapot and carries the steaming taonga to Koa.

"Yum. Thanks, Iri. Now cuddle in here beside me and I will bring you up to date." She lifts the covers for Iri to climb in and cuddle close. She loves it when Iri does this and calls her a limpet because Iri is able to wrap her long limbs around Koa so she feels totally embraced. Iri fits her like a limpet to a rock, so perfectly the water cannot seep in when the tide rises. And that's just what Koa needs right now. Iri is always warm – her own walking hot water bottle, Koa claims, and a brilliant talking one at that. Iri pours the tea and nudges Koa to start her story.

"Okay, okay, hang on tight, my little limpet." Koa nudges in closer. "Once upon a time, there was a wee girl named Koa. And she lived at Ohinemutu Marae near the shores of Lake Rotorua. Life was blissful and safe in those early years. We lived sustainably off the land, then the tourist trade all but spoiled our once beautiful wonderland. My parents then moved south to look after an ailing aunty and I recall the first time I ever felt ill. The local council was spraying Roundup while I was walking to school. They all used Roundup in those days, and never worried about the kids. Every day the man with his backpack would come nearer and nearer and every day we would play on the roadsides where he had sprayed, never thinking it was harmful. People used it to get rid of weeds in their lawns and gorse bushes on farms. I recall the plastic containers all over the show. It was a part of growing up Kiwi. Roundup was as Kiwi as Weetbix, and we ingested about the same amount through our tastebuds or lungs via the food and air without even knowing about it then. It was not until my cat, Wai, became desperately ill that we realised something was very wrong. The vet said she died from a lethal dose of poison – but we could never figure out how she got it. Not until I realised that she always lay in the catnip on the side of the road – the same stuff zapped by the council with herbicides over and over again."

"So how did it affect you?" Iri takes a sip of Koa's tea and then snuggles back under the covers.

"I was dizzy and very nauseous. My muscles would contract in the night and I would wake up with strange spasms. There was a terrible burning in my eyes. My

66

gums and mouth would bleed. Other kids were having similar sensations. They thought it was some kind of flu at first, then Wai died and slowly they began to put one and one together. Dad was furious and he went to see the council, but they just said heaps of tests had been done on Roundup and it was proven overseas to be safe. The government would not let it be used so widely if not, now would they? They made him feel like a stunned mullet, so Dad thought it must have been something else. At that time the council sprayed the kerbs every month. It was a never-ending process. Once they had finished our neighbourhood, they would start on another, and so it went on all over this clean green land of ours. Imagine how much Roundup was consumed on that basis. The pesticide companies must've been laughing all the way to the bank."

"Yeah, the bastards."

"Anyway, nobody took any notice of our complaints and we'd get the same official replies that it was authorised by the government and the government knew best. That's how they all thought back then. And people actually believed it. Unreal. Anyway, that's when the poisoning began. After I left school, as you know, I got a job in the botanical gardens and I never dreamed the sprays we used were so harmful. Nobody wore any protective clothing or masks and we regularly zapped the plants, the lawn, in fact everything in sight. It had to look beautiful for the public."

"I wish more people would appreciate natural gardens and bush without having to have everything like an English garden. It's a real colonial mentality, eh?"

"Sure – but we never thought like that then. I especially loved working with the subtropical and exotic plants. But even they got zapped with poisons. The entire botanical gardens were aerially sprayed with 2,4-D twice a year. The glasshouses were the worst. They were regularly sprayed with pesticides, and the poisons stayed in the air for days because they could not escape. It was very difficult for us as we had to do all the debudding and grafting by hand and it was too intricate for gloves, not that any were given to us, and we were constantly handling sprayed plants. After four years of this, our hands started to come up in blisters and bleed and get very irritated. By then, our eyes and noses were a mess and I was bringing up blood in my vomit. I had to leave the job, yet I loved my work. I was devastated." Koa sips her tea, tears welling in her eyes as she speaks. Iri hugs her closely.

"I went to doctor after doctor until I found one who diagnosed paraquat poisoning and after several tests, we worked with herbalists to try to cure the condition. I was diagnosed with ME first and treated as if it was all in my head. It took twelve years for the truth to be told, and I was so exhausted after that struggle that if I did not have ME at the beginning, I sure had it by the end."

Irihapeti strokes her hand tenderly. "Thanks for telling me all this, Koa. It is not the first time I have heard an ME diagnosis for paraquat and Roundup poisoning – in fact for pesticides and chemicals that they do not want to name. Much easier to put it all back on the sufferer. It's disgusting."

"I spent a fortune on doctors, acupuncturists, all kinds

of healers, but falling in love with you and coming here to the organic nursery at Te Kotuku marae has been the best treatment ever for me. Now I can still work in a nursery but feel safe doing so and rest when I need to. For the first time in ages, I feel I may fully recover from this poisoning. But I still worry about all the other kids who played on the roadsides over that time, and also anyone who has ever worked in a traditional nursery or with plants."

"Yeah – it's so strange that we like to work with plants and trees because they are healing and it makes us feel deeply in tune with nature. Yet the colonial view of gardening has tried to tame and commodify the plants and land so that great profits are made but at the expense of human health. The whole reason why we might garden in the first place is not only lost, but infected." Iri lies back on her pillow and sips her tea thoughtfully.

"Even now, Iri. Look at all those who follow TV programmes like *Maggie's Garden Show* and still zap their plants with pesticides under fancy and harmless names, little knowing what a terrible nightmare legacy they are leaving for their kids by poisoning the very land they hope to pass on to them."

"You're right, Koa. We need to educate people more carefully. Not just in how to grow organically – but how to avoid being sucked into the commercialisation of gardening so that it feeds into corporate profits rather than hungry mouths. And also how to recognise and handle poisoning when they encounter it. Thank Tane Mahuta most of the kids are safe living on the marae since we became organic."

"Don't be fooled, Iri. Some of the kids at kohanga come from land that is still being heavily sprayed, and all of them shop in town where Roundup is used as a herbicide. Look at little Mattiu, for instance. He's been down with colds and flu and had rashes and irritated eyes for over a year now. His mother has taken him to doctors who diagnose the flu. But I have suspected his father is spraying the land with Roundup, or worse, and once he told us so at the nursery. Their favourite outing is to go spraying with Dad. What kind of a legacy is that?"

Iri sits bolt upright. "Koa, I think you're onto something here. Mattiu and his bros have all been very sick. So have Kiri and Eruera's kids. And the tamariki from the outlying farms. Maybe we need to get someone like Matt Tizard up here to test them for herbicide poisoning? He's the best alternative medical expert in this field."

"It's a good idea. But we need to do so carefully. Many of the parents will be against it. Most people seem to think it is all a communist plot if you dare suggest that toxic chemicals sold to them as harmless weedkillers, like Roundup, could possibly harm them or their children."

"Right. We need to make this into a school science experience – until we get the results anyway. The kids will find it fascinating, and there's no harm if we are proved wrong, eh?"

"Glad I chose to tell you this today, Iri. I must admit, it has been in the back of my mind. But I am so used to being laughed at by professionals while enduring this long journey to discover what was wrong with me, that I hardly dared speak it."

Iri hugs her. "Well, you must never hold back from such things with me, Koa. We need to feel comfortable talking about the difficult things. And we will never ever laugh or make fun of another. Okay?"

Tears of relief run over Koa's wide cheeks and run down into the ridge between her brown shining breasts, just visible above her lavalava. "Thanks, Iri. Kia ora."

"You look exhausted, my love. Have a good rest and I'll take away the tea and have a wee walk and come back a bit later." Iri kisses her gently on her nose.

"Ka pae. I will." Koa snuggles back into the sheets and Iri cannot resist looking at her face as she drifts into sleep. Her eyebrows soar out from her eyes like the wings of an albatross in flight, her beautiful wide nose slopes down to her broad, high cheekbones and her dark tattooed lips. She recalls the strong women painted by Robin Kahukiwa in *Wahina Toa*. She strokes the side of Koa's face. Her wahine toa. She has been through so much, yet emerged from the ashes so powerfully. Her body is like the land, has been poisoned and yet still offers itself up for healing. Its hidden power gleams in the moonlight like the white bones of Muriranga-whenua, who told Maui to take her jawbone as a symbol of strength when seeking the new land. She is the land. And like her, te whenua will heal and become strong again. Koa is living proof that this is possible.

"Welcome to our first Rongoa Maori hui." Mere bends forward to hongi each of the women as they enter the workshop. They gather around the table in a ring and hold hands to do karakia to bless their ancestors and the kai steaming from a large woven flax kete which has been placed on banana leaves in the centre. After the prayers, waiata are sung to thank Mere for her blessing and to open the hui. Enticing and earthy aromas are wafting from the basket, and Cowrie is delighted that such a ritual hui will begin with food. What a blessing! Mere carefully opens the flax bag brought over from the hangi and extracts several parcels wrapped in banana and taro leaves from their garden. The steaming leaves are laid down in front of each of the women.

Mere continues. "I want you to open these taonga one by one, and each person must identify the plant that gave herself up for this feast by holding a leaf of that plant and naming it, thanking her, and sharing the contents around, so that by the end, you have all tasted the fruits of this bountiful land we have been gifted. This way, you will recognise each of the plants and be able to greet them as friends any time you walk into the bush. You will feel connected to them and thus will always appreciate what they have to offer us, as kai and as medicine. It has struck me very forcefully since Cowrie, Irihapeti, Koa and all of you working for an organic future for our land have been very vocal on these issues, that in fact this is exactly what our ancestors would have wanted us to do, and what they themselves knew. We may do this in different ways now, but the ancient knowledge made us intimately connected with the food we ate – and this is what we must once again do, and teach others to do. Ours will be a long and patient journey. This taonga was gathered over many years and it cannot be taught in one day. It is more a matter of learning to trust your instincts and rely on your inner knowledge."

She pauses to sip the fresh spring water. "As you begin to recognise the families of leaves and flowers, and the shapes and designs of the plants, you will understand how they are inter-related. In most cases, if one of that family can be eaten, then many can. If one is poisonous, then so are others in the whanau. You must always only harvest a small and sustainable crop. For instance, if the edible part of the plant is the root, then you must make sure there are many more rooted plants ready to take its place. You always plant more than what you take, so that future generations are provided for. If we had all done this globally, we would still be a sustainable planet, but greed took over as some came to control the production of food and profit from it. Strangely enough, it has been our indigenous ancestors and brothers and sisters globally who have held this ancient knowledge, but who have now been edged out of it by the corporate multinationals. Thus it is vital we learn carefully and hand on our knowledge to our mokopuna and tamariki so they can in turn pass it on to future generations. There has never been a more vital time on this planet than now to listen to the plants and learn from their wisdom. It looks as if those we trusted in politics in Aotearoa may be bought off by the multinationals, like International Seed Corporation, who now control the seeds and control genetic engineering – so we must each listen to our inner wisdom and the voices of our ancestors. Kia ora." Mere clears her throat. "Irihapeti, as guardian of our organic nursery, would you kindly go first?" Mere hands over the carefully wrapped taonga to Irihapeti and encourages her to open it.

Steam issues from the leaves as they reveal their enticing secrets. Finally, the last banana leaf. Inside is a fern frond, just beginning to curl. It is huge. Beside it sits what looks like the pith of the tree and a part of a frond. Iri knows from its size it must be the giant black treefern. "Is it the mamaku?" Mere nods and smiles. "And this looks like the inner pith and some part of the frond, but I am not sure which."

Mere grins. "Ka pae, Irihapeti." She holds up the core of the fern. "This is the koata, the pith of the upper trunk." Irihapeti smiles, loving that Koa's name, meaning joy, is hidden inside this strong and beautiful black treefern. "This part is the core of the beginning of the frond – the most tender part – and this is a new shoot. It is best to get this before it unfurls, or it can become too hard and bitter."

"But it feels so sad to harvest this exquisite spiral new birth," whispers Moana.

74

Mere nods. "Yes. It is. But this is the most nutritious part of the plant and is very high in vitamins and minerals. If we still lived in an Aotearoa covered in plentiful giant mamaku, eating some parts of the tree-ferns would not be a problem. It is simply that the colonial farmers burned and cut and buried millions of these ferns when creating farms for their cattle and sheep, and thus we now have a different level of resource and so each of us must make our own decisions around harvesting this kai. Generally, if you have a good supply and have a medicinal reason or shortage of good nutritious food, then you can harvest. But each time, you must make this decision and never harvest to stockpile or for greed."

"But there must be plants we can harvest which will not be destroyed by the harvesting too," suggests Koa.

"You are right – and we will concentrate on these later. Maybe you'd like to go next, Koa?"

Koa lifts her parcel, wrapped like a pyramid in taro leaves. Inside are several smaller curled shoots of the fiddlehead fern. "It's the hen-and-chicken fern but I can't remember the Maori name."

"Mouki. The young shoots were steamed in a hangi and eaten by my parents and theirs, like we might eat asparagus today." Cowrie licks her lips at the thought of such a ready supply of asparagus in the forests surrounding them. "It was a favourite delicacy of the Tuhoe iwi in the Uruweras and often eaten with potatoes. They also liked the feather fern, pakauroharoha, which was similarly harvested and steamed in a hangi overnight."

"Isn't this fern related to the *Dryopteris heterocarpa*?" asks Koa. They look blankly at her.

"The hetero-what?" asks Cowrie. "You turning into a shape shifter then, eh, Koa?" She laughs.

Koa grins. "No, Cowrie. It's a very similar shape to the feather fern and eaten by tribes in West Penang. I saw this on a botanical trip there several years ago and was fascinated. But back then I didn't realise our ancestors ate ferns as well, sad to say."

"That'd be right, Koa, and so typical that often our tamariki only realise our ancient wisdom after they have left home and seen it in other parts of the world. But we must now learn to harvest this knowledge and share it among all tribes for the healing of our planet."

"But surely that does not mean giving the knowledge over to the multinationals to buy the rights and misuse it?" comments Cowrie.

"Certainly not. This knowledge cannot be bought or sold. Like the land, it does not belong to anyone. We are the guardians of this knowledge and must look after it and use it well for the benefit of all. If we keep it to ourselves alone, or sell it for gross profits and do not use it wisely, then we are no better than those greedy corporates."

"What about our intellectual property rights?" asks Irihapeti.

"We have those by our sovereign rights as tangata whenua. And we do now need this enshrined in the law of the land. But that does not give us permission to misuse that knowledge. It's up to each of us to be ethical in this respect."

"Kia ora, Mere. And this is what we must teach our tamariki," Iri adds.

Little by little, each of the wahine opens her parcel, delighted at the contents, and they sample the kai one by one. Some of the leaves and fronds and roots seem bitter by today's tastes, but Mere explains to them that such tastes have altered since the sugar companies started bribing food manufacturers to put sugar into everything – even staples like tomato sauce – to get the tamariki hooked on sweet flavours which would then lead to their other sweetened products. "We must get used to these flavours again. Most of you like rocket in your salad – yet many thought that bitter when first tasting it. Now you would not be without it."

"True. And nasturtium flowers and borage flowers. We'd never have dreamed of eating them as kids and yet now even I, the queen of kai moana, adore them," admits Cowrie, grinning and biting into the delicious fiddlehead of a kiekie fern.

"Now you should work in pairs and identify the leaves and flowers of the plants you have just eaten and continue the process, noting any further memories you may have of them. We've begun today with eating certain parts of the plants our ancestors ate, and we will gradually move on to their medicinal uses as the weeks go by." Mere helps herself to some more spring water as the wahine gather up the parcels and retreat to their favourite places. Moana and Koa choose the table near the open window, which looks out over the black mamuku forest.

"We're so lucky to live here, Moana. It's such a restful

place. I give thanks for this each day when I wake up."

"Yes. It's great to be back here at last." Moana sighs.

"You lived on a farm nearby, didn't you?"

"True. But it began to be a nightmare."

"Why's that?"

"My husband, Tony, felt he needed to control the weeds all the time and he got obsessed with it. He was given cheap pesticides from that helicopter lot. Said they 'fell off the back of a chopper'. In other words, they were either stolen or dumped or sold cheaply. I worried a lot about our boys."

Koa stiffens. "And for good reason, Moana. When the government bans pesticides, then the suppliers seek to dump it anywhere rather than bear the costs of return. They prefer to hock it off cheaply rather than burn or bury or return the stuff. The same with big countries. The United States dumps its banned pesticides in the Pacific and other developing or Third World countries, who only ever needed them in the first place because their ecosystems were destroyed by the colonial farmers doing their slash and burn routine to make more farms for McDonald's and Co. Don't get me started on this."

Moana looks alarmed. "So what kind of stuff do they ban?"

"Stuff that they have found so toxic that they can no longer afford the cost of court cases against its use. It has to get that bad, usually."

"Sounds like the tobacco industry tactics."

"Very similar lack of ethics."

"So Tony is really playing into their hands, then? He thinks he's onto a good deal, but he's just a pawn to them, right?"

"Afraid so, Moana. And you need to tell him this, if you can."

"I need some distance from him at present. He's been harassing the kids."

And you, by the looks, thinks Koa, noticing the faded bruise on her cheeks. "Maybe Cowrie, Iri and I could pay him a visit?"

"I don't think he'd take any notice. See if you can send Piripi and the boys up to talk to him, eh?"

"Shall do. Thanks, Moana. But what about your kids? Have they been showing any signs of poisoning?"

"What should I look for?"

"Vomiting, diarrhoea, skin rashes, drowsiness, depends on what's been sprayed and how close they are to it."

"Tony takes them out with him when he sprays. They love to use the backpacks and sprayers. It's like Luke Skywalker with his laser gun to them."

Koa blanches. "Then you need to get them to a doctor fast."

"We've been to the local GP and they have had tests at Rawene Hospital. Said it could be a mixture of pollen and the winter flu."

"More like pesticides, if you ask me. Hang in there, Moana, as we're hoping to get a pesticide poisoning expert up to test all the schoolkids. But we do not want to alarm the parents yet. Would you be supportive of this?"

"I sure would. It'd be a load off my mind. Thanks, Koa. You and Iri are doing marvellous work at the nursery and I'd like to come and help out. I have more time now that I am not cleaning for Tony and since we prepare the food communally here on the marae."

"We'd love to have you at the nursery. Bring the boys after school too, 'cos we have a programme going for kids. Once they get involved in planting and harvesting from their own organic gardens, they will never want to use these sprays again."

"Thanks, Koa. That's brilliant. They wouldn't listen to reason on this – but if you can get them involved in experiencing something for themselves, then they will be open to it. Mattiu will be a starter for sure. Ever since he saw his father spray to death a small sparrow in his way, he never felt the same about him afterwards."

Koa grimaces. "I'm not surprised. I'll talk to Piripi about this tonight."

"Be discreet, Koa. Tony has his male pride and all that."

"No worries, Moana. That's a common problem. Nothing that a dose of love won't fix."

"Now I could get into that. Spraying more love about the fields is what we need. Maybe we could convince that Flyworks fella to fill his helicopter sprayers with Aroha, eh?" Moana giggles at the thought.

"Ka pae, Moana. Now what's that you have in your hand? We'd better get going or Mere will be back to us soon."

Moana pulls a luscious yellow flower with thick leaves like a cactus from the pile in front of them. "Looks like ice plant to me. Grows wild all over the sand dunes."

80

"Hottentot fig."

"Strange name."

"*Carpobrotus edulis*, actually. Its fig-like luscious fruits were eaten by the Hottentot tribes of Africa, and they used the leaves to make an excellent pickle."

"Yum. I could get into that!" Moana's eyes light up. "Mere, what's the local name for this ice plant?"

"Horokaka. Pig Face. See the snout inside the flower stems. Looks just like a kunekune pig!"

"So it does. Fascinating."

Next they are amazed to taste the rhizomes of the rengarenga rock lily, which grows near the sea and often hangs down from rocky ledges. Mere explains it was found in the early days near Maori whare and plantations. Koa adds that, according to her research, the sprouts of a very similar lily were eaten by tribes in South Africa, and that Aboriginals in Australia ate the roots of another related lily that resembles the rengarenga. Even the young shoots and pollen of the raupo are edible, and quite sweet. These bulrushes were once used in thatching the early whare and for making small canoes and rafts. Cowrie reckons they are also wonderful for making kites as well. "Edible kites, now that's a marketable proposition," she jokes. "The Californians would love that one!" They laugh. The pollen tastes a bit like mustard and they debate whether it could be used as a substitute.

When it comes to eating the tender shoots of the golden pingao, which grows over their sand dunes, Mere warns them that they are needed for weaving and to be wary when harvesting as this is now a resource that needs to be carefully protected. She shows them a delicately woven pingao bag by Toi te Rito Maihi, who has used the base of the shoots with flair in her design so that they fly out from the elongated kete as if wings. Cowrie imagines a sky full of such winged creatures, golden against the azure blue, shooting their way heavenwards, born of the earth but returning to the sky, as if bringing Rangi and Papatuanuku closer together by their daring act of levitation. She smiles, thinking of how Toi would laugh at the image and how Chagall would have loved to paint such flaxen angels alongside his flying blue violins and heavenly winged creatures.

Banners spike the air like flying fish. No Frankenfish . . .
Keep Aotearoa Clean and Green . . . Tino Rangitiratanga
. . . No Field Trials . . . Keep Aotearoa GE-Free . . . No
Nukes, No Genes . . . Bio Gro – Not Monsanto! . . . GE-
Free New Zealand . . . Ours for the Picking . . . Safe
Food, Sure Markets, Treasured Land – Aotearoa . . .
Bring Genoa to Aotearoa: Oppose Globalisation . . .
Save Our Sacred Toanga: Vote Green Now!

At the sidelines, three lonely pro-GE campaigners.
Bright Future or Dark Ages: Vote For GE or Be Doomed
. . . God Knows Best: Trust Him . . . Jesus for Genes: Our
Saviour. Nobody takes much notice of the loony-right
God Squad these days. They are left to their own devices
and people know there is not much point in even
debating the issues with such rigid fundamentalists. A
decade ago, they would have been pelted with rotten
eggs. Now they even receive a few sympathetic smiles,
as if at a wake for their own future.

Among the marchers, they recognise several other
Nga Puhi and Tainui families and even a few kin from
as far south as Ngai Tahu country. There are mothers
and fathers with their tamariki and mokupuna, doctors
and lawyers, farmers and organic growers, students,
scientists and even a banner proclaiming "Physicians

83

and Scientists for a GE-Free Future." Around them are stalls bursting with organic fruit and vegetables as it is their market day, and an atmosphere of celebration and rebellion surrounds tangata whenua and Pakeha alike.

There are Maori and Dalmatian, Samoan, Rarotongan, Niue Islanders, Aboriginal, English, Scottish, Welsh, Canadian, US, German and Ozzie Kiwis chatting and debating the issues and sharing kai before the marchers rally for the opening of the hikoi. Finally, as everyone is declared to be present, a karanga is called from the local marae. The marchers are welcomed with a blessing and karakia before they begin this long and arduous journey from Tai Tokerau. They will travel through the hills and lakes and shores of Aotearoa until they reach the parliament buildings in Poneke, the capital city of Wellington, where they will be greeted by politicians from all sides of the debate.

Cowrie, Kuini and several families from Te Kotuku marae are joining the hikoi. Some will go as far as Wellington, some back to the Hokianga because they cannot afford time away from work or their gardens. Iri, Koa and Mere have remained on the marae to keep the energy brewing and the tamariki and food supplies cared for.

"There is a proud tradition of hikoi in Aotearoa. We have marched as tangata whenua for our land, for our sovereign rights, for our sacred kai moana, and now we march to honour Papatuanuku and keep her free from GE interference." The crowd roars approval. "Many of us have sick relatives. We say to you all we do not oppose carefully monitored lab trials in order to find

84

cures for these diseases. But we are all opposed to the GE assault on Papatuanuku, just as we opposed her rape and degradation when US and French colonial governments invaded our Pacific Islands and used them to test their nuclear weapons." Another roar from the crowd and much hooting of approval. "And gradually we got the population of Aotearoa behind us to declare ourselves nuclear-free." A ripple of "kia ora" from the tangata whenua.

"Today is no different. We already know that 92 per cent of the submissions by Kiwis to the Royal Commission on Genetic Engineering are emphatically against its use." Cheers and clapping. "We represent many groups here today, and we are united in our opposition to GE and especially to field trials. We must make the government retain the moratorium on field trials and encourage Aotearoans to become the first entirely organic, GE-free country in the world. We will then be the sacred pearl in the oyster of the Pacific, of the world, and we will convince others to join us. This is our future: an organic GE-free Aotearoa by 2020. Kia ora."

Many more speeches by the Greens, Mana Motuhake, the Alliance, organic growers, tangata whenua, Soil and Health, and anyone who wants to have a say are heard between roars of approval and a few cries of doom from the God Squad. After a final farewell feast of kai moana and organic produce, they begin walking, singing waiata as they go, adults and children, scientists and dykes, doctors and gays, feminists and greenies, farmers and ecologists, hand in hand, joined in song. A native wood pigeon with green and brown feathers and a fat white belly flies over and looks down on the crowd, seeing a multi-coloured rainbow making its way magically down the main route to Auckland. She rises up onto a wind surge and then glides down over them, dropping a sacred red puriri berry that lands on the red, black and white tino rangatiratanga flag, held horizontally by the marchers.

The scarlet berry slides from side to side of the flag as they march, unaware they have been so appropriately blessed, until there is a pause and the berry drops down into the waiting kete of a kuia. She notices its arrival and smiles. The hikoi has been blessed. She now knows that, despite all the trials they may endure on the way, they will make it safely to their destination. But even that will only be a beginning. There's a long hard summer to come. Her dreams told her this and they must be prepared for all eventualities. Yet the berry taonga encourages her, urges her on. Tonight she will share this blessing with the others and sing waiata to the kukupa who flew over them, casting down safe food onto their flag of resistance, their future. A symbol of their potential.

Moana now spends her afternoons at the nursery, and the boys wander in when school is finished. They have established their own gardens alongside those of the other tamariki, and Moana is delighted that they are so into it. They were reluctant at first – but once they saw how enthusiastic the other kids were and got to sample some of the fruits of their hard labour, they became very keen. Mattiu is entranced by the orange, yellow and red bell peppers and declares he will become a pepper farmer when he grows up. Hemi likes the small bright purple eggplants, though he reckons they look better than they taste. "Wait till you have some of my eggplant parmesan," Koa tempts him, "then you will want to grow them forever!" Hemi is not yet convinced, but he is hooked by the beauty of the plants and the transformation from bud to flower to fruit. Ropata likes the lettuces and the tiny mesclun mix full of mustards and small magical plants that finally make a salad taste decent. He wants to grow nasturtiums all around his plot as he loves their bright yellow and orange faces cheerily waving in the wind.

"Look at them, Koa. You'd never believe these tamariki were bedridden most of the winter, eh?"

"D'ya reckon they have fully healed yet or are there

still signs of the poisoning?" Koa drops a large bucket of fruit peelings into the compost heap and covers it with grass clippings and shredded recycled paper.

"They have not fully recovered. They get tired easily and their mood changes are in flux still. Could be to do with the separation from their dad. The older boys find it hard just seeing him on the weekends, but Mattiu seems relieved not to return to the farm unless he wants to."

"Ka pae. But how is Tony coping without you, Moana?"

"Sounds like he has it sussed, Koa. The boys say he has a girlfriend who stays over there from time to time and does his housework for him. Daughter of that Flyworks fella, actually."

"Heaven help him then. I bet he is still taking all their reject poisons."

"Dunno. How did it go with Piripi and the boys when they visited him?"

"They didn't get far. He took out his .22 and said he'd blow their brown faces to hell if they came any further onto his land. Accused them of stealing his missus and he'd get even."

Moana stiffens. "This is what I most feared."

"It's okay. You're safe here on the marae, Moana. We'll protect you. He will not get near and we can leave him alone to poison himself and his land. When he finally gives up the land, we'll buy it back and begin the long process of cleansing it and letting it return to bush. Some of it can be planted eventually, but only after it has healed."

"You don't know Tony. I don't think he'll give up that

easily. Too bloody stubborn. He'll hang in there until the end. He's like the tough Kiwi fellas that Bruno Lawrence plays in our films. I could imagine him barricading himself in and fighting back with over-sized double-barrelled guns, or burning the land so that nobody else can enjoy it." Moana sighs. "But I am glad I got the kids away from that energy. They are finally beginning to relax again now."

"Ka pae, Moana. And you." Koa heaps up the compost with another layer of cut kikuyu grass.

"You don't want to use that stuff, Koa. It is a devil to get rid of when it springs to life in your garden. It spreads like wildfire and runs along under the earth and invades everything else you try to grow."

"You're right, Moana – but it also makes an excellent mulch. It's an African grass that is actually quite grace-ful. It's just that we have come to always think of it as a weed, or an invader. Your Tony would zap it with chemicals, no doubt. But if we manage to understand how it works, we can make good use of it. Most of our compost heaps comprise at least a quarter of shredded kikuyu grass. And look at how rich they are. So long as you keep turning them over and letting the air circulate, you have some of the best compost on earth. The worms love dancing through the kikuyu, and the shredded paper gives them air to breathe. Then they feast on the fruit and vegetable peelings. Not a bad life, really."

"Yeah – perhaps you're right, Koa. Maybe if we altered our view of human invaders and thought how we could transform their activities to be of some use on this earth, we could change them too."

"Perhaps, Moana. Let's hope so." Koa turns over the compost with her pitchfork and the feasting earthworms wriggle and dive back into their warm, steamy pile. "See all that land at the edge of the forest? It was originally clay and kikuyu grass where the early farmers burned the trees for their farms. We reclaimed it with clean, recycled cardboard and paper and added layers and layers of kikuyu mulch, sand and compost until we had raised garden beds to plant the kumara and potatoes and urenika. Now look at them thriving."

Moana admires the mounds covered in various shades of green foliage, from the heart-shaped leaves of the purple and red kumara to the furry fat leaves of the Maori potatoes and urenika, with their beautiful white and yellow flowers. "Beats roses any day. At least you can eat them as well as admire them."

"Some people eat roses too. The petals can be used for jams and preserves and are quite luscious, actually." Koa grins.

"You having me on?"

"No, it's true. Ask Iri." Moana turns around, but sees that Iri is bent over her laptop powered by the generator.

"Come over here, you two," calls Iri. "There's an email from Cowrie and Kuini." She reads:

Kia ora Te Kotuku. Cowrie and Kuini here. Just found a great email café in Kaiwaka, can you believe it? The march is going well. You'll never believe what happened the first day. One of the Nga Puhi kuia found a puriri berry dropped by a kukupa in her flax kete. She told us it was a blessing for our protest and it meant we would be safe, though she had a

90

premonition that this protest would only be a beginning. Some interpreted that as Helen Clark giving in to the multinationals, but we cannot believe that she would do this. Anyway, we've had an awesome time. Everywhere we go, there are people clapping us on and tooting horns as they go past. Every town we reach, tangata whenua are there with delicious kai for the journey.

People in Kawakawa told us that there was a helicopter spill of dangerous chemicals two weeks ago. Get Maata to check the books and see if it was Flyworks. The local council say it must be aerial spray drift or pollen and there's nothing they can do about either. But the locals are convinced it was more than that as the whole town was dusted and people had to go indoors all afternoon. It lasted for days and yet nobody has taken any responsibility. There was a protest outside the town loos as we passed. We stopped to join in. They had laid flowers for the passing of Hundertwasser, which they do each year now, and people were singing waiata and praying karakia. They also vowed to set up a fund to fight any agro-chemical battles in the region, in honour of what Hundertwasser and local iwi had given to the township by putting it on the map with their wonderful loos made from recycled materials which look more like a Turkish bath house.

The Kawakawa loos have an awesome atmosphere. Rounded earthen walls with brightly coloured bottles inlaid into the clay, beautiful basins crafted from porcelain and handmade tiles by the local tamariki as well as artists. Imagine a place to recycle human excrement being turned into a palace of celebration of the earth and of art. What a radical thing has happened here, where the best of European alternative energy has been combined with a genuine respect for working with tangata whenua, local artists and the people of the township. At first they were suspicious of it all, but now they praise the day Hundertwasser came to town and the tangata whenua embraced his ideas.

Now we're in Kaiwaka and we are going up to visit the Otamatea Eco-Village to stay the night on their marae and see how they are building sustainable houses, and the next day we go to the Kaiwaka Organic Green Market and Koanga Gardens. We'll spend another night there, after Kay Baxter takes us around, and then head on down through the Dome Valley. We'll email you again from Kaiwaka after our visits. We are having some great korero on the way and learning heaps. More soon. Hope you are all well.

Kia kaha

Arohanui

Cowrie and Kuini xx.

The bright moonlight guides her way as Irihapeti throws more manuka logs onto the fire, then joins Koa in the hot tub. It is fed by heat from the fire through recycled hot-water cylinder pipes, into the wooden wine barrel which they love to soak in at night. Iri floats into Koa's arms and lies there, cuddled into her warmth, both of them facing the moon as it rises above the mamaku, its sprouting fronds like an orchestra of violins facing the sky.

"You sad you didn't go on the GE protest march, Iri?" Koa looks down into her face lovingly. "I know you stayed here to look after me as well as the nursery. You knew I was not yet up to such a gruelling pace."

Iri laughs. "Doesn't sound too gruelling to me, Koa. According to Cowrie, they are having plenty of rest and really enjoying the trip as well as learning about GE-free organic practices on the way. That is exactly as it should be. No point in stating we are GE-free without showing what real alternatives we can offer. The more they discover about what is actually happening out there, the more we can truly envision a GE-free future and share this with other Aotearoans."

"Yeah, but I bet you wish you were there too."

Iri looks up into Koa's face. "A part of me does – but

I would never leave you here alone either, Koa. The nursery is not ready to look after itself, and we need to be here for the tamariki and their gardens. No, truly, I can say I am very happy to be here with you, my love. Besides, I'd miss cuddling into these luscious large breasts at night and you telling me stories."

"Me too. Glad you stayed here. Thanks, Iri. Besides, Cowrie and Kuini will keep us posted via the email cafés. They are dotted all over Aotearoa now, even in small towns like Kaiwaka. It's great."

"And so are you." Iri kisses Koa on her cheek, then her lips. They snuggle close as the wekas cry their shrill sounds into the night air and the morepork calls from a puriri at one end of the forest to the large kanuka in the distance. Another morepork replies, and they keep up their communication at regular intervals, with scruffling sounds in between as the water rats and possums go about their nightly business. A perfect crescent moon moves slowly higher and lights up more of the treetops. The bright eyes of a fat possum stare down at them from the closest kanuka. Iri sighs. "All those stories about a man in the moon when I grew up. How did they know it was a bloke? Maybe it was a luscious, large wahine toa."

Koa laughs. "You might be right, Iri. My sister is married to a fella from Hilo, Hawai'i, called Kane, and he told us about Hina-hanaia-i-ka-malama. Her name literally means the woman who worked in the moon. Kilinahi Kaleo reckon Hina is Pele's name when she in the sky, and she is Pele when on the earth. Anyway, as one version of the story goes, Hina is the grand-daughter of Kai-uli and

94

Kai-kea – that's the Dark and the Light Sea. Her parents can take the form of pao'o fishes. They have ten kids, some in the form of fish and some birds. One of the kids neglects his sister and escapes to the heavens, leaving her the calabash, Kipapa-lau-lau, which contains the moon and stars for her vegetable and fish food."

"Imagine eating the moon and stars. Incredible." Iri snuggles closer into Koa. She loves her talkstory in the hot tub at night.

"Settle down, my kotuku. Now, where was I? Right. So the sister meets a chief and they have another ten kids – five boys and five girls . . ."

"They breed like rabbits . . ."

"Shoosh, kotuku, d'you want to hear more or not?"

Iri nudges ever closer in response. "Okay. One of these kids is banished to Maui for sacrilege and he dies, but from his dead body the wauke plant springs, which is used for bark cloth – like our Pacific tapa cloth here. Anyway, his sisters search for him on the island of Oahu and they get turned into fish ponds, each stocked with special ika for which the island was famed. So, from Hina, the woman in the moon, and her offspring, we have magnificent tapa cloth from the wauke plant and a constant supply of fish waiting for us in their ponds."

"So there was a woman in the moon after all?" Iri looks pleased.

"According to Kane."

"Have you ever told Cowrie this? She'd be rapt. You know she has Hawai'ian blood also?"

"No. We've not spoken of this."

"Her grandfather, Apelahama, lived on the Big Island

and she went back to visit and meet her cousin Koana a few years ago. She returned full of the warm richness of the islands and said that the Maori and Hawai'ian languages and mythology are so similar that it is clear we are deeply connected. A fisherman, Keo, even took her to the spot where he said the first canoes left for Aotearoa. Ka Lae, I think."

"Kane talked about that place too. Said some fishermen were killed there while protesting US nuclear involvement and the desecration of the sacred island of Koho'olawe for their military installations."

Iri splashes water up her arm. "You have to korero with Cowrie about all this. She knows the fishermen who were murdered."

"Incredible. Maybe she and Kane are cuzzy bros?" Koa enjoys the thought.

"It wouldn't be the first time, eh?" Iri lies back in Koa's arms. "Is the calabash a kind of gourd?"

"Yes, it was usually made from coconut. Another story has a wahine sending for her coconut gourd and its contents fly up toward heaven in the form of a perfect crescent moon, just like we have tonight, the bright part called kena, the darker side, ana."

"So maybe that's how the moon was said to be made from cheese, only it was really coconut cream?"

"Not so crazy, Iri. I'd never thought about that. Magic, eh?" Koa holds Irihapeti and caresses her shoulders as Hina smiles down on them from her heavenly home, capturing the sparks of water on their bodies and making them glisten like stars dancing on the galaxies of their arms which float on a mythical ocean.

Maata peers through the Flyworks' window at the tarmac as she makes a late afternoon cuppa. Raymond is talking to a tall, large fellow she has seen him with from time to time. He must be one of the chaps that takes away unused and empty cans of poison as he has a big truck and she's seen them loading the plastic containers onto the back of it. She checks the front office. Barbara Dixon is collecting the kids from school and her daughter is inside the truck cab. Maybe this is the new boyfriend her daughter has been gloating over? He didn't sound too nice to Maata – but you never can tell from the outside. She makes sure nobody is in reception then slips into the back office to check the files. Out of her breast pocket she takes the slip of paper bearing a time and day that Irihapeti has written down for her and carefully goes back through the rosters and flight schedules. Finally she finds it. *Tuesday 18th, 2–5 pm. Farm #308. Due for DDT drop. Turn right over Kawakawa and start past the tall poplar grove. Dust fields 3-18. Marked with red crosses. NB. Flight abandoned. Sprayer buggered. Had to drop load over Zone B. Reschedule drop for next Tuesday.* The right date, the right time. She carefully takes the sheet from the folder and photocopies it, just as Raymond enters the lunchroom with his guest. She freezes, hoping he will not come through to the office. She hears their voices over the hum of the machine.

"Jeesus, Tony. Ya don't wanna freak out over a few brownies coming to dust you up a bit. You were right to point yer .22 at them and tell 'em to go to hell. They have no business stealing your wife and kids and then intruding on your property to tell you what to do with it. Next thing, they'll be landing you with some Treaty of Waitangi claim. Just stay put and don't give up your ground." Raymond thumps his cup onto the table and throws in a bag of gumboot tea. "Hand us the billy, will ya, Tony? Dunno where my waitress is hanging out today – but she's a good worker so I'm not complaining." He laughs.

Maata stiffens at being called a waitress and vows to show him she is not just his tea server when she gets the chance. But not now, while still holding the evidence. She slips the paper into her breast pocket, places the folder back into its file and closes it. Just in time. Raymond pokes his nose through the door. "Wanna cuppa?"

"No thanks. Still more filing to do."

"That's my girl. You won't mind if we shut the door then. Bit of a breeze here today."

"No worries. Thanks, Mr Dixon."

Raymond returns to the lunchroom and closes the door behind him. Maata suspects it must be private, but by now her suspicions have been aroused, so she gets up on a chair and leans up against the back wall where the open windows of both rooms are less than a metre from each other. Not very bright, these boys. After a while, their voices rise to a pitch. She can hear them clearly.

"But how do I get rid of the evidence? I've now got a barn full of used containers of bloody herbicides and pesticides that have been banned for years and I can't just take them to the dump."

"Then do what I do. Just get your digger and dredge out a bloody huge hole once a month and dump the containers in and chuck some earth over them. You are more isolated than us. Nobody will ever know. You could do it in broad daylight. We have to do it at night or before 5 am."

"But won't people notice the mounds and the digger always being used?"

"No worries, Tony. Every now and again we burn a few tyres to put people off the scent. If anyone says anything, we deny it. Then if they get ratty, we admit we burned a few tyres that day and they are so impressed by our honesty, it shuts them up for a while."

"Does that work?"

"Sure as pigshit, mate. Puts them right off the scent. One greenie fella even took some photos of us burning banned herbicides. That freaked us out for a minute. But luckily he was too far away and it could've been any field in the end. We zapped the lawyer onto him and that shut him up. He has no money and he was freaked out that he'd end up with large legal bills. That usually works with greenies – so long as they don't have Eco-Nazis like Greenpeace or Friends of the Earth behind 'em. They have the bikky to pay lawyers. That's when you have to get really clever."

"Whad'ya mean?"

"I learned a few tricks when flying choppers for ForestsFirst. Their lawyers and their PR spinners were like a Saatchi and Saatchi of the Underworld. They'd lean on a few supporters and get them to write emails and letters against the protesters, form groups that seemed to comprise interested Coasters but they were just being used for their cause. They'd hype up the scare of losing jobs and get the locals on board. That way, they had most of their workers and all the councils and public on their side against the greenies and conservationists. Sometimes they'd even write letters in wriggly handwriting on scraps of paper pretending to be old Mrs Gumboot of Okarito who was worried 'cos her son was going to lose his job, etc. Worked a treat."

"Really? You're not just makin' this up, are ya?"

"If ya don't believe me, Tony, I'll lend ya a book that proves it. Some eco-nut called Nicky Hagar. He's into Greenpeace and all those eco-groups. Anyway, he documented it all after ForestsFirst was finally exposed and it was even better than I thought. Clever buggers, all the way. Me eyes were poppin' out like organ stops reading it."

"Not so clever they didn't get caught out though, eh Ray? And that's what worries me. I'd never get Moana and the kids back if they nicked me using dumped toxins or if I ended up in jail for it. Been there before, just for passing on a few cheap CDs and VCRs to some of her own cuzzie bros too. You'd think she'd be pleased. But Moana said if I was ever dishonest again, she'd leave and take the kids with her."

Raymond smiles. "Tony, mate. Now you have a free

run. You should be thanking your lucky stars. I'd do anything to be a bachelor again, only I need the missus and the kids to help run the business. But I long for the good old days with the boys. The only fun we get now is up in the chopper. We do a few tokes of Northland Green, best dope in the country, while we're flying. Gary reckons you get higher on dope in the air. Haha. Bloody right too. It's a real buzz. We'll take you up and give you a toke. Maybe dust your farm for free once a year since you're helping us out a bit, eh? How'd'ya like that?"

"Be great, mate. I'm on anytime."

Raymond pauses. He's on a roll now. And he's been waiting for this moment. "Whatya gonna do with that huge farm now the missus has gone, Tony?"

"Dunno. I can't run it on me own and can't afford to hire anyone, either."

"I might be able to help yer out a bit there, mate."

"How come?"

"Got some friends in high places. When at ForestsFirst, we got to have a few tokes with the best of 'em and mixed with all these government dudes and scientists. Not as bad as you'd think. Anyway, one of them works for a group funded by MagicMilk, International Seed Corporation and backed by FarmCorp, and he said they are after some isolated blocks of land, well away from main townships where greenies hang out, to run some trials to test genetically engineered plants and animals."

Tony's eyes light up big time. "Like Dolly the Sheep and all that? For real?"

"Yep. You got it. But much better than Dolly. They're onto some sort of cross-gene stuff. I dunno the details.

101

Maybe sticking a pig's head onto some mutton for a lamb and bacon treat – who knows. But they could use those burial caves on your land and nobody would ever know, eh? Plus the old barns. They are after places that cannot be identified 'cos they reckon after the GE Royal Commission decision comes out, they might have to go underground, literally, to do their tests. They wanna be prepared. You on?"

"Shit, Ray. This sounds massive. I dunno."

Ray slaps Tony on the back. "You'd be mad to turn 'em down, mate. It'll mean big bikkies. Cash in the hand. And more than you'd ever earn slaving your guts out as a farmer every day – gettin' up early to milk those bloody cows."

"How much, Ray?"

"Can't tell you exact sums, but it's more than you'd ever imagine. Especially if they get a world first on your farm. You could be part-owner of Porky-Baa, the first baaing pig, which tastes delicious for all I know! C'mon, Tony. You in?"

"What's in it for you, Ray?" Tony is suddenly suspicious.

"Just a few back-handers. Bit of a commission, as agent, just as you'd pay a real estate broker. Besides, we'd fly these government dudes up and down, and then there's all the PR people and foreign investors. Could keep us both rich for a while to come, mate. It'll bring money into the Hokianga for others in business and we'd get rich and be heroes for it too, once the experiments are done and over. But it's gotta be top-level secret for now. Ya can't tell anyone. I won't even tell the missus. You'll have to sign a pledge and if you break it, you'll lose everything."

Tony sips his tea quietly, mulling it all over. Just yesterday, he felt helpless and wanted revenge because Moana and the kids had left him. He'd even thought about seeing if the brown fellas could talk her into returning. But now, he has an even better future ahead. Once he could get rich quick, he'd be able to get a lawyer and get the boys back off Moana. If she would not come back – he'd force them home and then she would follow. He knows her maternal instincts would be to stay with them. Then they'd all be sweet. His anger was only when he was pushed up against the wall, too many bills to pay, not enough help on the farm. This way, he'd have everything, and fast. "Okay, Ray. Bring it on! When can I meet some of these fellas and talk over a deal?"

"As it happens, we're flying them up here next week. They're keen to get some land sorted before the GM Royal Commission makes its rulings and before that bloody left-wing Labour–Alliance–Green lot get their mitts stuck into it. They could ban field trials and ban GE altogether if the greenies can convince them we should be organic and GE-free."

"It'll never happen. Too many sensible farmers out there."

"That's what we all said about nuclear power and nuclear weapons as a deterrent, Tony. But look how those lefties got mainstream Kiwis on board. Never did trust that Marilyn Waring sheila. What's a lefty lezzie like her doing in the National Party anyway? We're a party of farmers and politicians. If she'd never walked over the floor of parliament and joined the Labour opposition over the nuclear-free issue, we might never have gone down that path."

"Na. The lefties had Muldoon by the balls anyway by then, Ray. He lost it on whisky that night and it was the beginning of the end. The greenies and eco-activists and gays have run the country ever since, even when the Nats were in power. They've been whittling away at the edges, and we'd all hoped the GE decision would come when the Nats were in power. We'd have no worries then. Federated Famers are all for genetic engineering, bar a few greenies. Now we have MagicMilk, we'll be looked after by the Big Boys, so long as they can get the government to come to the party."

"No worries, Tony. Money and power always win out. You'll see."

Tony finishes his tea and burps. "Looking forward to that meeting, Ray. Give me a bell soon, eh? I think I'll go down the pub and celebrate tonight."

"Okay. See you there. But no blabbing. This has to remain top secret or you'll never have a chance in hell of getting a rich, fat lease on your land."

"Mum's the word then, Ray. See ya." Tony saunters out of the lunchroom, feeling better than he has in ages. Finally, some light on the horizon.

Maata steps down from the chair and closes the window. She's still in a state of shock. Raymond and Barbara have been really nice to her since she started work and she never dreamed that he'd be into something underhand until Irihapeti had asked her to check the records for the day of the Kawakawa poisoning. And now it sounds as if he's into some subterfuge. But what can she do? She'll lose her first ever job if she lets on – and maybe it could be even more dangerous for her. She cannot tell Barbara, because she does not know about it. Who'd ever believe this, apart from Cowrie and Iri and the others at Te Kotuku?

She decides to keep quiet for a while and just monitor the situation carefully. Maybe it's all above-board anyway? Maybe Kawakawa was a genuine accident. And perhaps the scientists do have to keep their work secret for fear of trials being interrupted and crops destroyed. She'd seen heaps of examples of genetically altered rape seed and corn trials being ripped out by activists in Europe and England on TV and on the net. And people suffering from terrible diseases that could be cured by genetically engineered solutions. Maybe the others at Te Kotuku are so set against GE that they do not understand some of the good it will do? Maata breathes a sigh of relief. She does not have to give up her job. Not yet. She'll see what actual harm happens, see with her own eyes, now she is an adult herself, before jumping on a bandwagon for anyone. She takes out the sheet of paper copied from the files and puts it through the shredder.

Irihapeti reads the next email from Kuini and Cowrie to the Te Kotuku nursery workers:

Tena koutou katoa – We're back at the email café in Kaiwaka after an amazing two days. Firstly, we went up a long winding road to the right of the Three Furlongs Pub leading up to the Otamatea Eco-Village. We were greeted in an old barn with an earthen floor full of broken, coloured tiles and sunlight gaping through the holes in the walls. It was very quaint, but bloody cold later that night when we slept on the floor!

The collective explained their philosophy and their vision in building from eco materials and using solar and wind energy. They each have five-acre blocks of land sloping down from the ridge into the calm waters of the upper Kaipara Harbour. Beautiful land. We could picture a pa on those slopes and wondered how our ancestors may have lived there once. The group is mostly European ecologists from Germany, Holland and other northern countries, often married to Kiwi men and women. They seem highly educated and very genuine. But once we got to look around their houses and discover what materials they were using and how they'd learned by experimenting, we also realised that most of them had plenty of bikky to start with. No shacks or huts like home. Some of these places have two or three main buildings, and the timber alone would be worth a fortune. However, we still liked their courage and their vision. Some have erected wind turbos for their power – though they said it makes the internet pretty slow and they have to negotiate time on-line! A bit like us with our old generator. Wouldn't mind trying some wind power at Te Kotuku, and one of the women said she'd help us design a system, so we're rapt.

Another wahine had a house which she described as Fairyland. She's very creative and a real character. We liked the wooden houses best, and we're impressed by the work they have done on the land already – transforming clay and kikuyu back to bush and a working organic garden by composting and mulching. But it was a shock to see so few trees up there. The land has been raped by farmers and it'll take some time to heal. They were very interested in our work at Te Kotuku and asked if they could come and see the nursery sometime. We said any time after the GE march would be okay – unless you want them earlier, Iri. We've given them your email address anyway. The German woman who sells cheese at the Kaiwaka Organic Market is pretty cute. Turns out she's written some organic cookbooks too. We should check these out. We liked her – a real sparkle in the eye and very sharp. Kuini teased me about liking her and how I go for those women from the north, but I assured her I am very happy to be single and focused on our work right now. [That's her version – I'll tell you the rest when I get back – Kuini] . . .

Anyway, it was fascinating seeing how they are using alternative ways of designing and constructing their houses using Permaculture principles. They're deeply into this Permaculture thing – but really, it's pretty much the ancient principles our ancestors used, adapted to modern ways. Letting intuition make the design. What they lacked in organic gardening, simply because they are still building their homes, was made up for by our visit to Koanga Gardens the next day. It endorsed all your work at Te

Kotuku nursery, Iri and Koa. Kay Baxter and the people there have built up impressive vegetable gardens and orchards using old heirloom seeds gathered on Kay's trips around Aotearoa, and they are now wanting to utilise the native forest more, learn about Rongoa Maori. We told them of your workshops, Mere, and they were very interested.

Another woman explained the gathering of heirloom seeds and the people they have all over the country now collecting and saving seeds. There's a whole Pakeha network out there and we could combine this with our own programme for tangata whenua and see which partnerships can benefit all. Last night, we stayed in their workshop space. They are also building a marae next door. We talked late into the night, shared knowledge about our experiments in working with plants and, of course, all the issues that concern us around genetic engineering. Spoke to another woman who got dusted in Kawakawa. We're wondering if Maata has had time to check out the flight schedules at Flyworks yet? I guess we'll find out on our return.

Gotta go. There's a busload of German backpackers trundling in here now and we wanna check out the whitebait fritters and kingfish at the Kaiwaka takeaways before heading on. We're going to trek through the ferns in the Dome Valley now and we're making a diversion through Matakana to visit Jo Polaischer's Rainbow Valley Organic Farm. We've heard heaps about it and are really looking forward to it. More later. We've found out there's another internet café in Warkworth and the kai is good too – so we'll try emailing from there. Hope you're all well and thriving. The energy on the hikoi is great. We might be up against the multinationals but we sure have strength within the ranks. We need to do this for the good of future generations also.

As we said to the Otamatea folks: Toitu he kainga, whatu ngarongaro he tangata: *The land still remains when the people have disappeared.*

This is now our emblem and we've painted it onto a large sheet to carry with us, in Maori and in English, for all to appreciate.

Kia kaha

Cowrie and Kuini.

Maata's best friend is Waka. He's always been a good mate to her and she knows she can rely on him. Today they have trekked to the highest dunes and now stand in the wind looking down over the Hokianga Harbour, their sandboards under their arms. The blue-green water stretches out beneath them, swirling towards a rip at the harbour entrance where ancient sailing ships from England went aground, unable to negotiate the rough and treacherous Hokianga Heads. Maata recalls the day they farewelled the *Manawa Toa* from here to join the peace flotilla to protest nuclear testing at Moruroa. She feels a pang of guilt that maybe she has not fulfilled the wishes of her Aunty Cowrie in carrying out the task to spy on Flyworks. Then again, how could they ask her to betray her own employers who support her to bring money and resources back into the marae? The decision has not been easy. They look south towards the far dunes, Omapere and the mighty Waipoua Kauri Forest in the distance.

"Race you to the sea," yells Waka.

Before he has had a chance to move, Maata throws her board down on the sand and lunges onto it, lifting her legs, bent at the knee, in the air, knowing she needs an advantage as his heavier body will propel him faster.

Waka grins, diving onto his board, and they shoot down the largest dune at a fast pace, sending some pied oyster-catchers squawking to their side. The thrill of the run is exhilarating as the sand whips their faces, the dunes flee past and the water comes closer by the second. Waka catches up with Maata and nearly overtakes her, but one of the torea flies right in front of him and he swerves to avoid it, losing precious seconds. Maata screams with glee as she surfs down the dune and into the waves and Waka swooshes in next to her, sending his wake over her body. She splashes him and they use their boards to spray each other with wave after wave of refreshing water after the long dune trek, laughing and relieved to be in the sea again.

Afterwards, they stretch out in the warm sand, their arms behind their heads, and talk. Waka describes to her the design he has in mind for his part of the marae workshop extension. "I wanna use traditional designs, but also my own imagination. I'll work with the theme of the kotuku, but interweave fern fronds into the design with some of the creatures of our bush featured also – like the giant cave weta and the bush weta. I love those insects – they are so ancient and powerful. Kind of primeval, really."

"Ugh. I'm not that fond of wetas but I can appreciate their beauty from a distance." Maata grimaces. "D'ya know that they're s'posed to be one of the two insects, along with the cockroach, that'd survive a nuclear holocaust?"

"No kidding? That's pretty heavy for such a beautiful day, Maata."

"Yeah. Maybe so."

"You got something on your mind?"

"Why d'ya say that?"

"You've been kinda distracted the last few days."

"Mmm. Just work."

"You sure?"

"Yep." Maata turns over, her back to Waka. They lie like this in silence for a while. Maata goes into a deep sleep in the sun. She has not been resting well at night. She dreams she is walking through the forest gathering flowers and leaves and berries, and a bird is caught in a trap over a pond. She wades into the pond to free the bird but begins to sink. She is in quicksand and it is getting deeper by the minute. The bird screeches and screeches until she can bear it no longer. She is being buried alive as the thick black sand comes up to her waist and then over her arms. She screams.

"Yo, Maata. What is it? You're here, safe with me." Waka bends over her, smoothing her hair. He sees the fear in her eyes. Gradually, Maata comes around and realises she is in the sun on the beach and there is no quicksand. She thanks him and rubs her eyes. "It was just a bad dream, Maata. Wanna tell me about it?"

Maata tells him what it feels like in her body to experience this fear and Waka listens quietly. "I reckon it's a premonition or something. That's why you've been so strange lately. You sure everything is okay? Are they working you too hard at the chopper base?"

Maata sighs. She's known Waka for years and can trust him to keep a secret. She tells him about the assignment from Iri and Cowrie to check out the books and then the conversation she overheard between Ray and Tony. Waka looks thoughtful throughout. "What would you do, Waka? You must promise to tell nobody about this, okay?"

"Sure. I think you are wise to just wait until things progress. There's no real evidence of anything yet, and you'd look like an idiot if you blabbed at this stage. Maybe we should hang out at Tony's a while and see what we can find out? We'd need to get photos of this stuff he's spraying and be able to identify the poisons too. No point in acting until we have all this. And then we can see if the Big Boys want his farm for their GE experiments. Sounds pie-in-the-sky to me. I reckon that Raymond fella is a bit of a bullshitter. Always likes to think he is in with the important people."

"He's been okay to me actually, though he can be a bit sexist at times."

"Older men are like that. Must be in their genes." Waka grins.

"Yeah – well maybe those are genes that could do with some interference. What is it Iri talks about – horizontal gene transfer. Maybe they could lay all the blokes out in the sand and transfer the anti-sexist genes of women into their makeup?" Maata laughs at the bizarre idea.

"One problem there, Maata. What about those sexist women who try to keep their power and betray other women in the process?"

"Goes to show that the methodology just doesn't work, eh Waka?"

They snuggle together and talk about their mates,

their ideals, and the complexities of not always being able to come down one side or the other on issues like those confronting Maata. They resolve to do a bit of detective work themselves and see where it leads them.

Tena koutou katoa – Cowrie and Kuini here. We're now
hanging out at Heron's Flight vineyard – not bad for a
GE-free march eh? The owners, Mary and David, have let
us camp between the café and the vineyard – and use their
email today. The Dome Valley walk was stunning – tracks
through fern forests full of mamaku, kauri, rimu and some
very large kahikatea. We took a side track and came out
in the Whangaripo Valley, and walked on a clay trail to
Rainbow Valley Organic Farm. It's a subtropical
wilderness. It was once dry clay and kikuyu grass and
we can see from the neighbouring farm, which is still
sprayed all the time, how dry and cracked the land had
become. Jo and Trish began replanting and mulching and
inventing new ways of adapting Permaculture and organic
growing principles just over a decade ago, and in that
short time, this lush valley has responded with love.

We were greeted by their kunekune pigs on arrival –
gorging on bananas. They've used Ethiopian banana palms,
with trunks as wide as a waka, as shelter under which to
grow all manner of crops ranging from vegetables and
herbs to Californian date palms. Everything responds to
the heat, and in our Northland climate it needs the shelter
to keep the mulch moist and the plants from drying out.
We've now seen how we could extend the banana
plantation at Te Kotuku and plant beneath the bananas. Jo
has given us some seeds to grow these majestic Ethiopian
bananas too. They only have one huge trunk, which helps

for using them as shelter since our Hokianga bananas are ladyfinger variety and they sprout everywhere. We tasted the bananas – better for cooking than eating – hence the kunekune gets a great feast – but the leaves make a luscious mulch. We've had lots of talkstory over GE-free issues and Permaculture too. Then Jo showed us how he has invented new farm tools hewn from recycled wood, to make organic farming easier. He's even adapted an old washing machine wringer to extract sugar juice from the sugar cane. It's delicious! Yum!

There's an extensive nursery growing all kinds of heirloom varieties – plums, apples, pears, tangelos, and mandarins, tasting like fruit tasted when we were kids. They've built a rammed-earth house which uses solar energy, with a wild garden on the roof, and an earthen oven for outdoor cooking. Inside are superbly crafted colourful tiles and a sense of peace and abundance. Outside the kitchen window, a spiral herb garden with rocks to retain the heat of the sun, and basil, Vietnamese mint, coriander, thyme, peppermint, lemon balm, garlic – and many others – looking more like trees than herbs. Like Kay Baxter at Koanga Gardens, they make good use of local fish and seaweed as a fertiliser in addition to mulching with plant material.

But what most blew us away was the sense of being in a true subtropical paradise with the planting of palms which take the place of our mamaku and ponga. Both of us were surprised at the lack of typical Aotearoan bush – which we have adapted successfully to use as a shelter for our organic gardens at Te Kotuku – but maybe this is because Jo is Austrian and works from a very global perspective when planting, not keeping to natives alone or falling into any of the usual stereotypes. Trish and Jo have together created an utterly unique atmosphere at Rainbow Valley

Farm and we'd love to bring Te Kotuku workers over to see it sometime. They want to visit Te Kotuku also.

After a day-long seminar, we walked down to one of the most beautiful and quiet vineyards we have ever seen to sample some of the local organic produce. Heron's Flight have won several awards for their wine and recently have moved to Sangiovese – an Italian variety which they have found does very well in the heat here. We tasted their wines, and their barrique-oaked chardonnay is hard to beat, accompanied by salmon and roasted pepper bruschetta with Mary's red pepper jelly – to die for! It was such a treat after all the walking and we had the best rest so far. It is hard to leave this place. The vineyard stretches out below us and they grow their own herbs and really make use of the very best local organic produce from the area. Some of the poets and writers in the group did a reading based on a celebration of nature, and several local GE-free experts spoke to us. We wish you could have been here – but we took notes for you, Iri and Koa! More on our return.

Today, we are setting out for Mohala Gardens at a local Takatu beach to see how some women have been converting a native bush and clay section to organic Permaculture garden, to show how it can be done on a sustainable level with a small section of land – using local seaweeds for mulch and also for sushi and for edible treats. We're looking forward to this. We'll camp out at the beach overnight – doubt there will be any email there – sounds quite isolated – then head off for Tamaki Makaurau. Talk to you again soon. We are thinking of you daily and also celebrating the abundance of this land of Aotearoa we are so lucky to live in.

Enough! It sounds as if we are on the road again. Hope we can get a swim at this beach – and maybe catch some fresh kai moana before heading off to Auckland. Love to all at Te Kotuku.

Any news on the chopper front? Kuini says we should be careful in giving away too many details over the net – so it's Flies or Choppers from now on!

Give Mere a hug and tell her not to have another Rongoa hui until we return – we do not want to miss out!

Kia kaha – Arohanui –

Cowrie and Kuini.

"Well, how did the meeting go?" Raymond clicks open a beer and offers it to Tony. Tony refuses, preferring a cold one from his fridge. He brings over a sixpack and plants it down in front of Raymond as they sit around his kitchen table.

"Bloody fantastic. Cheers mate!" They click cans. Tony guzzles down half a can in one go, spluttering the last mouthful out onto his dirty singlet. Raymond, who is very particular about cleanliness, winces. "They thought the farm was perfect – very isolated and only a dirt track off a long and difficult clay road. They reckoned the barns need a bit of work so they gave me cash in hand to get them up to scratch. Not bad, eh?"

"Reckon that paid for the sixpack, eh, Tony?"

Tony grins. "Yep. Got it in one! And plenty more where that came from too."

"So, what'd they think about using the caves?"

"Some of them worried a bit about their Maori significance. Said they would be protected under the Treaty of Waitangi. But I said that nobody knows about them except a few old tohunga who've probably carked it by now. None of the local brown fellas have been up here poking about, so it's likely it's been forgotten. Anyway, they are not on any of the Department of

Survey maps, 'cos we checked when Moana mentioned they should be marked. Said there was some tapu or other on 'em, but I don't believe in all that spiritual nonsense."

"Me neither. Goes against a good Christian up-bringing. Holds their whole race back, I reckon." Tony burps.

"D'ya reckon Moana will remember? Couldn't she kick up a fuss?"

"Only if she knows about the deal. We have to keep it quiet."

"Right on. But didn't she want the caves marked on the map for future generations?"

"Yep. Told her I'd do it. Took a day off, went to town, downed a few brownies with the local boys, took a bet on Cheater at the TAB, ate three pies, two bags of chips and two fried hoki, then returned home. She was real pleased I'd gone to Lands and Survey and rewarded me with a huge roast dinner." Tony laughs. "I had a hell of a time eating it and my dogs had a good meal. Managed to spoon it out into their bowls on the pretence of clearing the decks for dessert, and they wolfed it down before anyone got the wiser."

"Close call, Tony. Hope we don't have too many of those." Raymond wipes his brow.

"No worries, mate. Took your advice the other day and have been enjoying being a bachelor again."

Raymond looks around at the clutter of dishes in the sink and on the counter and old clothes piled up on every available chair, underwear and singlets flowing out of a large basket in the corner of the room, and nods. "I can see that. But Bella tells me you two are having a nice time also."

"Yep. She's a good girl, Ray. Very nice." Tony grins lewdly.

"Well, you make sure you look after her Ray. She's a bit young for you."

"I'll look after her like a father. We're just good friends." Tony suddenly recognises the protective look in Ray's eyes. "Not that I could ever replace you, mate. But you know I'll take good care of her."

"You've been a good father to those kids and a fine husband to Moana, so I trust you, Tony. Get her to do a bit of tidying up around here, eh? You wanna keep the place clean if it is to be used by the scientists. They like everything to be clean."

"No worries, mate. I never show them in here. Just the front room which is as clean as when Moana left. I can hire some local chick to do the shitwork now that I have some bikky." Tony pulls a wad of cash from his back pocket, his eyes gleaming. "Thanks, mate. Hope you get your cut."

"Have it already, thanks. And there's more to come."

"Great. Anyway, back to the caves. They said if I could ensure that there would be no hassles from the local tangata whenua, then it would be perfect for their top-secret operations. Nobody could ever find out about experiments underground, and they will fit out the caves with lights, cameras and all they need to monitor their work. Some of these guys will be living in the old shearers' sheds near the caves, so that's perfect."

Ray bites into one of Barbara's muffins he's brought

along. "But how can you guarantee that, Tony?"

"Showed them pictures of me, the missus and the kids. Told them I was close with the local Maoris and married to one of them. That seemed to satisfy them. I even managed to convince them that Moana was daughter of one of the chief fellas who was guardian of the caves and that as guardian, she could say how they could be used. Said there'd been a vote on this ages ago and everyone agreed to leave it in her hands to protect them. Besides, we ain't gonna do no harm to 'em. Just use the space. Nobody will know about it. As I say, most of the local sooties have forgotten about them."

"Sure thing, Tony. You're a bit of a beaut. Wish I'd known you in the ForestsFirst days. We could have done with a few more like you down the Coast then." Ray grins.

Tony is very pleased with himself. Things are really looking up. He's managed to get some income, a future for the farm, a bit on the side, and the respect of Ray who runs the local business association. Choice. Moana will be begging to come back to him soon. But he'll let her stew. At least he has Bella to screw in the meantime. Not a bad bit of flesh, and sweet to boot. No ties, no hassles. Just what he likes. In fact, he might get used to this new life. He grabs another tinnie and hands a cold one to Raymond, clinking tin upon tin. "Here's to a rosy future, mate. Genetic engineering and all."

"Cheers, Tony. I'll second that." Raymond downs his beer. As he does so, he notices that a pair of Tony's undies, which is hanging over the edge of the chair and touching the table, is sunny side up, showing he's had a

122

bit of a diarrhoea problem. Raymond nearly gags on his beer and turns his chair to face the other direction, noting he must make sure that Tony gets in a cleaner and does not rely on Bella to do his dirty work for him. Maybe Maata would appreciate the extra work and cash? She'd keep quiet about anything she saw because she needs the cash so much. She said that in the interview. And then he could keep an eye on Tony as well, just to be sure everything runs to plan. Not a bad idea. He'd get Bella to do it but he does not want Bella implicated if anything goes wrong. In fact, he'd prefer Tony to get another girlfriend outside his family and he'll work on this too. All in good time.

Raymond muses as Tony slurps on his beer, ranting on about how good life has become since Raymond offered him a hand and that's what mates are for. Raymond lets him burble on. He's a simple fella, this Tony, and that's good for business, he muses; the less he thinks, the better it is for us all. That's the way good corporates work. It's important to rely on the workers remaining ignorant of your real goals and focused on always trying to please you. He learned that with ForestsFirst and is happy to apply it now. Poor bugger. He looks at Tony. He's so insecure, he'd shit his pants to please you. He grins.

"Hey, Koa. Check this out." Iri reads from the screen of her laptop. "There's a message from the co-leader of the Green Party, Jeanette Fitzsimons, to all greenies and supporters over their stance on the GM Commission – what they can and cannot do."

"Read it out while I finish planting these seedlings." Koa dips her finger into the row of loo-roll containers filled with soil and sand, and drops a seed carefully into each one while Irihapeti reads:

Dear Green Party member

This message explains the Greens' options in relation to the ongoing discussions with the Government over GE so there is better understanding of what is going on. If you know members who are not on email please share this letter with them.

The Green position is that we do not accept GE outside the laboratory. That will remain our position and that is what we would ensure happened if we were the Government. However, there is a widespread perception that if we just hold fast to this position and threaten to withdraw support ("confidence") we can achieve a GE-free future now. It is actually much more complex than that.

The Government doesn't have to get our permission to do anything. They can go right ahead and allow all releases

124

and field trials and they don't need legislation to do it because the law already allows it. There will only be a vote in parliament if the Government decides to restrict GE, not if it decides to continue to allow it.

When they have made their decision, we then have to decide our response to what they do. If the decision is bad we have the option of voting against them on the next confidence vote. There is the opportunity to initiate a confidence vote only a couple or so times a year. The next scheduled confidence vote is not until February of next year.

If we say we will withdraw confidence, the Government could rely on Winston Peters of New Zealand First for confidence and continue to govern but without consulting us on anything. Alternatively they could call an election any time after we announced we would not continue to support them on confidence.

Winston has already said he would abstain on confidence and allow the Government to operate as a minority government. Whether and how long the Government would want to do this is an open question. In any case, the decision of what to do is the Prime Minister's decision. We can withdraw confidence but we cannot force an election now.

Even if there were an early election, Labour might well secure enough seats to govern without us, even if we get more MPs. In that case there would be nothing stopping them allowing GE to proceed as they wish. Or, worst of all, the Nationals with the help of the ACT party might be able to form a government and give the full go-ahead to GE. Labour knows all this and knows we know it as well.

We are talking with the Government to try to move them closer to our position. The TV1 poll, released on

Wednesday night, showed 62 per cent opposition to field trials outside a lab. This confirmed our own polling a few months ago, which showed that two-thirds of the public don't want GE outside the lab. The strong stand by the Maori caucus and (we think) by the Alliance has added strength to our position.

There is some chance of shifting the Government towards our position but it is unlikely to go all the way we want. We would then face the choice: do we express our great displeasure and disappointment in a range of ways but continue to give them confidence, knowing we have achieved a great deal towards our goal, or do we withdraw confidence and maybe have an early election?

If they have come most of the way to our position but not as far as we would like, we risk losing those gains if we have an election and they no longer need us. That is because legislation is needed to implement any improvement to the status quo and legislation takes many months to pass. Having only the status quo would be bad for the GE-free cause.

If the Government does not even come close to our position, then we have little option but to withdraw confidence and then deal with whatever the Government decides to do in response. As I said publicly this week the Green Party will not support a government that takes us down the GE road. The Party will of course have a plan ready to kick-in if an election is called at short notice.

So you see the issue is not really about compromise at all. It's not about weakening our position. It's not about accommodation. It's about how far we can persuade them to go. It's about them having the power to do what they like and us having the power to withdraw confidence if we don't like it, with unknown consequences.

Thanks to all of you who have worked so hard over the past months and years. I hope this letter clarifies the present position a bit. Our decision must be about how to best protect and preserve the GE-free option right now. As I hope I have explained above, that is a much more complex calculation than simply "do we withdraw confidence?"

We had all hoped the Royal Commission would be the end of our struggle for a GE-free New Zealand, but it is clear it is just one step along the road. Victory will come but it will take ongoing work, now and in the future.

We will write to you all again as soon as there is more concrete information to share.

Yours for a GE-free New Zealand

Jeanette Fitzsimons
Co-leader
Green Party Aotearoa-New Zealand.

"D'ya reckon she's selling out, Koa?"

"*No* way. Not half as much as Helen Clark might be by the sounds of the leaks so far. I think the Greens have no option but to go down this path. None of us can rely upon Winston Peters as tangata whenua because he whistles like the wind and moves the way he thinks his best votes will go." Koa drops the last seed into the containers and begins another row.

"Yeah, maybe you're right. Besides, I trust Jeanette. She's never compromised for the sake of ambition and she's clearly here for the long haul." Iri scrolls through the supporting material on screen to see what other responses there are. So far, all are in support of Jeanette's stand and the way the Greens have reacted. Ever since the Royal Commission made it plain that New Zealand might as well abandon the possibility of being GE and it would be a compromise whatever the government finally chose to do, the internet has been buzzing with responses, and newspapers, television and all media have been jammed with irate New Zealanders demanding to know what is going on. Helen Clark, as a feminist Prime Minister known for her socialist leanings, is under incredible scrutiny and she realises it. She knows full well how strongly Kiwis voted against having nuclear power, nuclear weapons and nuclear-powered ships in their ports; she knows that the submissions against genetic engineering registered 92 per cent against, and the 8 per cent in favour were groups and researchers paid by International Seed Corporation and MagicMilk and other multinationals who had everything to lose by the decision. Even in the general electorate, 62 per cent of Kiwis are against any form of genetic engineering, and that includes the conservatives, even by their own polls.

Iri hopes these numbers will force the government into a decision against GE and a reversal of the findings of the Royal Commission. But will big business put on so much pressure that the government cannot afford to turn its back on the economic opportunities offered here? Only time can tell. Iri sees that Koa has nearly completed the pohutukawa seed planting. She logs off and quietly tiptoes behind her lover, wrapping her arms warmly around her large and beautiful body. Koa snuggles into her embrace. "Wanna hot tub, Koa?"

Koa turns around to face her, hands covered in sand

and dirt. She smiles. "Sure do. Does that include a back rub and massage?"

"Only if you tell me some more stories tonight."

"That depends on the quality of the back rub." Koa smiles. Irihapeti loves her talkstory and is always hungry for more.

"I can guarantee that in advance," whispers Iri into her ear. "I start here, like this . . ." She runs her fingers down Koa's spine and rubs out from the backbone toward her sides. This always sends delicious shivers through Koa's body, and she finds it hard to resist Iri's sensitive touch. Her green fingers, caressing plants and soil like a lover, have prepared her to be so caring to others. It's so integrated into her being that it would be hard to separate the grower from the lover, the activist from the spiritualist, the carer of the land from the carer of the body of land that is Koa, Papatuanuku, Earth Mother. Our heritage.

Minutes later, they are sitting in their wooden hot tub, Hina smiling down on them. Iri massages Koa's back while Koa sings a waiata to the moon, crooning into the crisp night air.

"Now, my kotuku, comes your treat. I'll tell you a tale and you tell me what it is really about." She begins: "This story is called 'The Woman in the Moon Cries Foul'.

"In Pape'ete, women gather around a fire to finish designs on the tapa mural they are making to protest nuclear tests at Moruroa atoll. A corner of the tapa reveals a child praying. A pattern of stars erupts through the sky of the tapa at the top border, one star for each detonation since nuclear tests began. Maeve begins to count the stars. One, two, three . . . one hundred . . . one hundred and fifty. Tears fall down her cheeks as she marks the final stars. She dips her fingers into crushed berries, the colour of ochre, and adds a star from last month's underwater explosion. All eyes are on her as she presses the imprint into the cloth through the bark stencil.

"At the atoll, a white explosion erupts from the ocean and spans out towards the canoes. Clouds part and the moon glares down on the broken waters. In the distance, a thunderous drumming. Eyes rise to the heavens as waves echo out from the centre of the explosion towards the waiting canoes.

"The last panel is completed on the tapa mural. It depicts Tureia Island after the nuclear tests. Inedible coconuts fall off the trees. Maohi get sick from the fish, vegetables and water. They fall into the sea and become stars, forming the border at the bottom of the tapa cloth. Waves bang against the canoes near the atoll. They threaten to swamp the paddlers, who beat their paddles against the side of the canoes in protest. Thunder rolls out of the skies with a terrifying power and crashes down over the heads of the workers at the nuclear base.

"Fire blazes from the land as the Maohi women show the finished tapa-cloth mural telling the stories of their lives from when they could still eat fish and coconuts to the diseases and contamination that prevent this now. Yet there is determination and power in their faces. As they hold the tapa high, the moon shines onto the bark cloth, illuminating its stories.

"Maeve looks up to see Hina-nui-aiai-i-te-marama, Great Hina beating in the moon. The Goddess who refused to be silenced when she kept beating her tapa cloth at night was sent into the heavens as penance, and tonight she returns to avenge her people. As Hina holds her mallet high and thumps against the tapa cloth, the men raise their paddles in protest and the Maohi women raise their mallets in defiance. Punua bursts thunder onto the nuclear base, shattering the towers in two, and Hina smiles down from the Moon."

Iri stops her massage a moment. "Well, it's about the protest against nuclear tests at Moruroa, and it's voiced through the retelling of the myth of Hina."

"Yes, partly right. It's a Tahitian version of the story but I have adapted it to honour the protesters at Moruroa. But how do you think it is relevant here?" Koa grins as she imagines Iri scrunching up her face in thought behind her.

A while later, Iri replies. "Is it about not giving up? That sometimes you have to beat your drum hard to get the message out, in this case, on the tapa cloth, that we must not ever give up the fight just because it gets hard or there are sacrifices along the way? And about protecting the earth and not devastating her with poisons and nuclear waste."

"Not bad at all, my Clever Earthworm." Koa and Iri have reclaimed worms for their goodness to the soil and their knowledge they could not do their work without these soil savers. Iri grins. "It's about not giving up, no matter what. We have to support each other, you and I and all those against GE, because there is no going back once the decision is made. We need to draw on all the stories and mythology and lessons we have learned down the years or we will be doomed to repeat the same tired lessons of history all over again. And we simply cannot leave such a legacy to our tamariki."

"Ka pae, Koa." Iri holds her lover close, whispering into her ear. "I love you for being so strong. And for always bringing the joy back to my tired spirit."

"That is the meaning of my name and why I was called Koa," her lover replies, running her hand slowly around the back of Iri's neck and down to her breasts floating gently on the moon-washed water. She bends to kiss her, drawing Iri towards her, folding her legs around her waist as they float under the protective eye of Hina, who knows they will complete her work eloquently on their earthly plane. The stars dance on the moonlit waters, reflecting Hina's light into the faces of the women.

"You'll never guess what happened at work today, Waka." Maata watches as Waka follows in his father Piripi's steps as a talented carver, curving his hand-hewn chisel up the trunk of the totara log, tracing the swirling design of his fern-leaf pattern. Waka looks up, encouraging her to continue. "Mr Dixon suggested I finish work early on Fridays as he wants me to clean the house of a friend. Said he'd pay really well for it, but it'd be a real mess. At first I was reluctant, as I need the time for further study, but then he told me it was the home of that Tony fella. I figured that I could spy on him much easier if I was working in his home, and then you could come and collect me at the end of each session. That way, I could let you know if the way was clear for a bit of a rekky." Maata grins, pleased with herself.

Waka looks up from his work tentatively. "You sure you want to get that close to this fella?"

"No. But cleaning his digs isn't such a big deal. I do this for Mere already and it'd be a breeze. I'd have access to all his records and hear his calls and really find out if anything is going on there after what I heard when he and Mr Dixon were talking at Flyworks that day."

Waka still looks unsure. "I like the idea of you having this access but I don't like the feeling that this dirty old man might have further access to you."

Maata blanches, realising that Waka is being protective of her. "Thanks, Waka, but I am sixteen now and perfectly capable of looking after myself. Besides, if you come and collect me each time, you'll know if anything is not right, okay? Then you can let the others know. Mere will be so furious that she'd be more than a match for him!"

Waka grimaces. "I've no doubt of that, Maata. Your grandmother is very gentle, but she can be fierce when she needs to be."

"Too right, Waka. So you don't mind then?"

"What if he hits up on you? I'd mind that."

Maata smiles to herself, knowing he loves her even though they have agreed to be good friends for the time being. "He already has another girlfriend – Dixon's daughter – so that should not be a problem."

"Okay then. Only if I can be there each time to fetch you. I must admit, it's a bit of a coup, Maata, after our decision to keep an eye on him. Must be someone looking after us, eh?" Waka smiles broadly, sweeping her to his side and planting a kiss on her cheek. "So whad'ya think of the koru so far?" he adds, blowing the shavings away from the design and showing the graceful spiral which reaches up toward the heavens.

"It's inspiring, Waka. Huatau." Maata runs her finger along the coil and feels the smoothness of the cut and the rough edges of the indented wood. "Piripi will be really proud of you."

"I am already," booms a voice behind them as Piripi walks in, carrying a carving under his arm. He lays it on the table for them to admire.

Maata looks at the work of art, not quite sure what it is. It resembles a musical instrument, but she has never seen one quite like this before. Two long, narrow gourds tied together at the top and bottom, with a face at the head, its tongue leading down to a green and white feather that decorates its shiny, brown body. There are holes either side. Piripi explains it is one of the early Maori flutes, putorino. He places it delicately against his lips and plays and Maata is entranced by the haunting sound that floats out from the hollow belly of the instrument. She has never felt this way since first hearing the bone flute played by her uncle and this moves her deeply.

"I've been working with Ta Haumanu, a group dedicated to the revival of Maori flute and instrumental playing, and this flute was made by a very special carver, Brian Flintoff. His taonga puora are singing treasures that pay homage to Hine Raukatauri, the Goddess of Music. I can see her in his work."

"Me too," replies Maata. "This feels like the rounded body of a beautiful woman."

"Yes, but one who calls for her lover. D'you know the story behind her?" Piripi asks.

"Just that she inspires musicians."

"All our instruments, especially the flutes, are descended from Hine Raukatauri. She's represented on our earth as the casemoth. The caterpillar of this unique moth spins an intricate bag, then covers it with tiny leaves from the forest so she can hang from the branches in safety. The males pupate and fly away, but the females stay within their womb-like cases. At night they can be heard crying for their lovers, and this wailing sound is

135

the inspiration for all Maori flute music."

"Wow! That's amazing! Do they miss the males that much?" asks Waka, knowing he'll get a reaction from Maata, who is always under the influence of her Aunty Cowrie.

"Who says they are wailing for their male lovers, Waka? Piripi just said wailing for their lovers. Could be anyone."

"Ah, maybe, but the balance of male and female is important in creating any of the instruments," explains Piripi. "The putorino also has a male voice within its body."

"Could be trans-gendered then," adds Maata, not to be outdone.

Piripi shakes his head in disbelief. These young kids, they need to have it their way.

Maata suddenly recalls a story her Aunty Cowrie once told her. "Didn't the kokako bird once ask Maui to grant the ability to sing like Hine Raukatauri? I remember Cowrie telling me something about this."

"Ka pae, Maata." Piripi looks pleased. "Maui told the kokako to eat the casemoths. The result was that the bird was able to sing like magic, as if it had swallowed and then recreated the sound of Raukatauri, making this even more mystical and musical in the process. Hence the kokako now has such a haunting melody and a tonal scale like no other bird."

"Do kokako still eat the casemoths?" asks Waka.

"Sure. That's why they sing so sweetly," adds Maata, who has seen them feasting lusciously on the moths and singing to their heart's content.

Piripi takes a carved bone flute from his chest pocket and shows it to them. "See this end? You blow from here, like this." He raises the flute to his mouth at an angle and gently whistles into it. A soft cry comes out, like the wailing of a baby kakapo in the distance.

"Wow. Amazing. What's the carving at this end?" Maata points to the head of the flute near his lips.

Piripi holds the koauau toward them and places his finger at the mouth of the flute. "This end we blow into represents the face of the flute. The eyes, nose and lips are carved around the open mouth. When you blow into its open mouth, then the nose comes close to the musician. See." He demonstrates.

"Just like you are giving the flute a hongi by touching nose to nose then?" asks Waka.

"Ka pae. Just like that. Now – look here at the other end." Piripi turns the instrument to face them with the part that is furthest from the lips.

"But that's also got a face on it," pipes up Maata.

"Ka pae, Maata. But look more closely. What do you notice that is unusual?"

Maata examines the koauau for some time before she discovers its unique qualities. "The face at this other end has two noses, one above and one below. But why?"

"That's because this end represents the face of the music and it takes two breaths to make the music, the breath of the musician and that of the instrument, the koauau," replies Piripi.

"So both rely equally on the other for their existence and their spirit?"

"Yes, Waka. Just as you with this koru carving of

yours. Both you and your instrument for carving are one spirit. Just like we are tangata whenua – people of the land. If we abuse the land, we cannot live on it. We are one with the land, just as a musician is one with his or her instrument, and breathes the spirit of Hine Raukatauri with every breath taken."

"And since the land is Papatuanuku and the spirit of music is Hine Raukatauri, and both are female, then you blokes need our spirit to survive, eh?" adds Maata, looking very pleased with herself.

Piripi looks at Waka and raises his eyebrows. "Whad'ya think, bro?"

"Ah, let her have her way," laughs Waka, secretly proud of Maata for standing up for her sex. He knows she was abused as a child and the extent of the harm to her then. It has been a long journey to repair her broken spirit. Sometimes she can overreact, but he adores her for her strength in making this journey and her assertiveness now. He can see her as wahine toa, as strong as Irihapeti or Cowrie or Mere in the future, so long as she does not let the past submerge her, as it did when she nearly drowned a few years back. When Maata glimpses his affection, he looks down to his carving and pretends to inspect it more closely.

"So what's this wavy carving which curves around the finger holes and down over the body of the instrument?" Maata points to the waves of bone.

"The carver calls it *te ata o te rangi*: the pathway of the music. It depicts our music spiralling into the world."

"I like that. It looks like soundwaves, rolling across the ocean to the horizon." Maata fingers the deep curves in the bone lovingly. Waka notices her touch.

"There are usually three finger holes or wenewene, but sometimes there can be five. Most of our music consists of a very compact scale of microtones," explains Piripi, lifting the koauau to his lips and moving from note to note in a sliding glissando. Maata recalls the voice of Diane Aki from Hawai'i on the tape that her Aunty Cowrie brought back from her other homeland. The sliding notes are hauntingly similar, but here they sound as if from another world, one that knows more than this earth, one full of mystery and wisdom, a world beyond this where an inner knowledge lies in waiting for the soul explorer to discover. Maata never talks to anyone else about this world, but she has known it since she was a child. She was always captivated by the description of the music of the spheres at school, and she associates these haunting melodies with that unknown sound inviting us to a world beyond this. One day, she'll discover for herself what this truly means.

They are walking through the Waipoua Forest, hand in hand, dwarfed by the giant kauri, kahikatea, the weeping leaves of the rimu, strong black mamaku sheltering the smaller kohuhu, and nikau palms waving their fronds toward the waiting heavens. Piwakawaka flit around their heads, grateful for their presence so they can catch the insects which jump out of their way, their fanned tails allowing them to hover and pounce at just the right time. A stream slithers along beside them, offering up her clean water for their thirst. Just as they bend to drink the water, the ground shakes. A mighty thundering rolls toward them from the sky in waves. They look up to the giant twinned kauri towering above them. Suddenly, out of nowhere, an albatross with a gigantic wingspan flies toward one of the kauri. They can hardly believe their eyes. It looks as if the giant seabird will crash straight into the trunk of the tree, shattering itself. The sun glints across their vision a second and the bird smashes into the tree, sending branches raining down around them. They are saved by a rimu which stands in its path. They gasp, stunned, and hide within a nearby cave to recover. A few twigs have gashed the sides of their faces. They bathe the wounds with their wet towels, refreshed by the stream. Just as they emerge from the cave entrance, another mighty thundering. The sky is shaking and birds are falling from the heavens in their droves. To their left, another mighty albatross swoops down and heads for the second giant kauri. They jump back into the cave. This time the bird hits the tree with such force that the tree is shattered into pieces and crashes down around them, taking the kahikatea, rimu and nikau palms with it. The thundering debris sends up a spray of dust into the forest, clogging their noses and fogging the cave. They run toward the cave entrance, afraid of being trapped in by the branches crashing around them, but there is nowhere to escape. The forest around them is devastated. Huge trees lie moaning like wounded soldiers, their branches crushed or poking imploringly toward the silent heavens. The dust from their impact has created a fog so thick it resembles the aftermath of a nuclear holocaust. The ground begins to shake in shock. They run, blinded, right into the body of the dead albatross and are suffocated by its feathers . . .

Irihapeti wakes with a start, gasping for air and shocked by her nightmare. Koa lies beside her, still asleep. Iri rises and walks toward the window. There is a heavy mist over the Waipoua Kauri Forest and she cannot see if it is still standing. She shivers. It's unlike her to have nightmares. She usually sleeps so well after all the hard work in the nursery. She lights the gas stove and boils the billy for a cuppa, watching the sun begin to rise over the hills and melt the fog. Gradually, the tops of the trees appear mysteriously from the mist and she breathes a sigh of relief. For now.

Tena koutou katoa – Today we walked from Heron's Flight Vineyard through rolling green pastures and native bush on the Takatu Peninsula. To our right, Kawau Island and further south Motuketekete, Moturekareka, Motutara and Motuora Islands. One of the walkers told us that the outer islands are being replanted with native trees so they can be sanctuaries for saving rare bird species in Aotearoa. She'd sailed out to Motuora with a group from Forest and Bird Association and they'd planted trees and had a walk and a picnic there. Already, several species of rare birds have been raised there, as on Tiritiri Matangi Island, where wild parrots now breed. To our left side, as we walk toward Tawharanui, is the majestic Hauturu Island, rising out of the jade-green and aqua waters like Tahiti. The local Pakeha call it Little Barrier Island, and in the distance, its big sister, Great Barrier Island. Kaka, who knows this area well, tells them that the kakapo have been successfully bred on Hauturu Island and that her great-grandmother, whose ancestors were buried on the island, has swum out there to visit them along with other relatives. That the island is sacred and it is right that it is now protected as a breeding ground for native birds.

Although some of the peninsula is used for farmland, many farmers want to return to organic methods of farming used by their ancestors. The end of the peninsula is a marine park, and fishing and the gathering of shellfish is forbidden. This allows more fish species to breed and multiply. We walked down into a beautiful bay, treeferns to our left and an enticing glimpse of the sea between their waving fronds. To our right, alas, was an ugly set of buildings and a huge tract of land concreted over as a tarmac for helicopters. The bush and grass had been heavily sprayed and the buildings housed a company whose business is spraying the land with pesticides, herbicides and poisons. Kaka told us they'd only applied for a licence to run one helicopter, as most farmers can do, and then secretly built up the company so the local council would find it hard to refuse them a resource consent once they were successfully established and the farmers, police, and even the council were dependent upon them. She said the small beach communities include many organic gardeners, like the two we were about to meet, and that the community had once been supportive and happy. That the helicopter eco-vandals have destroyed all that, and now the bay is divided into those supporting the poisoners and those against the devastation of the land.

She handed around photographs of the company burying toxic waste and pointed to clearly visible burial mounds on the land leading down to the beach estuary. We asked how they could get away with this on land that was, we understood, zoned as a pristine and protected coastal area, home to many rare native bird species. She laughed, saying that money could buy votes and that the owners were related to some of the richest investors in the country. Everyone sighed, knowing the game. The Poisoners, the locals call them. You reckon they are cuzzie bros of Raymond Dioxin at Flyworks? We wouldn't be at all surprised. Who needs International Seed Corporation to fight when we have mini International Seed Corporation clones dusting the earth with their poisons and making a living from devastating the land. When will people wake up to the fact that we cannot keep doing this and survive

143

on this earth? Kaka said that a survey had been done and one-third of the people in the bay had been hospitalised or suffered from some form of cancer or poison-related disease in the past decade. Pretty telling really. One employee there even thought she had multiple sclerosis from the muscle spasms she experienced, typical of toxic chemical poisoning. But she stayed on for years out of honour and loyalty to her employers, until she was finally offered a position with another company. Her health improved after that. Surprise, surprise! The best thing was, she started smiling again and acting like her real self.

We've heard so many similar stories on this hikoi and know this is a battle being fought all over Aotearoa at present. Land zoned as protected for its unique native vegetation and bird life is slowly being turned over to commercial use, as more and more people want to shift into the country and bring their businesses with them. So many rural areas need the money and thus are easily exploited. Local councils are begging for more business, so they are easily bought off by unethical operators. It's time the people of this land woke and realised that the clean, green image of this country is just that – an image, that needs to be fought for and protected and truly cherished if we are to become a rich source of organic food for Kiwis, and for the world in the future. We need to do our bit too and make sure Raymond Dioxin does not blight our sacred Hokianga with his toxic choppers. I hope Maata is safe working there. Maybe we'll invest in a gas mask for her. He'd get the picture if his receptionist wore protective gear, and so would his clients! Kuini and I like the image! But seriously, Mere, do keep an eye on Maata for us, eh?

After a while, we rounded the bend of the bay and walked into a beach paradise. A sleepy inlet nudged by gentle waters, an estuary full of matuku moana. We've never seen so many sea herons at once. They nest in the mangroves

144

and a stand of ti palms beside the sea and share their salty homes with pied oystercatchers, sooty shearwaters, swallows and red-billed aki aki. In the trees surrounding the bay – kahikatea, kauri, rimu, puriri, manuka, kanuka, giant mamaku and a range of treeferns, as well as large yellow-flowered kowhai hanging out over the water – are rare native birds. Flying above us as we walked along beside the bay were large white-breasted green-coated kukupa, swooping up on currents of air and diving back down again, white-throated tui with their coats the colour of paua-shell flying swiftly through the trees. Dancing piwakawaka greeted us as we entered Mohala Gardens, flicking their tails in delight, and one of the women played her sacred pumoana, the sounds of the seashell resounding out over the waves below and back into the forest above. I felt the voice of the sea in her playing, smelt the salt air as vibrations surfed through me.

The women of Mohala have about half an acre of land, most of which is mature native bush with the same trees as when we entered the bay. They cleared a small patch to build their own settlers' cottage from cedar, lined with recycled rimu dug from the Dome Valley swamps when the land was being reclaimed. The house sits on stilts amidst towering black mamaku and silver treeferns, and you walk up wooden steps to enter it. It is truly like living in a tree house. You can touch the ferns from their hot tub on the deck. We never found out their given names as they call themselves Turtle and Selkie. Very cute. The Turtle is short and round and dark and called herself a "literary activist" and gardener. Her Selkie is tall and svelte and blonde and is a writer, translator and eco-activist. Both write on ecology issues and are devoted to organic gardens here in Aotearoa and in the Orkney Islands off Scotland, where they also have a seaside cottage and garden, gifted to them from the fruits of their hard work. We liked them and their vision and they were amazed I'd been to Orkney so recently with the storytellers from the Edinburgh Festival. We shared some wonderful korero.

They showed us pictures of the land before they began their work. Apart from the native bush covering the top part of the land, the rest was clay, thick with kikuyu grass. By luck, some neighbours were building and dumped a huge pile of trees and clay onto their yard. They mounded the clay as a barrier to the roadside and planted it in bananas, feijoas and guavas, with flowering shrubs and lilies and native grasses beneath. The kikuyu was harvested, year after year, as mulch and gradually they covered the remaining ground in recycled cardboard from the local supermarket. They had also used shredded paper from The Poisoners, donated by a local employee, until they found out it was covered in toxic ink. Then they discovered an alternative supply via TEPS, the Takatu Environmental Protection Society, formed to fight The Poisoners and to challenge all kinds of commercial development on the Takatu Peninsula that was harmful to the bird life or the environment in any way. The group comprised the more enlightened members of the bay community, many of them long-time environmentalists and working as scientists, academics, writers, eco-tourist operators and local residents, who had bothered to read the Resource Consent Act and think about the future of their bay for their descendants as well as themselves.

We were fascinated by the way the women developed the land using their instinct rather than from any strict plan. They said that Fukuoka, author of *One Straw Revolution*, also did this, and that many modern forms of Permaculture were too rule-bound. We were encouraged to trust our inner sense of design and let the landscape talk to us, rather than us imposing our will onto the land. We felt this really accorded with our vision of how we have developed

Te Kotuku nursery. They had a small orchard on land sloping toward the stream with old heirloom varieties of grapefruit, tangelo, mandarin and even a pippin apple, which tasted delicious, just like when we were kids. Yum! Under other fruit trees like Meyer lemon, Tahitian lime and Ethiopian bananas (from Rainbow Valley seeds which Jo gave them!) they planted herbs which thrived in the semi-shade. Mint, peppermint, lemon balm and tea herbs were allowed to roam wild over their mounds, nudging up to the luscious leaves of the wild Vietnamese mint which loved the shade by the stream. Thyme, oregano and massive bronze and green fennel sprouted from every crevice, and lush pregnant leaves of comfrey filled every available hole – they steam the comfrey and eat it like spinach, or use it for mulching or add it to their compost.

No fancy compost bins for Turtles and Selkies! Each compost mound was turned every time new vegetables were layered onto the clay, sand, green mulch, and the worms were like snakes! After three months, the compost mounds were covered with more sand and seaweed from cleaning the local beach and ready to be planted in rua and Maori potatoes, purple urenika yams, golden, red and violet kumara and anything from their local organic supplier that looked as if it might sprout. Their vegetable garden boasted the largest spinach leaves we have ever seen, fed by seaweed mulch and gigantic flowering artichokes, their leaves sheltering smaller baby spinach. They'd recycled old wooden trellises from Mr Warehouse, who lives in the same bay, generously donated by his builders when they did renovations, and up these wooden arms grew asparagus beans and scarlet runners with their bright red flowers waving in the sea breeze. Next to them, cherry tomatoes, tied with flax to the trellis but hovering near enough to be supported by the same structure. Great use of space. The entire garden is surrounded by a canopy of banana palms which provide much-needed shelter in the hot Northland sun in midsummer, and whose leaves form watery nutritious mulch for all the plants.

Where old pongas had fallen, they'd planted bright red, yellow and pink-green bromeliads into the ponga logs, too heavy to move, and an entire community of bromeliads poked their tropical noses out from their ferny homes with glee. A recycled loo building, now used as a garden shed, provided rainwater from its roof to fill the garden tank when the stream was low. A narrow path took us into the rear of the garden where huge native puriri, kahikatea, mamaku, kauri and smaller kawakawa plants presided over a nursery of nikau palms and ferns, leading to a waterfall which fed a pond full of native fish and trickled down towards the sea below. We walked through their native bush, noting medicinal herbs which they make into remedies for themselves and their friends, including much use of the kawakawa which Turtle uses as a tea. She swears it has the same properties as tropical kava, used as a relaxant in Fiji and many Pacific islands. She made a tea from the plant and I went to sleep immediately – which Kuini reckoned was a miracle!

We had the best night's sleep ever, out under the stars in their garden, and Turtle let me use her email. I told her I was also called Turtle by my family in Hawai'i and it turns out we both share Nga Puhi, Hawai'ian and Pakeha ancestry. Amazing. I think we'll stay in touch. Tomorrow, we head off to the Tawharanui Marine Reserve and one of the local Kawerau iwi who once lived on this peninsula will take us to their burial caves and on a day-long coastal walk around Takatu. We're relaxed and ready for it. This hikoi has made us aware that so many Aotearoans are really looking after their land, from large projects like Koanga Gardens and Rainbow Valley Organic Farm to small plot holders like Turtle and Selkie at Mohala Gardens.

Nice redemption for The Poisoners of this country, eh?
I knew mahalo meant "thanks" but mohala means "gently
unfolding creativity" in Hawai'ian. How appropriate for
their work – and ours. We need to keep unfolding, trusting
our instincts and our inner vision, to ensure the land
remains sustainable and bring others on board our organic
waka.

It's been great to find email almost everywhere we go –
another key to our survival, with the GE-free coalition,
the Greens and almost all activist and ecological groups
on-line. This is incredibly encouraging to us. For so many
isolated organic growers, the net provides support,
information and a way to protest on ecology causes while
not entering the cities to get nuked by their fumes as we
used to have to do. Nobody can sit back and say the issues
are too huge and we cannot be effective any more.
We've heard on line that Helen Clark and the Labour
Government have been bombarded by more emails
protesting the GE issue than ever received before.
Right on – keep it up, Te Kotuku – and others!

In farewell, Turtle shared this saying with us all:

Te toto o te tangata, he kai;
te oranga o te tangata, he whenua
Food supplies the blood of our people;
our welfare depends on the land.

Kia ora!

We don't know when we'll next be in touch –
but take care of yourselves – all of you – and stay strong.
Kia kaha – arohanui

Cowrie and Kuini xx.

"Yo, Koa! Meriel Watts, Director of Soil and Health, has sent us an advance copy of Jeanette's speech to be delivered in parliament within the hour, via Sue Bradford. Here's a copy fresh off the net!" Irihapeti hands over the pages to Koa, who settles down in an overstuffed armchair, bought cheap from Rawene secondhand shop, and reads:

From: "suebradford.warkworth"
<suebradford.warkworth@xtra.co.nz> "Meriel Watts"
<m.watts@auckland.ac.nz>

Date: Wed, Sep 6, 2000, 4:54 pm

JEANETTE ABOUT TO SPEAK ON SPRAY DRIFT
IN PARLIAMENT – WITHIN THE HOUR –
HERE'S SPEECH

Embargoed until delivery
(please also check against delivered speech)

Jeanette Fitzsimons

I want to speak today about a Member's bill which is not on the Order Paper. It was on the Order Paper last Member's day, having just been drawn from the ballot, and it would have come up for debate today, but today it has gone. That bill is the Agricultural Chemical Trespass Bill, first introduced to the ballot by Jill White some five

150

years ago and finally drawn in the name of Nanaia Mahuta last month. And now it has gone because the Government didn't want it debated.

There is a perception in this country that agri-chemical spraying is a relatively harmless practice vital to the rural economy. This is a myth, which has led to an acceptance of breaches of individual rights that are unacceptable in any civilised society.

The number and variety of cases coming across my desk convince me that there is a growing underclass in NZ of chemically damaged people who, after exposure to toxic substances from their neighbours, are never the same again. I want to mention just two.

First, the family who set up a motor camp in a quiet rural area surrounded by paddocks, then found those paddocks converted to grape growing and were subjected to intensive spraying with herbicides and insecticides. The child was eventually confined to a wheelchair. The parents suffered a wide range of debilitating symptoms that required them to give up their business, go on sickness benefits, lose their livelihood and capital investment, and eventually separate under the strain. I eventually pursued their ACC claim to appeal and lost.

In a notorious incident, a Northland farmer, Lawrie Newman, along with his home, property and drinking water, was sprayed with 2,4-D herbicide from a helicopter. He became extremely ill with skin rashes, blinding headaches, racing heart episodes, muscle cramps, emotional instability and night sweats. Occupational Health and Saftey experts found that these illnesses were the result of 2,4-D poisoning, but did not express a view on whether this also caused his later heart attack, weakened immune system, weight loss and lack of energy.

Mr Newman is now suffering from the early stages of Parkinson's disease due to his exposure in 1995. Prior to then he was in excellent health.

He has no legal redress.

It is a dysfunctional society that can allow this to happen to an innocent person on his own property.

There is also, of course, the effect on the livelihoods of other farmers. Anyone who had organic certification and suffered this level of trespass would lose that certification and with it much of their income.

The Minister for the Environment has offered to form a working group of stakeholders to consider the issue. But her faith that the Hazardous Substances and New Organisms Regulations soon to be announced will address the problem is misplaced. Those regulations will in fact legalise spray drift below a certain threshold based on what officials will decide is an "acceptable daily limit" of exposure. Too bad if several different neighbours spray on the same day and you get several times the acceptable daily limit. Each of them will be legally protected, but you won't be.

The Chemical Trespass bill is back in the ballot in the name of Ian Ewan-Street. We will drop it if the Minister's working group comes up with actual legislation to protect the chemically sensitive and their children from chemical trespass. But so far we're not holding our breath.

Koa looks up from the pages, tears in her eyes. "I sure wish Jeanette and the Greens had been about when I got poisoned by toxic sprays and herbicides. Nobody believed us back then. They thought it was me being over-sensitive."

"Yeah, well, many still think this – and people like The Poisoners that Cowrie mentioned in her last email have supporters who still collude with their lies and covering up. It's not as if these fellas don't know the story. I recall when Meriel Watts' book, *The Poisoning of New Zealand*, was first published. There was a huge outcry from farmers, helicopter companies and multinationals and they even tried to shut her publishers down. Said it was all 'conspiracy theory stuff'. She was personally threatened and there were even death threats. That's how serious these guys are. They know their livelihood is at stake and they will stop at nothing to bribe people to follow their cause or tar and feather their opponents. Look at the whole ForestsFirst debacle. Nicky Hagar's book shows the black and white evidence of their campaign to devastate anybody opposing the logging of native timber. Anyone who dares speak out on such issues faces death threats – and they will not be the first or the last ones in history to be obliterated at the hands of The Poisoners and the multinationals who benefit from selling and distributing their poisons." Irihapeti bangs down her cup on the table in defiance. "This is why so many are joining the fight against GM and globalisation. Both go hand in hand and both are engineered by the multinationals, whose *raison d'être* is greed, not sustainable living."

"Well, I'm sure grateful to Meriel for my survival. Reading her book allowed me to find out so much that even my doctors and the health system were unable to tell me on my journey to discover what my illnesses were and how to recover from them. I had no desire to be a victim, despite their trying to paint me as such, and as soon as I got the knowledge she provided with her research and insights, then I was able to start this long healing process." Koa wipes back the tears that flow from her face in relief.

"Hey there, Koa." Iri cuddles her closely, wrapping her arms around Koa's lavalava. "We will not ever give up on these causes. They are connected to the GE issue. While the genetic engineers say that GE means less spraying, we know it's not true from the overseas research. It just means different poisons and mutations entering into our food source and the air we breathe. Bugger them, Koa. I will fight this battle for you and for all of us if it is the last thing I do and so long as I have breath on this earth."

Koa looks at her lover, her friend, her soulmate, her eyes again filled with tears of relief, joy, sadness, happiness. "I know, dear Iri. You are my saviour too."

Iri snuggles closer. "I wouldn't mind another hot tub session right now."

"In the middle of the day? We'd never get any work done afterwards."

"Who said anything about work?" Iri has a gleam in her eye. She takes Koa by the hand and leads her to their caravan. As they play and laugh, the piwakawaka go strangely quiet, sensing a storm lies ahead, while the women of Te Kotuku bask in their blissful happiness.

Maata bangs loudly on the door of their caravan the next morning at dawn. "Come. Quickly. Mere needs you!" She disappears before they have time to ask any questions. They wrap their lavalavas around their bodies and flee to the nearby cottage, expecting to find Mere on the floor with a heart attack or having had a fall. Instead, they witness the flickering of her television, so seldom used, through the curtains. Inside, Mere points to the television screen, as if in a trance. "I knew their greed and treatment of indigenous people would come back to haunt them. But not like this, it's terrible." On the screen, people fleeing, dust around them. Firemen and police everywhere. A pizza sign on a blackened shop, a bagel symbol smashed in the rubble. Looks like New York. Then, suddenly, an eerie shot of the twin towers at the base of Manhattan. From the right, a black dot appears, flying toward one tower. It disappears into the building and flames flash out the sides. Seconds later, a replay of the second tower with what looks like a passenger plane heading toward it in slow motion. The plane smashes into the building, as if in a terror movie, and then it collapses, like a pack of cards, in dust and rubble. They cannot believe their eyes. It's then that Irihapeti recalls her dream. Maybe it was a premonition? Maybe she should have told others about it? She feels guilty before reminding herself it is absurd to feel such an emotion now.

For the next few hours, they remain glued to the screen, stopping to make tea and discuss the issues. They are torn, feeling for their friends and whanau in New York and on Great Turtle Island, yet knowing why this has happened and being amazed that the announcers have so little awareness of their own government's history. Not so long ago, the United States supported the Taliban into power, when it suited them, and now the Taliban are the enemy because they have supported Osama bin Laden, believed to be the perpetrator of this atrocity. Between repeated shots of the giant birds flying into the twin towers, which the news corporations know is compulsive viewing such as they have never had handed to them on a plate like this, are glimpses of Osama bin Laden. Such a graceful and beautiful man with soft eyes, about to be turned into the devil incarnate by the United States and world news media. The women can never excuse such acts of violence, but it makes them sick to see it happening. Yet again. Before long, talk of war, of revenge against Afghanistan for harbouring bin Laden and the Taliban.

"Please no. Not another Vietnam," urges Mere, pleading with the screen image of Colin Powell, a black brother who would turn on other black brothers for the US cause. They sit in stunned silence as the images flow, as the anger grows, as more and more information comes out. Over the next few days, they watch events unfold, bringing the new seeds inside to plant in their packs and sharing korero. They feel for the New Yorkers, strangely humble in their hours of terror. Yet they also feel for the tangata whenua of Afghanistan, who have been the victims of perpetual warfare over the last few decades, their land being reduced to rubble and their fields to dry dust. That the world powers could even think of attacking such a devastated country besieged by atrocious poverty and malnutrition, before the onset of yet another harsh winter, fills them all with anger.

"Why the hell can't they bring the Taliban and Osama bin Laden to justice using the court system? If they can do it with the Serbian and Bosnian tormentors, then surely they can do it now," argues Mere. "I have seen too many wars, too much devastation. There is never, ever a reason for war. We have to find better ways to resolve our oppression or anger or suffering. Surely?"

Her questions hang in the air like balloons, float into the sympathetic ears of her listeners, already on her side of the fence. But they do not reach into the screen to the announcers and the police, firefighters, angry at their lost brothers, the people bound in their grief at this moment.

"Is it unholy to say that this kind of suffering happens at the hands of the United States daily and yet is never on our screen in close-up focus as now?" asks Koa. "And thousands of children die of malnutrition every day without any media fuss."

They nod in agreement with her, in sympathy for all those suffering, on both sides of the world. But as the hours go by, more and more US evangelism and warmongering irritates them, angers them. They return to their daily tasks, weighed down by the battles they are now fighting on local and international fronts, but even more determined not to give up. As Mere stated on the first day of their viewing, "We cannot collude with depression, with anger. We must always fight our causes in the belief of creating and leaving behind a better world than the one granted to us. We owe this to our ancestors and our descendants. To those who went before us and those who come after us. Such wisdom, such grace." She ends on a note of warning: "*Ka tahuna te ururua ki te ahi, e kore e tumau tonu ki te wahi I tahuna atu ai: kaore, ka kakatoa te parae.*" To Maata, who does not understand all her words, she explains. "Literally speaking, this means that when the bush is set on fire, the flames will not remain in the dry brushwood; no, they will spread right over the plains."

"So what does this mean for Afghanistan?" asks Maata.

"That war can never be confined to a few people. It will spread like wildfire."

"Well, we need to tell that to the United States."

"Too right, Maata. And all of you need to get on the internet and get writing to your local papers. We need to support those tangata whenua in Afghanistan right now and also fight our battle for the land here too. But they need us more right now." Mere is wahine toa, standing proudly in her defiance.

"What a powerful woman," whispers Koa to Irihapeti, as they depart for bed.

"Kia ora. Cowrie will be proud of her too. I hope they email soon and let us know how they are." They wander out into the night air, so grateful for this land they live on, so grateful to be near the sea and to have a land capable of nourishing them when used sustainably, a land that they are willing to share so long as it is respected.

"So what's it like working for Mr Creepy?" Waka opens the van door for Maata.

"Nothing weird. Real messy place. But apart from that, he was okay." Maata climbs into the van and plonks her backpack onto the seat beside her. "Let's have a swim. I'm hot."

"Got the surfboards in the back. Wanna head for the dunes?"

Maata grins. It's their favourite place and they do not always have the use of the marae van on loan from Piripi. "Sure."

They drive out to Mitimiti Beach and carry their boards over the high dunes until they get to the wild West Coast breakers, thundering in on the sand.

"You game to join me?" challenges Waka, knowing she has not been in this rough surf since she was nearly drowned a few years back.

"Yeah. Why not?" Maata rises to the challenge, realising she has to do it sometime. Besides, after the September 11th explosion, she knows that anything could happen to anyone anywhere and it's up to everyone to live life as fully as possible and appreciate every moment. Somehow, this strange act of vengeance has given her even more courage to stand by her principles and the bravery to take risks and appreciate life as never before. Mere said they owed it to themselves to give thanks for every moment on this earth. She'd heard this stuff before, but never really believed it. Now it has flown home to her, as sure as those giant birds flying into those twin towers.

Maata and Waka run down the beach and into the raging waves which curl into large watery caves and crash over the pair as they paddle out on the surfboards, their heads tucked down, their feet like fins. The first wave hits Maata hard so she digs her fins in deeper and thrusts through the belly of the second wave, emerging on the other side, triumphant. She gasps out the salt water that filled her mouth and draws a huge gulp of air into her lungs before the next wave curves over her body. Suddenly, she is exhilarated. Her body is strong again, her will determined. Waka paddles alongside her until they clear the rough water and can float a while in the rolling sea beyond the breaking waves.

"We made it! Choice!" yells Waka, admiring the strength in Maata's arms. Her eyes light up a chestnut brown when she is excited and her voice deepens. She fins through the water like a sleek seal. Something in his soul is aroused by this woman emerging from her child-hood cocoon, something that is rare. A strength of spirit and an ability to keep fighting despite the odds. Maybe the abuse she endured as a child has in some way prepared her to cope with anything life throws up for her? Maata paddles alongside and dangles a fin into the water, touching his fin. A wave of energy surges through his body, stronger than any of the waves they have dived through today. He looks away, unable to meet the rich intensity of her eyes. It's then that he sees a fin circling around them. His heart beats like a Pacifika drum in his ears.

"D'ya reckon the herbs will have enough sun here under the banana palms, Iri?"

"Sure. It's the heat they want and most of them do better in the semi-shade. Remember what Cowrie said in her email about Jo's planting under the Ethiopian bananas?"

"Yeah. I hope she brings some of those seeds home to us as well." Koa makes a nest in the raised earth, sand and fernleaf mulch for her Vietnamese mint. The leaves, striped dark and lime-green, wave in the wind, delighted to be back in warm earth nurtured by mulch and prepared by worms.

"We can always email and get Jo to send some if not. I'm really looking forward to visiting his farm. D'ya reckon he'd be into us taking the kura kaupapa kids as well?"

"Only one way to find out. Sounds like he's into educating others and sharing his experiences." Irihapeti places some dead ponga logs around the outside of the raised beds under the bananas.

Koa notices this. "What if the new bananas want to spring up and the treefern log is in the way?"

"No worries," grins Iri. "See that log over there?" Koa looks in the direction she is pointing. "It was moved an arm's length by the baby banana to the right. They are incredibly powerful when they sprout new shoots and they manage to surge through almost anything in their way.

"But won't it destroy the garden edging?" Koa looks puzzled.

"Then we'll adjust to fit nature's whim," smiles Iri.

"Fukuoka would like that!" Koa stands upright, rubbing her back.

"And it's easier to go with the flow. That's what gardening with nature is about. Staying flexible all the time and adapting to new challenges. None of this Italian Renaissance design crap for me."

"Yeah – it's fine in its place. But I like Te Kotuku gardens much better." Koa stretches and admires their day's work. They have made raised beds under half the banana plantation and planted out the new herbs they had sprouted last season. Now they scatter organic mustard seeds all over the plot to take the place of any weeds that might have the errant desire to thrive there, and plant a few nasturtiums. Both will be great for salads, and they seem to wend their way around the other plants without too much hassle.

"Can't understand why so many gardeners hate nasturtiums and root them out at the first chance." Iri especially loves the new dark scarlet nasturtium sent to her by Cowrie after their visit to the eco-village in Kaiwaka and takes great care in planting it at the edge of the plantation, nurturing its new home with a few cockle and mussel shells from their last feast.

After a brew of fresh manuka tea with pohutukawa

honey, Koa settles into her favourite tatty armchair while Iri dives into the internet to catch up on emails. Koa is rereading Rachel Carson's *Silent Spring* and finds it still speaks to the current ecological issues vibrantly so many decades after the writing. Every now and again she recites a passage to Iri, and Iri reads from the emails to her. They debate the issues and soak up the support from the local organic gardeners who are using the net to find out new methods or share old ones. Irihapeti scrolls through a number of anti-GE petitions and responses to the Royal Commission's report on GM. Then she finds an email from Cowrie's friend Sahara, in the UK, who has sent an article from the magazine *Resurgence* which she subscribes to.

"Hey. Listen to this. It's about the importance of women in organic and GE-free farming."

Koa looks up from her book. "About time too. What's the essence of it?"

Iri sips her tea and scans the screen. "Mainly that the desire for organic food has grown out of the rejection of GM products and that over half the organic farmers are women compared with about five percent farming chemically."

"Women have always been involved in farming and still are in the Third World. It's mostly industrialisation and the corporatisation of farms that changed all this. But ecology pioneers Eve Balfour and Rachel Carson warned us against what we are facing now with GM."

"Too true." Iri scans the article and prints it off so that Koa can read the details later. She is encouraged and fired up by the strength of the article. "This inspires

165

me to want to keep up the pressure against GM. Imagine what Rachel and Eve would have thought of the Commission's report?"

"They'd've thought it a sell-out if they'd lived to witness what we have by now."

"I still find it astounding that we were not taught about them at school and they were never mentioned in my botanical classes. I only discovered *Silent Spring* by chance in a secondhand bookstore in Kawakawa."

"I only discovered them on the net and through *Organic New Zealand* magazine. Never heard of either of them before that."

"Disgusting, eh?"

"More planned than that. They were, after all, a huge threat to the multinationals producing agro-chemicals, just like Meriel Watts' book in Aotearoa."

"Cowrie mentioned that Meriel is working on her doctorate on pesticide use in Aotearoa. Be great if we could ask her for a copy when it's finished. Have you got her email?"

"Yep. It's on file here. Ya want me to zap her a request?"

"Ka pae."

Koa and Irihapeti talk late into the night, debating the issues of GE and discussing excerpts from the article and from Carson's book. They decide it is time that they passed on this knowledge since it was missing from their own education, and they start to plan a hui based around a sharing of such information and resources. Maybe the people Cowrie and Kuini are meeting on the hikoi would be willing to talk and share their discoveries,

166

alongside those from the strong Maori Coalition against GE.

"We need to include Carson's book as essential reading for the hui and also for our kura kaupapa courses. We could summarise some of the main issues for the tamariki. They are hungry for knowledge and wisdom in these areas and so disillusioned with the blindness of globalisation. Their new heroine is Naomi Klein with her *No Logo* book. If they could link the issues of GE to those of globalisation, then they'd have a ready audience of young people willing to get on board and fight to keep Aotearoa GE-free." They work late into the night, fired up by the article, inspired by the work of the women who came before them. "We have to make sure the tamariki work across race lines here, Koa. Rachel Carson is tangata whenua on these issues. We have to judge people by how they act in saving our earth, not just on their words and the colour of their skin."

"Too right, Iri. What was it that the Navajo elder told Cowrie on Great Turtle Island? The land belongs to those who look after it best. We are all caretakers of Mother Earth. None of us owns the land. It responds to those who look after it best. Something like that."

"I agree. But the issue of land rights goes beyond this. It's vital we retain much of the land taken away from us in order to look after it appropriately. That process has to take place at the same time."

"But what happens if we get greedy Maori leaders wanting to sell portions off to the multinationals for gold mines or genetic engineering?"

"Then buggered if I will excuse them for the colour of

their skin. No. It has to go deeper than this. The Navajo are right. It has to be about who looks after the land with the most care. That's our future, Maori and Pakeha."

"Ka pae, Iri. Reckon it's too late for a hot tub tonight?" Koa looks exhausted.

"Never too late for that, my love. You get the towels and I'll throw another log on the fire under the tub."

"Thanks." There is a full moon tonight, beaming down on them as if affirming their korero. The giant mamaku lifts her arms toward the heavens, black against the light behind, magnificent in her strength and power. Her ferny fronds wave in the gentle night air and send shimmering fingers over the water, mimicking the dances of the wahine where their hands move like ferns in a breeze.

Behind Maata, Waka sees the fin moving closer. He knows a disturbed or hungry shark can lunge from fifty metres away and attack in a matter of minutes. It's too far to surf to the shore. There's no choice but to wait and remain as still as possible. But if the shark looks up, their feet dangling off the edges of their surfboards will appear to the mako like enticing food, two seals waiting for the crunch. It's just a matter of which one first. Maybe they should try for the shore.

Maata is still blissfully unaware of the shark or Waka's weary watching. She's seen him gaze into the far horizon so often that it is second nature to her now. Yet this time, his eyes are very focused. Closing in on something. Maata turns around but does not see the fin. She thinks he is fixed on the driftwood floating past. Waka is always collecting interesting pieces of driftwood for his artworks.

Waka is not sure if Maata will panic, given her past experiences and especially her near-drowning when the current took her out to sea while collecting kai moana with Cowrie. If she does, then the shark is likely to panic also and attack. But how can he get her to remain still enough that it may get closer and decide they are not a good feed after all. Waka leans over carefully and takes Maata's head in his hands. He gently strokes her face, watching the shark circle nearer and nearer.

Maata is touched by his gentleness. She wonders what has suddenly inspired him out here in the oceans, while she'd hoped this might happen in the warmth of the dunes or the comfort of his bed. Stay present. Enjoy the moment. Stay with it. She hears the voices of her counsellor in her ears, the affirmation of the kuia who took care of her. Don't question the place, just affirm the feeling being shared. She balances carefully on her board so that she does not fall in.

The shark moves closer. It's now about twenty surfboard-lengths away. Waka holds Maata's head in his hands, crooning to her, whispering into her ear, as if these might be the last words he ever gets to share with her.

Tena koutou katoa – Kuini here. Cowrie is out bodysurfing with a few others on the hikoi from Ahipara. The Tawharanui Coastal Walk was stunning. We hiked across the farm, over several fields and a stream to a beach. From there, up a cliff path and over the far hills, looking out into the wide Pacific Ocean with Kawau and her sister islands to the right of us. The local community are replanting the hills in natives: pohutukawa through to manuka and kanuka. There's a working farm on the land and they have many visitors from schools and people from overseas as well. One of the community helpers also works two days a week at the Goat Island Bay Marine Reserve in neighbouring Leigh, and she told us how they are trying to convince the government to retain at least 10 per cent of the total New Zealand coastline in marine reserves like these two. The water is teeming with fish from blue maumau to piper and red schnapper and they say the whole coastline of Aotearoa would have been like this once. They asked for our help in their cause as the issues we are fighting for are so similar. They are opposed to any kind of genetic engineering of fish species and to the cruel and polluting methods of fish farming and have already lodged submissions on these issues to the Royal Commission.

We had some great korero but went to bed very late. I asked the park ranger if I could do a brief email to you today while the others surfed before breakfast, then we are off again. Talk to you again. Hope you are all well.

Mere – please contact Ahi for me and let her know we'll try to email her and meet up later on the hikoi. Thanks.

By the way, we're all in a state of shock over the US invasion of Afghanistan. The park ranger's wife, Sheila, read out a wonderful article by novelist Barbara Kingsolver. Remember how much we all loved the political power of *The Poisonwood Bible* and her dealing with the issues of colonisation? Well – wait till you read this. Best we have seen so far – and we surf the net at every break when we email you. It's empowering and enlightening. I'll copy it into the end of this email.

Kia kaha- Kuini [and your Turtle in the Waves!] xx.

LA Times Headlines 10/14/01

No Glory in Unjust War on the Weak
By Barbara Kingsolver

Barbara Kingsolver is the author of, among other books, "The Poisonwood Bible" and "Prodigal Summer." This article will appear in a forthcoming collection of essays.

TUCSON – I cannot find the glory in this day. When I picked up the newspaper and saw "America Strikes Back!" blazed boastfully across it in letters I swear were 10 inches tall – shouldn't they reserve at least one type size for something like, say, nuclear war? – my heart sank. We've answered one terrorist act with another, raining death on the most war-scarred, terrified populace that ever crept to a doorway and looked out.

The small plastic boxes of food we also dropped are a travesty. It is reported that these are untouched, of course – Afghanis have spent their lives learning terror of anything hurled at them from the sky. Meanwhile, the

172

genuine food aid on which so many depended for survival has been halted by the war.

We've killed whoever was too poor or crippled to flee, plus four humanitarian aid workers who coordinated the removal of land mines from the beleaguered Afghan soil. That office is now rubble, and so is my heart.

I am going to have to keep pleading against this madness. I'll get scolded for it, I know. I've already been called every name in the Rush Limbaugh handbook: traitor, sinner, naive, liberal, peacenik, whiner. I'm told I am dangerous because I might get in the way of this holy project we've undertaken to keep dropping heavy objects from the sky until we've wiped out every last person who could potentially hate us. Some people are praying for my immortal soul, and some have offered to buy me a one-way ticket out of the country, to anywhere.

I accept these gifts with a gratitude equal in measure to the spirit of generosity in which they were offered. People threaten vaguely, "She wouldn't feel this way if her child had died in the war!" (I feel this way precisely because I can imagine that horror.) More subtle adversaries simply say I am ridiculous, a dreamer who takes a child's view of the world, imagining it can be made better than it is. The more sophisticated approach, they suggest, is to accept that we are all on a jolly road trip down the maw of catastrophe, so shut up and drive.

I fight that, I fight it as if I'm drowning. When I get to feeling I am an army of one standing out on the plain waving my ridiculous little flag of hope, I call up a friend or two. We remind ourselves in plain English that the last time we got to elect somebody, the majority of us, by a straight popular-vote count, did not ask for the guy who is currently telling us we will win this war and not be "misunderestimated." We aren't standing apart from the crowd, we are the crowd. There are millions of us, surely, who know how to look life in the eye, however awful things get, and still try to love it back.

It is not naive to propose alternatives to war. We could be the kindest nation on Earth, inside and out. I look at the bigger picture and see that many nations with fewer resources than ours have found solutions to problems that seem to baffle us. I'd like an end to corporate welfare so we could put that money into ending homelessness, as many other nations have done before us. I would like a humane health-care system organized along the lines of Canada's. I'd like the efficient public-transit system of Paris in my city, thank you. I'd like us to consume energy at the modest level that Europeans do, and then go them one better. I'd like a government that subsidizes renewable energy sources instead of forcefully patrolling the globe to protect oil gluttony. Because, make no mistake, oil gluttony is what got us into this holy war, and it's a deep tar pit. I would like us to sign the Kyoto agreement today, and reduce our fossil-fuel emissions with legislation that will ease us into safer, less gluttonous, sensibly reorganized lives. If this were the face we showed the world, and the model we helped bring about elsewhere, I expect we could get along with a military budget the size of Iceland's.

How can I take anything but a child's view of a war in which men are acting like children? What they're serving is not justice, it's simply vengeance. Adults bring about justice using the laws of common agreement. Uncivilized criminals are still held accountable through civilized institutions; we abolished stoning long ago. The World Court and the entire Muslim world stand ready to judge Osama bin Laden and his accessories. If we were to put a few billion dollars into food, health care and education instead of bombs, you can bet we'd win over enough friends to find out where he's hiding. And I'd like to point out, since no one else has, the Taliban is an alleged accessory, not the perpetrator – a legal point quickly cast aside in the rush to find a sovereign target to bomb. The word "intelligence" keeps cropping up, but I feel like I'm standing on a playground where the little boys are all screaming at each other, "He started it!" and throwing rocks that keep taking out another eye, another tooth. I keep looking around for somebody's mother to come on the scene saying, "Boys! Boys! Who started it cannot possibly be the issue here. People are getting hurt."

I am somebody's mother, so I will say that now: The issue is, people are getting hurt. We need to take a moment's time out to review the monstrous waste of an endless cycle of retaliation. The biggest weapons don't win this one, guys. When there are people on Earth willing to give up their lives in hatred and use our own domestic airplanes as bombs, it's clear that we can't out-technologize them. You can't beat cancer by killing every cell in the body – or you could, I guess, but the point would be lost. This is a war of who can hate the most. There is no limit to that escalation. It will only end when we have the guts to say it really doesn't matter who started it, and begin to try and understand, then alter the forces that generate hatred.

We have always been at war, though the citizens of the US were mostly insulated from what that really felt like until Sept. 11. Then, suddenly, we began to say, "The world has changed. This is something new." If there really is something new under the sun in the way of war, some alternative to the way people have always died when heavy objects are dropped on them from above, then please, in the name of heaven, I would like to see it. I would like to see it, now.

Tony has reroofed his barns with clear plastic as instructed by his new lease-holders. He'd got a good deal from a mate in some truckloads of the stuff discarded because they were the wrong lengths for a government job, bought it cheap and pocketed the rest of the bikky. Felt they owed it to him really, taking such risks with his property. If the GE freaks found out what was happening here, they'd be down on him like a Greenpeace rubber ducky onto a whaling boat.

"So whad'ya gonna grow here?" he asks one of the botanists.

"We're not s'posed to say, really. Top-level secret and all that."

"Well if ya can't tell me, who the hell can ya tell? I mean, I'm not about to blab and stuff up my future income, am I?" Tony takes a plastic packet from his chest pocket, unfurls it and begins rolling some tobacco into the paper. "Wanna rolly?" he asks the chap.

"Haven't smoked in years. Then again, I miss it like hell. Why not then, eh? The missus'd never know."

"Too right," smiles Tony, handing over a rolly and making another for himself. He pokes the end into his mouth, lights up with a match, then holds the other fella's ciggie against the tip of his own.

"It's rituals like these I most miss. And the mateship that goes with them," admits the fella.

"What's yer name, mate?"

"Steve."

"Stevie Wonderboy, eh?" Tony laughs.

It's lost on the young man who has no idea what Tony is on about.

"So what's the big secret then, eh Steve? Ya gonna clone the body of Marilyn Monroe onto the head of Helen Clark and fuse the two together?" Tony guffaws. "I know which bloody half I'd take."

"No. Nothing like that," answers Steve, drawing in the sweet taste of the tobacco. "It's actually much more simple. We're experimenting with more productive patterns of growth. We've transferred genes from the fast-growing *Pinus radiata* into the native kauri tree to see if we can increase the pace of growth a bit."

Tony looks disappointed. "Why the hell d'ya wanna do that? Bit of a letdown after all that Frankenfish stuff, eh?"

"You don't want to believe all that rubbish the Greens put out. They're all into conspiracy theories."

"Yeah, bloody academics and liberals. Too much time at university on our bloody taxpayers' bikky, eh?" Tony puffs his smoke into Steve's face, little realising he is talking to a PhD graduate.

Steve decides it's best not to reply to this one. Tony's not very bright, but he seems a decent enough chap. "The point is that the timber of the kauri tree is worth ten times that of a *Pinus radiata*. If we could increase the growth rate, and still produce giant trees, then we'd be growing gold in them there hills, mate."

Tony looks out toward the Waipoua Forest. "Ah, now I see what ya mean. You could have another Tane Mahuta in ten years and rope in heaps more tourists as well as flinging the axe at the other thousands of trees around it. Shit. Not a bad idea. I could be interested in planting a few trees at that rate. Got a few spare acres out the back. Keep me posted on the progress, eh?"

"So long as you keep it quiet. I could lose my job over this."

"No worries, mate." Tony winks at Steve. "Me too!" He laughs, picking up his newly acquired cellphone and sauntering off to his new four-wheel-drive. "See ya later. Off to town for a while." He grinds the silver car into gear and drives off, leaving a cloud of red clay dust behind him.

He cradles her head in his hands. "I love you more than I've ever loved anyone on this earth, Maata. Remember that, no matter what happens, always remember that," whispers Waka into her ear. Maata wonders why he is so intimate, balancing on their surfboards, out here on the sea. Behind her head, the shark circles in closer. Then again, Waka always did like the sea and maybe this is his chosen place to be so romantic. She loves hearing his words, but tries hard not to giggle because the surf keeps pushing their boards away and she has to cling to him to remain so close. Their lower bodies swirl in and out as their heads remain locked together. She's grateful for this embrace that she has waited so long to experience and thought might never come. She melts to his touch, her senses swimming with the sea, her soul leaving her body, as if winging its way up into the heavens and looking down on them from above.

"Gidday, Ray. Howya goin', mate?" Tony slaps a tankard of Lion Red onto the counter and burps appreciatively.

Raymond pretends he has not heard and tries to pass him to get to the toilet and have a wash before his Friday night wine in the quiet without the family. Tony grabs his arm and yells into his face "You deaf from flying all those choppers too long, mate? Or too much hanky-panky with the missus? They say it zaps yer hearing like DDT on a field of cabbages." He laughs, proud he has come up with an appropriate metaphor for his new flying friend.

Raymond realises he cannot escape. "Hi Tony. I didn't see you there. Too much on my mind."

"Well, I can relieve you on that front." Tony swigs another drop. I'll bet, thinks Raymond. "I gotta preposition to put to yer. Might bring in some good bikky too."

Raymond's ears perk up at the mention of money. He decides not to correct Tony on the pronunciation of his proposition. "Fire away. No – let me buy you another tankard and let's take a booth over in the corner. I presume this is of a sensitive nature?"

"Yep. Lion Red. See ya there." Tony is pleased he has managed to garner such high company in the local pub.

He saunters past his old mates, making sure they all see him heading for a private booth and will watch Ray following behind with their beers. That'll show 'em who's boss, now. All those fellas who doubted him after his missus left. All those rumours about him abusing her. Well, wait'll they find out how important he really is, being courted by scientists, genetic engineers, FarmCorp. And mixing it with the head of the Rawene Business Association, Mr Chopper himself.

He sits himself down and splays his legs out wide, taking up as much space as possible. He lights up a fag, dropping the ashes onto the table, then remembers to wipe them away with his sleeve before Raymond arrives with the beers. Bit of a fussy fella, this Ray. He'd noticed this before. Raymond negotiates his way past many of the association's members before arriving at the table, much to the delight of Tony. In a loud, booming voice he announces, "Thanks Ray. Very good of yer. Cheers, mate. Here's to better business deals!"

Raymond clinks his glass of wine against Tony's tankard but whispers in his ear at the same time. "Keep it quiet, mate. D'ya want the whole pub to find out? If we botch this job, we'll never get another chance. My future relies on this."

"Sure, mate. No worries. Mine too." Tony takes a few swigs to calm his nerves.

"So what's the big deal?"

Tony lowers his voice. "I found out that these botany fellas are going to breed giant kauri trees by crossing them with pines. You know, so they grow even faster. Probably gonna stick in some eucalyptus genes too. They grow like ruddy Ozzie rugby players, two a bloody minute," he adds for good measure. Just to make it sound more impressive.

"Yeah? And?" Raymond is not sure he believes Tony. Maybe he's winding him up.

"Well, I'm already the chosen farmer to grow these monsters."

"Who sez?"

"The botany fella – Steve."

"Okay." Raymond decides to humour him. "So how does this connect with me?"

"Ah, my boy, that's where I'm indisposable to you." Indispensable, translates Raymond in his head. "'Cos who d'ya think they're gonna fly in to cut down the trees, eh? Bloody Flyworks Choppers, mate! We've got it sewn up by the balls! I grow the FrankenKauri and you fly in and take 'em out."

Raymond starts to get interested. "Are you sure they said you'd get the contract if it worked out?"

"Sure as there's piss in this brewery." Tony slurps his beer and lays a hairy, dirty hand on Raymond's clean, ironed shirt sleeve.

"So when do they reckon this might be happening?" Raymond is keen to know because he wants to expand his helicopter licence and this could be the opportunity he has been waiting for. He's already flying way over the limit of his licence for a private chopper, but if the big boys of genetic engineering with the big research funds want to inject some money into the ailing Hokianga council for an expanded resource consent, then he'll be as sweet as rain on a hot tin roof. He grins.

"Dunno. Looks like they are very close to financing it big-time. They just need one further trial." Tony has made this last bit up – but he does not want to put off Raymond now he has him eating out of his hand.

Raymond looks pensive for a while, weighing his bets. He's also hoping that Tony will remove his filthy hand from his freshly laundered shirt. There's no telling where that hand might have been. He recalls the dirty under-wear on Tony's chair and nearly gags.

"So whad'ya reckon, Ray. You in? Plenty of other chopper pilots who'd jump at the chance if you don't."

This brings Raymond back to earth with a thud. "Of course I am. I'd already discussed this with the boys earlier. I forgot to tell you. They want us to have the work since we are all in on the deal already. So, here's to our future, Tony. May it continue to be rosy." And clean, he thinks, clinking his delicate Heron's Flight chardonnay against the heavy metal tankard of Tony's Lion Red.

Maata has fainted into his arms. She's collapsed, like a puppet once held up by strings. Waka is not sure if she is still alive. It all happened so quickly. One minute he was holding her, the next she was head down in the water. He grabbed her and propped her up, folding her legs onto the surfboard and making sure all of her body was out of sight of the shark as it circled closer and closer.

He now has his own legs tucked under him and is shaking, still holding onto Maata and keeping her board close, as if they are both on a life raft drifting on the open sea. The fin circles the two surfers. Waka has been hoping he might be wrong, that it was a Hector's dolphin who'd lost its way. He'd hoped against hope this might be so. But he also knows that dolphins seldom circle in this way and it is typical behaviour for a shark, especially one who is hungry or one who might attack through fear or because it is ill. He utters all the karakia he can remember and stays as still as possible. At least Maata passing out like this has ensured that she will stay quiet and immobile. But he is aching to check her pulse, to make sure she is okay. He dare not do this – yet. The shark is too close. The mako slashes its tail, breaking water, and heads toward them. Waka closes his eyes and prepares to die, holding Maata in his arms.

"Yo, Koa. Where did the marae get the bulk corn for the last hangi?"

"From a Northland grower, I think."

"Was he organic?"

"Dunno. We've asked that all kai for the marae be GE-free and organic, but you know what the old fellas are like if they think they're onto a good cheap deal. They may have got it off a farmer who they trust but who sprays for all I know. We really do have to do more work on this with them."

"Sure do. Listen to this. It's from Chris Bone of the GE-free Register." Irihapeti reads from her screen:

In light of the good response to the last e-mail that i sent to the GE-free registered group i have taken the liberty to alert you all to the following.

This is an important issue for all of us i expect. Do you want to eat corn products that have been sprayed by Roundup Herbicide?

Application A446. An application has been received from Dow Agrosciences Pty Ltd to amend the Food Standards Code (in NZ and Australia) to approve food derived from a corn line 1507 genetically engineered to produce a Bt protein (CRYlF) that confers protection against attack by certain lepidopteran insect pests, and a PAT protein for

tolerance to glufosinate-ammonium herbicide
(i.e. Roundup Ready and Bt producing)

If you would like to make a submission to ANZFA please
go to

http://www.anzfa.gov.au/foodstandards/applicationsandsub
mi461.cfm

You will need to write your submission as a document that
you can attach. It need only be brief.

Best wishes,

Chris Bone
GE-free Register
PO Box 1803 Whangarei
Phone/Fax 09 4388 649

Website www.gefreeregister.co.nz

"Go into their website and get more info, and I'll ask
Mere if she knows where the corn came from."

"Ka pae." Irihapeti dives back into the net and pulls
up the screen. She's lost in detail and hardly notices Koa
slipping out the door to go to Mere's cottage. Koa arrives
to find Mere in quite a state. It turns out Maata and
Waka have not been seen all afternoon. "He collected
her from work and they borrowed Piripi's van to go
surfing at Mitimiti Beach. But nobody's seen them since
and it is getting dark already." Mere is beside herself.

"I'll never forget Maata's fear when Cowrie brought
her back from the surf after she'd nearly drowned. She
was carried out in the strong Tasman current and was
incredibly lucky to make it back safe. It's lucky that
Cowrie was there to save her. But this time she isn't.

186

Maata and Waka are just tamariki. If she gets caught in a rip like that, even Waka could not save her. I'm afraid for them both. I'd be devastated to lose Maata, and Piripi would never be the same again if he had to let go of Waka. He's invested so much energy in handing on his ancestral skills and whakapapa to his son. What can we do?"

Koa is not used to Mere, the wahine toa and kuia of their group, asking her for help. She hesitates for a moment. Then swings into action.

"Okay, Mere. Let's use Irihapeti's old motorbike. We've been to Rawene and back on it – and if you're game to let me drive you, we could be there in no time. Most likely we'll see them coming home safely as we head out. There's only one road we can take – so we cannot miss them."

Mere hesitates only a few seconds. Then she nods, pulling on her warmest cloak and following Koa out the door. She takes a moment to write a quick note so that Irihapeti and the others will not worry – and for Maata if she arrives home first.

"Maata and Waka gone. We're off to collect them. Mere and Koa." That should be enough. No point in worrying others too much.

Koa kickstarts the motor twice before it slurps into gear, and checks they have enough petrol. Mere climbs on behind her and they take off into the darkening dusk. The road is bumpy and the air cool as they make their way towards the coast through the forest and over the road beside mighty dunes. No sign of Waka and Maata, nor the Te Kotuku van. Finally they reach the beach. It is pitch dark by now, the moon hidden behind a thick layer of clouds. The surf thunders in toward them. No van. No tamariki. Just an empty, deserted beach.

Back at the cottage, Irihapeti examines the note left behind by Mere and Koa. It is so strange for Koa to go off like this without telling her. And how would they get out to Mitimiti? Maybe they have the marae van? She treks over to the workshop to see if Piripi is around. Nobody in sight. Then one of the tamariki appears from behind a large waka carving.

"Tena koe, Irihapeti? You wanna see our work?" Iri admires the exquisite carving which has taken them months to get this far.

"You seen Waka at all?"

"Na. Not since this morning. Just a tick – he was gonna collect Maata from her work this arvo. Maybe they went into town?"

"No – I think they went out to the beach. But perhaps I should check Flyworks first. Maybe they'll know."

"Dunno. Good luck." Hemi goes back to his carving.

Irihapeti returns to the cottage and calls Raymond Dixon. He's just home from the pub and picks up the phone after two rings. He likes to be known for his punctuality and efficiency. "Flyworks Helicopters. How can we be of service to you?"

Irihapeti explains that Waka was supposed to collect Maata from work and asks if he did so.

"No. I didn't see any boy from the marae come here." Raymond munches on a thick beef sandwich. He's hungry after too many chardonnays while humouring Tony and resents he has had to do this. On the other hand, he is pleased about the prospect of more money and a resource consent in the hand at once. He talks between bites. "Come to think of it, she left here and went to finish work at Tony's."

"Tony's. Where's that?" Irihapeti wonders if Maata is moonshining at a restaurant by night to earn extra money.

"Tony. You know, the fella with the farm on the hill overlooking the Waipoua Forest. His missus comes from the marae. Mona, I think."

Irihapeti gulps. "But why would she go there? She doesn't even know him?"

"Yeah she does. She'd got a job cleaning for him." He does not add that he organised it, hearing the tone of the woman's voice. She does not sound too pleased at all.

"Shit. Since when?" Iri is furious.

"Why the hassle? He's an okay fella." Raymond bites into the last of his beef sandwich and crunches on a bit of gristle that Barbara forgot to remove. "Damned woman."

"What damned woman? Don't you know about Tony? Moana left him because he beat up on her and the kids."

Raymond winces. This is not what he needs to hear. Not when he is about to go seriously into business with this man.

"Na. Ya got the wrong fella there. He's as clean as a whistle, that Tony. No worries. You got his number?"

"No. Can you please give it to me?" Irihapeti is by now deeply concerned and knows she must get to the farm as quickly as possible. She takes down the cell-phone number and calls immediately. No reply. She tries again. A blurred voice answers in the distance with much disturbance around. Sounds like a pub.

"Kia ora. I mean hullo. Is that Tony?"

"Yep. Who's calling? You wanna make an offer for some FrankenKauri?" He laughs.

Irihapeti recoils. She has no idea what he is on about but she is sure he is drunk. "Where are you, Tony?"

"At the Rawene pub, of course. Where should I be?"

This is getting nowhere fast, thinks Iri. "Is Maata there with you?"

"Who? Mother? Me mother carked it years ago."

"No. Maata, Martha – from Te Kotuku marae."

"Oh, the brown girl? No. She finished her cleaning and got picked up by some brown fella, Walter or something."

"What time was this?"

"About six o'clock. Said she was heading out for the beach."

"Thanks, Tony." Irihapeti hangs up the phone and strides to the shed to find her motorbike. It will not take her too long to get to Mitimiti. She needs to make sure they are okay.

Cowrie skims the waves, elated. It has been some time since she has bodysurfed like this. Not since Maata nearly drowned in the rip. That put her off for a while, and then she'd been so long overseas in Orkney. Far too cold to swim there, though she did have a skinny dip one time – much to the shock of the local Orcadians at Waulkmill Bay – when she was out collecting spoots for their dinner one night. Kuini watches her from the top of the hill looking out over the beach. She adores the way Cowrie is so graceful in the sea, like a turtle finning her way through the waves. It's as if she was born to be in the water rather than on the earth, yet she relates to both with the same passion she brings to all she does. Kuini loves her for this.

Cowrie is some way from the other surfers, nearer to the rock cave they explored at low tide the day before. Kuini looks on as Cowrie sizes up a strong wave and surfs in toward the cave. Surely she is not going to try to surf through it and out the other side? It is far too dangerous. Cowrie heads at breakneck speed toward the hole in the rock and disappears into it. Kuini holds her breath waiting for her to appear out the other side. Just as she fins her way into the cave, a school of kahawai break water on the surface and scoot past her, as if on a rescue mission at great speed. Cowrie has still not appeared out the other side of the cave. Kuini runs down to the beach to try to scale the rocks and get to her. But she knows she could never reach her in time. She's used to her friend taking such risks but cannot understand her judgement this time. The wave was far too strong, the current too fast, the cave too narrow. It has a twist in the middle, and if Cowrie did not swivel around in time to get out the other side, she'd be smashed against the wall. What could Cowrie have been doing? Kuini grits her teeth in fear as she runs toward the rock face, then she pushes down her feelings and concentrates on action.

Koa and Mere scan the dunes, calling out for Maata and Waka. They wait while the wind whistles back at them, but hear no human voices, see no sign of their van or surfboards.

"At least this is a good sign, Mere. If we'd found the van and trace of the tamariki, I'd be a lot more upset."

Mere is very quiet, as if listening to the sea. The birds are settling down for the night and having their last korero. She strains her ears, as if they might provide some clue for the disappearance of the kids. But she can only hear the wailing of the wind, the thundering of the surf, and the cries of the aki aki as they glide over the waves, every now and then swooping down for their prey.

"Maybe they didn't even come out here? You know what kids are like. Perhaps they changed their minds and went on into town or to visit some mates? We might be barking up the wrong tree altogether." Koa hopes to appease Mere's worries, but deep in her own mind she is not sure either.

"We must explore the entire area while we are here, comb the beach for any sign of them so we can get help from the *Manawa Toa* crew if we need to go out to sea." Mere is clearly expecting the worst and preparing for this possibility.

Koa winds an arm around her kuia and hugs her closely. She can feel the determination of the older woman and realises she will not rest until she has searched the beach and dunes. "Okay. Let's try. You walk the beach and I'll cover the dunes, then we'll meet near Tipo's cottage. We can ask him for help if we have no traces to go on by then. Are you all right with that?"

"Ka pae." Mere wraps her coat and shawl tightly and sets off down the beach.

Koa watches her, wondering how far they will go as the beach stretches out for miles. She's sure Tipo and his kids will have seen Waka and Maata because not much passes them by and they are the only ones living near here now. At least they can call back to the marae by then and see if the tamariki have turned up, since Tipo has a cellphone at Manaia Hostel.

Koa sets out over the dunes, keeping Mere in sight at all times. The last thing they need is a triple tragedy – if that is how the night is to pan out. Deep in her heart she hopes that the kids never came to the beach, that they opted to hang out with their mates in Rawene, but a small doubt still nags at her, eating slowly as a caterpillar edges its way around the outside of a lettuce leaf.

As she walks along the beach, looking for any signs of life or clothing, Mere recites her prayers, and the wind catches her karakia and spreads them over the sands like the winnowing of new seeds. She recalls giving some fernleaf, gum and speargrass taonga to Maata as a small child and her delight when Mere would repeat the words of offering:

Taku heo piripiri
Taku hei mokimoki
Taku hei tawhiri
Taku kati taramea
My pendant of scented fern
My pendant of sweet scented fern
My pendant of scented gum
My sachet of sweet scented speargrass.

Maata learned the words by heart and would make small offerings of silver fern, kauri gum and toetoe and bind them together with flax. She'd pour over sweet-smelling fragrances from native plants and then make offerings to all who came to visit, chanting this verse like a karakia. She always loved to please others and basked in their delight afterwards. Such an affectionate child to come from such early childhood trauma. She could not possibly be rescued from this fate and then placed into the hands of danger, not again. One close call with death by sea is enough. Mere is not sure Maata could survive another. She repeats the verse, over and over, as if it might call up this child, now growing into a woman, as if it might bring her back from the brink of death as the turtle saved her from drowning in the waves.

The wind is picking up as Koa battles her way across the dunes in the decreasing light. They have not brought torches with them, so Koa cuts some beach toetoe and lights it to guide her way. Then the moon comes out from behind the clouds and provides just enough light to ease their painful tracking over these sands. Koa remembers all the wonderful times she, Iri, Cowrie and

Kuini have had on this beach, gathering mussels, tuatua and toheroa before collecting was banned, and roasting them over a fire made from the ample driftwood that the sea offers up every day for their use. One time, Maata came with them and it was stormy like today. She was delighted to find fresh scallops thrown up by the pounding waves and gathered them in her kete and had them sizzling over a driftwood fire by the time the others returned with their kai moana from the rocks and sea-bed.

That day, Cowrie and Maata told the story of Maata's rescue from the waves, and in the firelight Koa had seen the deep closeness between them and the intimacy they shared through this experience. This was intensified by their life together with Mere, who'd adopted both of them and looked after them. Mere's guardianship of Cowrie trained her well to look after Maata. Koa realises how distressed Cowrie will be, having saved Maata once, to discover she has been lost to the sea again. She refuses to give in to such thoughts at this stage and focuses on searching for clues in the dunes. But it is like looking for a piece of kauri gum in the Sahara.

Suddenly, a wailing like a karanga pierces the night air, and Koa watches Mere sink to her knees on the wet sand. She is bent over a piece of cloth. Koa runs down the dunes, her feet digging deep into the thick sand and slowing her pace. The wind whips into her face and it seems as if she will never reach Mere, whose wails are spiralling over the dunes, up into the trees beyond, out over the waves. In the distance, a lone takapu cries back eerily from beyond the breakers, thinking its mother might be near, disturbed by the cries of grief it cannot identify as it is buffeted by the rough ocean, its beak still empty of fish.

When Koa nears Mere kneeling at the high tide line, she sees a pattern of green sea turtles swimming over the deep blue material locked in her grasp and recognises a piece of Maata's lavalava, ripped from the side of the cloth and covered in blood. She knows there is only one way this could be here on the beach, still intact, the blood still fresh. Mere holds the cloth to her face and moans into it, still uttering her karakia, still hoping there may be an answer other than the story the ripped lavalava tells.

Koa rubs her shoulders lovingly as the tears fall down her cheeks and onto the turtles, soaking into the blood and making it run into the blue sea of the lavalava. Koa moves from side to side with Mere as she wails and weeps, holding her as tightly as Mere holds the cloth, her only reminder of her little Maata, the child she'd raised as her own. The green turtle, whose fin has been ripped off with the material, turns red as the blood soaks into its flesh and drips down onto Mere's knees below. The wind howls into them from the sea as if joining their grief, and the waves pound the shore in anger. Or maybe it's defiance, that they have finally claimed this child who was once grasped from their reach just as she was offered up to them by Tangaroa, God of the Sea.

Kuini scrambles desperately over the rocks, heading for the sea cave that Cowrie disappeared into minutes ago. No sign of her emerging triumphant out the other side, nor her crumpled body thrown up by the waves that smash violently against the inner walls of the cavern and spout like a surfacing whale from the cave mouth. The wind rages against her, slowing her progress, and she dreads what she may find inside the cave, that she may have to wait until the tide falls to discover its gruesome secrets. The other surfers have headed back to the ranger's house, and Kuini cannot leave the cave to get help. Her only hope is to find Cowrie, dead or alive. She slips across the wet rocks, struggling to find ledges wide enough to carry her weight, and clings precariously to the slippery cliff face, praying she will make it.

A rock slides out from her feet and sends a hoard of smaller rocks after it. Kuini grasps onto a thick pohutu-kawa root as wide as her wrist that is poking out of the clay cliff above the rocks. It bends with her body, but holds her in place until she can tentatively find another foothold, not daring to look down to the sea thundering into the rocks below her. A surge of water thick with kelp crashes over her, leaving a tangled mass of seaweed locked onto her hair and shoulders. She shivers with the cold and holds onto her sacred pohutukawa tightly. The sea recedes and smaller waves only reach to her knees, granting her a reprieve so she can make her way slowly to the cave entrance. She lies on a ledge above the cave and listens. Nothing but the roar of the sea, the swoosh of the waves as they enter into the cave, smash up against the back wall, swirl around violently and whirl with new fury out the other side. In the distance, aki aki screech their calls into the wind as they swoop past.

"Cowrie. Cowrie. Are you there? Can you hear me?" Her voice boomerangs into the cave and back again. The echoes resound several times before bouncing back to her as if mocking her calls. Kuini hopes that Cowrie might have found a hidden ledge inside the cave, just enough to provide an air hole – but also realises this is a very faint possibility. Perhaps Cowrie was smashed against the rock wall and hurtled back out to the open sea? Maybe her body was sucked under the wave and Kuini did not see this as she ran down the beach? Fears crowd her mind like bats crashing blindly against rocks in the wet, black night. All she can do is chant, again and again, in her head:

Ko Hinemoa, ko au . . . ko Hinemoa, ko au . . .

Like Hinemoa, I'd risk all for love . . . like Hinemoa, I'd risk all for love . . .

The underground burial cave on Tony Pratt's farm is like a body being wired for life. Its belly is rigged with intestines of coloured plastic snakes wriggling from one side to the other. Hooks are attached to the rock ceiling through which the wires can travel. Audio, video and computer wiring decorates the once dark cavern like a Christmas tree covered in gaudy lights, garish speakers and microphones. Steve looks on with delight as his men transform this ugly old cave into an experimental laboratory.

Then they begin work on the connecting caves, using all that are large enough to stand up in and hold their captive prey for the duration of their experiments. Not that they will be treated as captives. Far from it. These animals will have the very best that modern technology can offer and be monitored day and night, 24/7. Nothing will be spared for their comfort, from the best hay that International Seed Corporation and MagicMilk can provide, via their research funds, to the best vegetables available. The workers have already decided to buy from the local organic collective, just in case. It wouldn't be good for their cause if any of the animals died from a crop blasted with Roundup or any of its baby toxins.

No, this cave will look like a manger by the time they

have finished. And they will be the three wise men – Tony, Ray and Steve, who bring frankincense and myrrh and whatever the third thing was – to welcome the birth of the New Christ, the baby Jesus, the brave new world of cloning. This genetic experiment will be like none before. It will be breaking new ground, opening up new worlds, eventually bringing together humans and animals in a holy mergence, where one can save the life of the other. This moment, thinks Steve, will be the end of life as we know it and the beginning of a brilliant, shimmering existence. He is alive, humming, entranced by the enactment of his vision at last. All his training, study and research has led to this moment in time. Finally, he will be recognised as the New Creator, for he will hold the key to a pristine form of life on this planet, a better breed of creature than God or computer engineers could ever dream about, let alone create.

Mere refuses to stand, is still kneeling down, grasping her life-line to little Maata. The torn rag hangs limply from her hands, the wounded turtle bleeding from its shoulder where the fin was ripped off. She whispers karakia to the cloth, as if her prayers might make her beloved Maata appear magically from the withering piece of lavalava, like Venus from her scallop shell, magnificent in her living glory. Mere would give Maui her jawbone, her teeth, her eyes, her limbs, if only she could have Maata stand beside her now, if only she could surf in safely on the welcoming waves, right here into her arms. She'd willingly relive all those harsh years of coming to terms with her abuse, the hardships it caused her and others, the tears of grief, the hours awake in the dark when little Maata had violent nightmares. She'd embrace every moment of caring for Maata, washing her, her clothes, her dishes, until she was old enough to begin to take care of herself. She'd welcome back the times of stormy defiance as Maata entered into her teenage years, rebelling against the calmness and safety of Te Kotuku marae, of Mere's cottage, of Cowrie's care, wanting to sit for hours under those dreadful headphones listening to those awful wailing monsters that Mere had seen on MTV. Right now, she'd hug Maata walking into her lounge on the arm of one of those dread-locked wailing motorbike boys, helmet in his hand, fag in his mouth, so long as he was there with Maata, her Maata, her child, her grandchild, her tamariki, her mokopuna.

She feels the warmth of Koa's breath on her neck, hands gently massaging her shoulders, and slowly she stands, still clasping her torn rag. Koa guides her up the beach towards Tipo's cottage. From there they call the marae to see if Maata and Waka have, by some miracle, defied fate and returned. No such luck. Irihapeti is still at the cottage, waiting to hear from them, puzzled at her missing motorbike but realising, after calling Piripi, that the tamariki had the van and Koa must have taken Mere on the motorbike. Irihapeti wants to scold them for going alone, but knows she cannot, not in the face of this disaster. Instead, she tells them to come home and assures them she will call the *Manawa Toa* crew, the coast guard, the police and Rawene Hospital to make sure that they all know and in case anyone has found the bodies of the two teenagers.

Koa and Mere stay for a warm cup of tea with Tipo, who says that he saw the two earlier, that they'd paddled out beyond the breakers and then he'd gone to smoke some mullet he'd caught in his net. By the time he returned, the kids were gone. He assumed they'd finished surfing, packed up and headed home. There was no sign of them, nor their van, nor that anything was at all wrong. He always keeps an eye out for kids surfing or swimming here because the rip is so dangerous and there can be freak waves. But he knew the marae kids were used to the wild West Coast surf and never gave them another thought. Mere thanks him for his help. Tipo offers them a bed for the night, saying that they'd still be able to keep in touch with the marae, and fearing a trip back in the howling wind on the motorbike, but Mere insists that they must return home, be there for the others. Tipo knows better than to argue with a kuia and agrees.

Mere and Koa mount the old bike, huddled in jumpers provided by Tipo to keep them warm enough for the return journey. He waves them goodbye and immediately calls Piripi to let him know they are on their way. He's known Piripi since they were kids at school together and he realises just how frantic he'll be at this time. Just as well. Piripi is alone and has not yet heard the kids are missing. Tipo fills him in on what he knows and assures him that Irihapeti is doing all she can – and maybe he should join her at Mere's cottage and both wait for Mere and Koa to return. Piripi can do little else. His van has not returned and there are no other available cars. He talks as long as possible with Tipo, soothed by his voice and knowledge that he feels his son and Mere's tamariki will be fine. He just has this feeling. Piripi knows to trust this well and heaves a sigh of relief to hear it from a mate he loves.

The ride home to the cottage is bumpy and rough. Koa's eyes stream with tears from the cold night air whipping into her face and the grief she feels inside her. Mere is tensely holding onto her waist and her head is slumped into the back of Koa's neck. Koa has never seen the kuia like this. She's always so strong, such a wahine toa, that she never imagined anything would knock her back like this. Then again, Koa has no idea what it is like to lose a child you have rescued from abuse and then raised as your own. It's a special feeling that few could ever know. When they turn onto the clay road to the cottage, they see all the lights glowing and people inside. Mere dreads having to face them, but knows she must. She utters karakia and prepares herself for the long hours of the endless night that lies before them.

Cowrie is crammed into an upper ledge of the cave, her knee badly bruised and the left side of her body injured as she smashed against the rock wall. She knew she'd never get out alive if she let the wave take her further and clung to the rock crevice until the wave slurped out, taking a mass of sand and seaweed with it. She hauled herself up onto the ledge just as the next wave crashed through the cave. A large crab edged itself further into the slit as she did so, not keen to share its home with this strange creature surfed in by the wave.

Moments after she'd crawled into the air pocket, she felt a pang of pain as the injuries seeped through her body, and in seconds she was back in the sea in her mind on the day Maata nearly drowned in the waves. She recalled the energy as clear as light and tuned into the power that surged through her like a wave, giving her the courage to carry Maata safely to shore on her back, like a turtle swimming through the waves. She invoked Laukiamanuikahiki to protect her again, as she'd saved Maata then. In that moment, she felt a pang of alarm. Maybe it was Maata in trouble, in a rip tide again? Maybe the fear was not for her but for Maata? She curled into a foetal position, still clinging to the ledge, and focused all her energy on saving Maata. It felt like

Maata had collapsed, but she was not alone. Maybe she'd also found a rock ledge to keep her above the water? Maybe she was also waiting for the tide to recede to return to safety? Cowrie lost consciousness for a moment, was surfing in the waves, surfing into the beach at Mitimiti, her little Maata on her back again, safe from harm, safe from abuse, but exhausted and drained.

Minutes have passed. It could be hours for all Cowrie knows. The tide has receded slightly and, although the waves are still surging through the cave, they are further down the rock wall. Soon, she may be able to lower herself into the water and safely swim out. If her leg allows her to do this. She sends a shaft of light into her bruised knee, willing it to heal well enough to get her out of here. In the distance, she hears a faint voice. It sounds like Kuini. But it can't be. She left her behind at the ranger's house when they'd left for their swim. She listens hard. There it is again.

Kauri . . . Kauri . . . Kauri . . . Cowrie . . . Cowrie . . . Cowrie . . . She tries to answer, but her voice is weak and tired. It is muted and unable to carry that far. Queenie . . . Queenie . . . Kuini . . . Kuini . . . She gives up, laying her head awkwardly on her arm, and passes out in pain.

The lights are blazing at Mere's cottage as they drive up the clay pathway. It looks like a wake. Maybe somebody has died? It's very late for a gathering and must be an emergency. They park outside and peer in the window. There is Mere, her head in her hands, a piece of Maata's lavalava still dangling from her fingers. Irihapeti's arm is around her and Koa's arm is around Iri's. Piripi sits next to Mere, holding Waka's first-ever carving, fondling it and tracing the spiralling lines around the body of wood affectionately, sadly, as if he could conjure his son from the heart of the tree which once stood proudly near the marae before it was felled for their carving. Bill Noa, the local policeman from Pungaru, stands tall, his cellphone to his head, talking quietly as he makes his enquiries to the coast guard.

The couple walk into the cottage and there is a stunned silence. It's as if they have all seen a bunch of ghosts.

"Where the hell have you been?" demands Piripi. He runs toward them and pulls them both toward him, hugging his son with one arm and Maata with the other, tears running down his cheeks.

Over the next hour, Waka and Maata both try to tell the tale which comes out in bursts and each time the story seems different. It turns out that Maata fainted from exhaustion after her week's work, study at night, and from dehydration, as she had not had any water since the morning. Waka was relieved as a shark was circling around their boards and her fainting could have saved their lives. If either of them had moved, the shark might have decided to move in for the kill. Waka held Maata closely, keeping her head above the water and all their limbs above the surface so the shark would have to knock them off their boards if it wanted a meal. Just as it seemed to be circling for the kill, a huge school of kahawai surfaced to their port side and swam within a few feet of them. The shark, knowing it could have an easy feast from the swarming fish, and that the present catch would be much more than a mouthful, if tasty at all, veered to the left and in its first gulp hooked a kahawai. Once it had the taste of its dinner, it followed the fish out to sea, allowing Waka to get Maata onto his surfboard, tie her board to his, and surf in, albeit rather awkwardly.

Once ashore, he ripped her lavalava to cover the bleeding cut on his leg caused by the second board crashing into his shins while he tried to get Maata safely into the shallows. By this time she was coming to, and they both managed to walk and limp, arm in arm, back to dry sand. They then dressed the wound with a clean piece of towelling to soak up the blood and must have left the ripped lavalava behind. Once the boards were back in the van, they drove straight to Rawene Hospital to make sure Maata was okay and to get Waka's shin dressed properly. That's when the doctor, Clare Ward, their favourite, told them it was probably a mixture of dehydration and exhaustion that had made Maata faint and might have saved their lives.

"I felt as if some power larger than me was helping me paddle in," adds Waka. "I had a strength in my arms as never before. At first I did not think we'd ever make it. Then it was like a dolphin came under our boards and lifted us on its back and powered us in."

More like a turtle, thinks Mere, hugging Maata and crooning into her ear, not believing she is still alive, and castigating herself for ever thinking she would not be safe. She wonders where Cowrie is at this very moment. No doubt very pleased with herself for tuning in at the right time. Just as Laukiamanuikahiki protects Cowrie, so Cowrie protects Maata. Maybe this is the sacred taonga I receive for rescuing them both from their abandonment? Perhaps I just need to trust this and know they will always be safe in the end, thinks Mere, relieved neither Maata nor Waka is badly hurt. But she is unaware that her own daughter, Cowrie, is lying wounded on a rock ledge inside a sea cave, the waves washing around her.

The barn and caves are now ready for work to begin, and Steve invites Tony and Ray to have a look. Best he keeps them sweet and onside, only knowing what he thinks is safe for them to know.

"Wow! These caves look like Waitomo, all lit up like a bloody Christmas tree!" exclaims Tony, genuinely surprised at their work. Not bad symbolism, thinks Steve, but says nothing. "Maybe I could run a tourist operation after you boys leave? All those Europeans who click their ruddy cameras at that Tane Mahuta, ugly old bugger that it is with half its branches and leaves gone and just a ruddy big trunk to gawk at, they would think all their bloody holidays had come at once if they got to see this. Pity it's not bigger, or I could screen horror movies from the back wall and have them freakin' out as a few bush wetas land on their noggins just at the right moment." He laughs, enjoying the thought very much.

"Don't worry, Tony. If our experiments work as we expect them to, you'll be so rich from the results that you'll never have to work again. We all will be. Just relax, keep yer trap shut and leave it to us." Steve wants Tony to know just enough to keep him happy and out of the picture. Of course, he'll offer to buy the land if it works out for further experiments, and if not, he'll dump Tony and his farm like a mutilated lamb.

Ray perks up his ears at the mention of money. "What kind of riches are we looking at, Steve?"

"No end to that if we are successful, Ray. You'll be the chopper we use to collect the kauri if the barn experiments work. But if Operation Cave is a winner, then we'll all be rich men. I can't tell you more than this. It's top secret."

"I thought you'd agreed to keep me posted on progress?" Tony is hurt he is being shut out.

"No worries, Tony. You'll be the first to know once we strike gold." As if, thinks Steve, knowing he cannot trust this simple man with such knowledge when the time comes. He'll divert him with a few good stories. "In fact, since you are both mates," he adds with a carefully engineered grin, "I'll tell you that we are to do some cloning here. Highly regulated, of course. FarmCorp will be inspecting the results, so everything will be above board. We have to pass it all by ERMA – the Environmental Risk Management Authority – so it will all be very rigorous. You'll see them coming out here to inspect the premises and at the end to watch over the results." Both Tony and Ray nod appreciatively, delighted they are in on it thus far. They know they've hit the big time and no way will they sacrifice money for gossip at this stage of the operation. Though it is tempting.

Tena koutou katoa – Kuini here this time. We're still at
Tawharanui and the hikoi has moved on, but they will stay
in touch via email. Tariana from Kawakawa will be on line
when she can. Cowrie had a bit of a scrape on the knee
while bodysurfing at Anchor Bay and she's also got a few
suspected bruised ribs, according to the vet who works
here. We thought it appropriate for a vet to inspect a
turtle, eh? No need to worry, Mere. Your Turtle is okay.
It happened last night. We tried to call but your phone was
engaged. Bet Maata was on the net, eh? Tena koe, Maata.
Cowrie said she thought of you while in the water as she
got pushed about a bit by the waves. She sent you energy
just in case you needed it. I told her you could look after
yourself and it was time she took care of her own body.
She just had to get the biggest wave to the most rugged sea
cave! Typical Turtle!

We've decided to stay on a bit while she heals, and then
catch the bus from the nearby township of Warkworth
when she's okay. We have not considered whether to join
the others in Tamaki Makaurau yet. It depends on how
fast our Turtle recovers. There's a big anti-GE march
planned down Queen Street and a rally at Aotea Square.
Maybe some of Te Kotuku whanau will go down by bus?
Check out the details on the GE-Free Coalition website
we emailed to you recently. Kia ora.

Last night I dreamed about caves. Probably because
Cowrie was trapped in the Tawharanui sea cave. But this

cave was strange. A bit like Waitomo. All rigged up
with lights and wires. There was a body groaning in pain
and I tried to crawl forward to see what it was, but every
time I made some progress, I was being pulled back again.
I could not see who or what was pulling me. Creepy.
Reminded me of when I was trapped in some Maori burial
caves on the farm as a kid. Remember me telling you
about that? I fell down into them and lay with a broken
leg, looking at a line of old skulls, until Kuri, my alsatian,
alerted the whanau. It took me weeks to recover. I kept
hearing our ancestors wailing out to me for destroying
their peace. I thought they'd punish me until Aunty Poniki
told me that they'd know I fell in by chance and did not
mean to disturb them. That although burial caves are tapu,
our ancestors know who comes with bad intent and who
does not. I asked what would happen if I came with bad
intent? They said it did not bear thinking about, that
people had been cursed with illnesses and some even died
when they disturbed such sacred places. However, that
would not happen to me, they assured me. I was able to
get over it then. Strange how these feelings can return
with such force, eh?

Anyway, I'd better not rabbit on as Sheila needs to use
the net to check up on some seaweed recipes. They collect
a range of wakame from Jones Bay and she's promised us
a treat tonight. That'll cheer Cowrie up. You know how
miserable Turtles get when they cannot do all they want
to do! Some interesting kai moana should do the trick!
Hope you are all well. We love you.

Kia kaha – arohanui

Kuini – and Wounded Turtle! xx.

"Please don't ever do that to me again, Maata. I was so worried that the tide had ripped you away from me, that I'd never see you again." Mere is nearly in tears and holds Maata close the next morning.

"Sorry, Mere. I promise I'll let you know where I am. But even then – you still could not have helped. You couldn't have stopped the shark from coming, nor me from fainting." Maata hugs her warmly.

"True. But at least I would have known for sure you were there and not anywhere else. As it turned out, you did go off later to Rawene Hospital without letting anyone know."

"Yeah. I won't do it again."

"Well, it's taught me a lesson not to worry so much. You can look after yourself in the end. You sure knew how to beat that shark away, eh?"

"Maybe I'm following in Cowrie's footsteps? Perhaps I am protected by the turtle like she is?"

"Maybe so. We'll see. It doesn't sound like she was too protected out at Tawharanui according to Kuini's email. Then again, it could have been worse. Imagine if I had lost both of you on the one weekend. That would have been devastating."

"Can I make you a warm cuppa tea, Mere? That'll

cheer us up." Mere nods as Maata moves toward the small kitchen area.

Mere looks out the window onto the herb garden. The peppermint and lemon balm are lush this year, and orange and yellow nasturtiums wend their way around and over the leaves as if they are hugging the plants and nurturing them. At the border, lemon verbena are sprouting from their woody winter stems and the pineapple sage is sending up bright scarlet ribbons of fire. She watches Maata as she reaches out the window to pick the heads of lemon balm. What a strong and beautiful young woman she has raised. She is so proud of her. Despite the shock she went through yesterday, she seems to have recovered well. The young seem to bounce back like a tree branch held down by snow and now released into the spring air. She hopes her Cowrie fares as well. Soon after, Maata hands her a steaming brew of lemon balm and fresh ginger tea.

Maata opens the fridge and sees the whitebait that Piripi dropped by that morning. While Mere is sipping her cup of tea pensively, she decides to make her aunty's favourite whitebait fritters. She mounds up the stone-ground flour and tips in some milk from the marae cows. She then adds an egg from their own hens and mixes it all up with some kelp and pours in the small whitebait. When the pan has heated with a dob of olive oil, she drops tablespoons full of the mixture onto the hot surface, and it sizzles. About a minute later, she flips the fritters over, and her mouth waters for the delicious treats.

Mere comes back to earth from her reverie. "What's that you're cooking Maata? Smells like heaven to me."

"It is. Now you just relax and I'll bring them to you."

Mere is happy to do as she says and settles into her old chair with relish as Maata delights in preparing the treat for her. Whitebait fritters with fresh lemon slices and a salad of nasturtium and red mustard leaf. The perfect breakfast. Over this treat, they discuss Maata's work and Mere's upcoming medicinal plant hui.

"How are you finding it at Flyworks? That Raymond fella treating you okay?"

"Yeah. He's okay. At least he got me a job at Mr Pratt's farm. I'm glad of the extra money."

"You be careful of that fella, Maata. You know he's Moana's ex, don't you?"

"I figured as much. But he isn't gonna hurt me at all. He keeps his distance and just lets me clean up around him. Bloody messy fella though. You should see the state of his undies. Worse than a cow paddock on a hot wet day!"

Mere laughs. "Ugh! He doesn't expect you to wash them does he?"

"Yeah. But he has a fancy new washing machine and dryer. I don't even have to hang the clothes out. Just bung them in and then throw them into the dryer afterwards."

"How can clothes get clean if they are not properly aired? The man's a heathen. You just watch your back there Maata. Call me if ever you feel uncomfortable and I'll get Piripi or Waka to collect you immediately. Okay?"

"Yeah. You fuss too much. I'll be fine."

"Better fuss now than be sorry later. Got any more

whitebait fritters?" Mere licks her lips and places her fork onto her plate.

"Course I have. Another plate keeping warm under the grill." Maata fetches them and they tuck into a royal feast fit for Dame Te Ata, their Maori Queen. Outside the window, an orange and black monarch butterfly lands on a yellow nasturtium flower and tests her new wings by stretching them in and out, knowing she is safe in this sweet scented garden of Te Kotuku.

"Next time you decide to run away on my old bike with a kuia, at least let me know about it so I do not worry," Irihapeti admonishes, looking up from her laptop as Koa enters the nursery studio.

"Sorry, Iri, but Mere was deeply upset and she did leave you a note."

"Yeah – but just get me next time. I should have been there to take her out to the beach."

"Fair enough. I didn't think. I just felt the urgency of the minute. So – any more juicy responses to the government's cop-out decision on GE yet?"

"Yep. A stunner from a physics professor at Auckland University. Best piece I've read so far on it."

"Wanna share it with me? I've got a break before my session with the tamariki." Koa settles into her old overstuffed armchair to listen. "Is it long?"

"Na. Under two pages."

"Then read it to me and print it off later if we wanna share it with the others. Where did ya find it?"

"Was printed in the uni newspaper, *Craccum*, and on one of our link sites."

"Sounds a lot more political than when I was there," quips Koa.

Iri looks up. "I didn't know you had been there at all.

219

Thought you were a Mainlander by then."

"Was. But I did a continuing educational course in botany when I first came up to Tamaki Makaurau. Excellent too."

"Ya wanna hear it?" Iri's eyes are glued back onto the screen.

"Fire away."

"Okay, then. Here goes." Iri reads from the laptop: "Royal Omission – Great title eh? I like the way they spin off on the Royal Commission." She goes on:

Royal Omission
by Peter Wills, Professor of Physics, Auckland University.

The Royal Commission on Genetic Modification has recommended that things in New Zealand be left more or less just the way they were before it started its work. Except for one thing: we should abandon the possibility of a GE-free New Zealand, something that a large proportion of the parties who participated in the Commission's processes asked for. The Commission describes excluding the possibility of a GE-free NZ as "Preserving Opportunities."

The country's researchers, regulators and business people have been given the green light again, and the people who managed to get the light changed to amber while the Commission did its work have been told that they can have their GE-free New Zealand in bits. The Ministry of Agriculture and Fisheries will work out how far apart GE farms and GE-free farms should be and when disputes arise they will come in and mediate.

The gist of the Commission's attitude to genetic engineering can be gleaned from the second sentence of their report's Executive Summary: "It [genetic

220

modification] holds exciting promise, not only for conquering diseases, eliminating pests and contributing to the knowledge economy, but for enhancing the international competitiveness of the primary industries so important to our country's economic well-being."

Genetic engineering is cast as heroic, fitting perfectly into the fashionable view of human good as the creation of wealth and health through global capitalism. Furthermore, our academic and governmental institutions, cooperating with industry, so we are told, have got everything right, at least more or less. The system needs just a bit of a tweak here and there, but they have made no fundamental errors.

The report cites everyone and criticises no-one, but one has to look a little more closely to see whose interests and interpretations of the facts have been given weight. The recommendations make it very clear how interests vested in genetic engineering have been weighed against those somehow opposed to applications of the technology. In all of the major areas, research, agriculture, food, patents and liability, the Commission accepts the adequacy of the institutions and practices that have already been put in place by experts and makes only minor suggestions as to how things can be improved.

The unique circumstances of the "biotechnology century", as the Commission calls our times, are dealt with by setting up a Bioethics Council and a Parliamentary Commissioner on Biotechnology and asking the Ministry of Science, Research and Technology to develop a biotechnology strategy for the country. And then the Minister in charge of the Environmental Risk Management Authority is to have a "call in" power (that has never been exercised) extended so that it includes the significant cultural, ethical and spiritual issues that have been at the heart of the debate about genetic engineering in New Zealand during the last few years.

The wishes of those who went to the Commission and asked for New Zealand's GE-free environment to be kept the way it is, even for the time being, have simply been omitted from the substance of the recommendations. It is recommended that there be research into environmental impacts on soil and ecosystems, research support for organic farming, a strategy for the use of BT, protection of GE-free honey, special assessment of GE trees and so on, but all predicated on the progressive introduction of genetically modified organisms into our agricultural environment. Everything can exist side by side. It doesn't matter that mounting evidence suggests that humans are pretty well incapable of keeping GE farming and organic farming properly separate from one another. New Zealanders will work out, as no-one else has managed to, how to make cross-contamination impossible.

The main result of following the Commission's recommendations will be that organic farmers will just have to accept International Seed Corporation's and Aventis's genes getting into their crops. The Australia New Zealand Food Authority has already proposed that 1 per cent contamination with GE material in any product must be considered normal and should not trigger any labelling requirement. The Commission praised ANZFA, in spite of their blatantly unscientific support for genetically engineered food.

The Commission has accepted the word of the experts from the academic-governmental-industrial biotech complex and has set aside the concerns of people who want to retain the integrity of more natural ways of practising agriculture – free of wholesale wired-in manipulation for the short-term commercial gain of big biotech multinationals. What will our great-great-grandchildren think of the way we are treating our world?

www.safefood.org.nz/comission.htm

"He's really hit the nail on the head in that last paragraph. Our mokopuna will never ever forgive us if we let this madness go ahead. We must show this to Mere. She'll get it out to her network. Needs to be emailed on to the Green movement too." Koa is pensive a while, then adds, "D'ya reckon he'd come and talk to some of our elders? They said they'd like to hear a more scientific approach. If he spoke alongside the kuia in the Far North Organic Growers, I reckon they'd really listen to this fella."

"Maybe. I'll suggest it to Piripi and see what he thinks." Iri notes this below the article on the screen and copies the message into her email files.

"If we can convince them it is as serious a danger as the nuclear issue – and much more lasting as far as we are concerned as guardians of Papatuanuku, that there is no going back once the field trials begin – then we might be able to swell the support for our cause. Let's remember most of them were not anti-nuclear in the beginning either. They thought the protesters were a bunch of anti-Vietnam stirrers. But then when the wider issues became known, they were, like the rest of Aotearoa, vehemently against any form of nuclear power or warfare."

"Yep. I reckon if we can keep reminding them of this and making the connexions, then they'll really listen. At first, I never thought that over 90 per cent of the people would vote against nuclear power."

"But remember, we already have the vast majority of submissions to the Royal Commission against GE. We just need to make sure all the Aotearoans who voted against it are as educated by the time the government makes its final decision."

"Sounds like it is pretty much made up already. I can't believe that Helen Clark has sold out so drastically. Some see this as a compromise, but I see it as treachery, when we all fought so hard to support her as a feminist politician in power and our first elected woman Prime Minister."

"Yeah, but with MagicMilk and those creeps from the Round Table breathing down her neck, she has to make some compromises, even if we may not agree with her. Maybe she's just buying time until Jeanette and the Greens convince Aotearoa to go completely GE-free."

"I might have thought so once, but I am really beginning to wonder now. Hey – let's call a hui tonight and see what the others think of this news. It stinks."

"I'm with you on that. Ka pae."

Irihapeti burrows back into her work while Koa starts labelling the seeds they had harvested and dried at the end of last season, which now wait eagerly to fly off to their new homes in much-loved gardens and on marae all over Aotearoa as part of their seed-saving programme. A caterpillar roams over the bench below the seeds, aiming for the lush green leaves of the basil plants. She knows she has to scale the wall to the dizzying heights of the windowsill above the seeds, but that her trip will be worth while, for this is a garden without pesticides to poison her offspring, where she knows she can breed in peace and there is plenty for all of them to eat, insects and humans alike.

Maata crams the dirty washing into the gleaming new machine and sets it going. She has no idea what half the buttons are for, so hits some kind of superwash thing and lets it do its work. The machine rumbles with the weight once it starts spinning. From the room next door, she can hear that Tony is on the phone.

"Whad'ya mean ya can't advance more money? If this experiment is as world-shattering as you say it is, then it's gonna bring in heaps of bicky. What's the point otherwise?" Then silence, as Steve's accountant tries to explain it in simple terms. "Well, I'll check with Steve on progress and get back to you then. Yes, yes, I know we can't discuss details over the phone. I'll see what he says in person." The receiver is slammed back down on its holder. Tony sighs, then swings himself out of bed. He's taken to watching telly in bed these days, now he does not have to run the farm. Peter Tremain took on his jerseys and the few nutty sheep he had left and now he's a man of leisure – so long as the bikkies keep rolling in. That's all he has to make sure about. He dresses and saunters out to the kitchen to see if Maata has made a pot of tea.

"Martha. You made a brew yet?"

Maata yells out from the laundry. "Na. Ya want one

225

now?" Why can't he put on the kettle himself, the lazy bugger.

"Yep. One of them fancy teas you make. Can't do it meself." Tony has come to enjoy being spoiled, now that Ray's daughter has left town for a job in Kawakawa. This sheila from the marae isn't such a bad looker either. But too close to Moana to risk anything. Better that he acts on his best behaviour as part of his master plan to get Moana back home. None of these chicks can cook, wash or iron half as well as her. Besides, he misses having the boys around, especially now that he has more time on his hands.

Maata emerges from the laundry and begins grating ginger into the pot, adding a good dollop of honey because Tony likes his tea sweet. She's got him off sugar and onto the pohutukawa honey she brings from home. "'S'not bad, that stuff," he remarks, while she is adding the creamy white honey to his tea. "Hope I don't turn into a buzzy bee the way you keep feeding it to me, though. Or a bloody pohutukawa, with flaming red spiky hair!" He laughs, always enjoying his own weak jokes, and rubs his balding crown.

"No chance of that, Mr Pratt. More likely you'll grow a sting in your tail!" Maata risks being cheeky for once.

Tony is taken aback for a moment, then grins. "You little beaut. You're bloody right too. That's exactly what I need right now – a bit of a bite to my bark, make these fellas take more notice of me."

"Who are those men working in the barn?"

"Ah, just some fellas from FarmCorp. Developing

226

some new research to make kauri trees grow bigger or something. I dunno, they just hire the barn from me."

"That's great, Mr Pratt. Maybe they will be able to reforest parts of the Hokianga stripped of kauri by the early settlers? That'd be wonderful." Maata takes a genuine interest in his work. Tony is very pleased.

"Call me Tony. I don't go for that Mr and Mrs stuff meself."

"Okay. Thanks, Tony. Would it be possible to see what they're doing sometime? I did a school project on the Waipoua Kauri Forest and the significance of Tane Mahuta to the local community. I'd love to see what is being developed."

Tony clears his throat. "I'm not sure if that is possible. You know those sciencey fellas. They like to keep their research close to their chests. What they have of 'em anyway. Doubt most of those university leftie fellas could lift a lamb into the dredge if you asked them. Too much time spent studying. Makes their eyes grow too close. You noticed how little flesh hangs between their eyes?"

"No. I have not been that near to them yet."

"Ah, I get it now. You think there could be good pickings among those FarmCorp fellas, eh? Get yerself married to a rich fella and away from the dead-end life here? Well, maybe you're right. I sometimes think I should'a done that years ago." Tony rubs his chin, thinking it may be about time to grow his beard again.

"No. I love it here at Te Kotuku. But I am truly interested in the kauri forest and I would like to see the work. Surely they wouldn't mind if you showed me around sometime? Maybe you could ask them?"

Tony slurps his tea thoughtfully. Perhaps this would help him get back into Moana's good books? Add a few brownie points to his credit. Brownie points, haha, that's a good one Tony, m'boy. Shows you're still up to scratch. "Okay. I'll see what I can do. Why don't you come down with me, as I have to talk to their boss man, Steve, anyway. You could have a squizzy around the place while I detain him over the lease money."

"Thanks Mr Pra– ah, Tony. That'd be great." Maata pours him another tea, thinking how easy it is to get this man to come around. He is a walkover, really. She can't understand why they all find him such a bully on the marae. Maybe he just needed someone to understand him, spend time with him?

What a buzz, man, thinks Tony. This is gonna be so easy. All I have to do is let her have a look and ask a few stupid questions and she'll report back that I am doing good work for the district and Stevie Wonderboy won't mind. He says he has a public relations spin if anyone walks in off the street to ask questions, and the whole thing looks so kosher with their painted FarmCorp signs all over the barn. Steve's best friend and now business partner was a signwriter before he did his MBA and got into PR Spin. Mike. He's a real smoothie. Martha will like him, and he's down with Steve today so this should be sweet. Tony licks his lips and tells Maata to take off her apron and dolly herself up a bit to meet the boss men.

Maata cannot believe the simplicity of this Pratt, but does as he says, since she is about to get into the barn and check out this operation without even having to nick any keys or squeeze in at night. She can't wait to tell Waka how luck has turned their way. She takes off her housework clothes and climbs back into her Flyworks uniform. "Very professional. That's choice. You look like a bloody lady pilot in that gear with them epaulettes and all," sniggers Tony. "Okay, get in behind!" Maata winces at the farmer's command to his work dogs and suddenly realises that this is how he views women. No wonder Moana left him. Never mind, I need to find out what he's up to, and then I can ditch the job if it gets too difficult. I need the money for now, though, so I'll play it cool. She follows behind Tony, pretending to be one of his dogs, sniffing the kikuyu grass as she passes without him noticing. She'd love to lift her leg over his precious spray packs and littered Roundup containers as they pass, but thinks the better of it.

Steve and Mike are in the barn office which was once a horse stable. Light filters through the clear plastic roof and illuminates everything. Steve initially looks surprised to see Maata with Tony, but then again, he'd expected this to happen sometime. Lucky he's using Operation Kauri as a front for his real work – Operation Cave, where the human cloning takes place. It doesn't really matter what they see here as it looks like any traditional nursery to outsiders. Nothing unusual, except the very carefully monitored conditions and expensive computers that make sure it all ticks along like clockwork.

Mike, always the PR man, jumps in immediately. "I see you've brought a visitor along, Tony. How nice.

Can I show her around the nursery while you two talk business?"

"That's perfect. Thanks, Mike." How easily they play into my hands, thinks Tony. This will be a breeze. I could skipper one of the black boats at this rate. He smiles to himself, then remembers Maata's comment about the sting in his tail. He waits until Mike and Maata have begun to walk down the first aisle of tree seedlings, and then homes in on Steve, demanding more money or he will blow the skull off the whole operation. Steve, sensing danger, takes him further into the room and shuts the door so they can talk in private.

Mike and Maata get to the end of the first row. "So, why do you have all this computer gear just for a few seedlings then?"

"That's because we need to monitor their growth very carefully so we can present the work along with our research papers to FarmCorp. If the science is to benefit all, then we have to be very careful in documenting it."

"Yeah – but surely the plants need air to breathe? How come you don't have openings in the roof? Or doors open?" Maata asks. "You're not doing GE stuff are you? Where you can't let out the genie into the fields?"

Mike is taken aback by her shrewd deductions, then realises she is just concerned because of all that ridiculous Greenie Frankenfish stuff in the newspapers. She probably wouldn't know a kauri from a pine seedling if it bit her bum. "No way. I'm an environmentalist myself, actually." And adds, for good measure "A paid-up member of the Greens, in fact. I would not support that GE stuff. I reckon the country should be GE-free, actually." Mike wants to lay down his false credentials right from the start. This kid could blab anything he says back to the local tangata whenua, and then they'd all be in deep shit. He knows better than to alienate them. He did not do all those arty-farty Treaty of Waitangi Partnership courses paid for by his government department for nothing.

"Great. My Aunty Cowrie is a Greenie too. In fact, most of the marae and the Far North Organic Growers are against genetic modification. She's on the hikoi to protest GE which is marching from Tai Tokerau to parliament now. Well, she was, until she had an accident surfing on the way and got laid up for a bit."

Bloody good job, too, thinks Mike. He'd been warned about that Cowrie chick and her mates. Known eco-activists. He's got police files on them from the anti-Vietnam War and anti-nuclear protests, downloaded by a friend of his working for the Wanganui police. Easy to bribe these fellas. Just slip them cool hard cash and you have them downloading files on anybody. The National Party Government made it so hard for the workers that they all struggle in these jobs to survive financially. Any extra cash is a bonus. Mind you, not much better with Labour in parliament these days. You can hardly tell the difference between the two main parties, both edging more and more towards the centre to get more votes. Years ago, you'd never have thought that a liberal like Tony Blair would cosy up to a right-wing conservative like George Bush Junior, but now they are pissing into each other's pockets like Tweedledee and Tweedledum.

War is always good for retaining the status quo and their votes.

A fantail flits down in front of them and he suddenly comes back to earth with vigour. "Who the hell let that monster fly in here? Quick – get rid of it!" he yells. Nobody seems to listen. The nursery workers are outside the barn having afternoon tea. The fantail hopes they will kick up some insects for its meal, but there do not seem to be any insects about in this strange nursery. She lands on a stone nearby and waits for them to pass. Mike panics and grabs the spade. He whacks it down on the head of the fantail and lifts it to reveal a spattering of blood, flesh and feathers. Maata immediately bends down and offers karakia for the murdered piwakawaka. She is in a state of shock and acts intuitively as she has been raised to do. It's then that she notices a baby piwakawaka, not yet able to fly, at the side of the rock. Maybe the mother had been protecting her young? Maata wails her karakia and finishes with a proverb that Mere taught her: "*Mate i te tamaiti he aurukowhao, mate i te whaea he takerehaia.*"

Mike stands back, amazed at her outburst, but also annoyed he acted so swiftly and blew his cool. Not a good look. He asks Maata what she is saying.

Maata, annoyed at him, grumbles her reply: "The death of a child is like a leak in a canoe, but the death of a mother is like an open rent in the bottom of the canoe." She is thinking about how close she and Cowrie may have come to death recently, and how this has ripped their adoptive guardian, Mere, apart. How it would kill something in her if they died. How vital it is to protect the self, the soul, the aroha. To stand up for the causes they believe in. Here before her, it has been proved. It is literally a matter of life and death, and to these guys the death of another, be it fantail or human, means nothing if it comes between their research and their wealth.

Maata knows she has to remain calm, keep her cool, in order to do what she came to do. This may be her hardest test yet. Mike has not seen the baby bird, nor does he realise what he has done. She stands tall, towering over him and lies. "It's okay, Mike. I know how much this research means to you and that one bird could destroy it. Let's move on." Mike is delighted he has won her round so easily. Good he let her mumble her superstitious mumbo-jumbo stuff. Now they can get on with the rest of his PR spin. He'll make damned sure it's stronger from here on. Maata begs forgiveness of the mother piwakawaka and sends aroha and karakia to her and her baby. "I think there's a baby bird too. Let me take it and look after it." She bends down and gathers up the small bird in the palm of her hand, holding her fingers protectively over it.

There's nothing Mike can do to stop her. Besides, he reasons, the small bird is not yet at the stage where it can gather food for itself, so it will not be dangerous in spreading GE seeds about the place. Not that he really cares. He'd love to see how long it'd take to develop another Tane Mahuta in the wild – and this would be just the place to do it, so close to the mighty Waipoua Forest. But the timing is not right – not yet. He wants to test what they can do in the lab first, then release a few into the wild. Once the forestry industry sees what wealth it is onto – there will be no questions about the ethics of it then. He knows that. The International Seed Corporation clones have even won over a left-wing Labour Government with their spin. He never thought he'd ever see that day come. The corks have been flying off bottles of their most expensive champagne ever since. Like the heady days of the 1980s when shares skyrocketed and you could turn a hunk of dirty real estate into a goldmine in just a week with a good spin on it in Auckland.

But this time, it's lasting. This time they are on their way to massive riches. If they can make the entire world dependent on GE seed, then they own the most valuable resource on the planet. Who cares about gold or silver when you can't eat? And, if it all goes sour, then they'll hedge their bets by investing in organic farming to clean up the mess. Not that it'll be truly organic by that time, but with a good enough spin, people will believe it's okay. He grins to himself as Maata is preoccupied with trying to get the wretched bird to drink some water from the cup of her hand. I'd smash it with the spade if she wasn't here, thinks Mike. But there's no harm in letting her think she can save it. Most birds do not survive without their mothers, so it'll probably die anyway.

The great white heron at the apex of the whare nui shakes with anger. She is the sacred guardian of Te Kotuku marae; she is protector of the birds and creatures and land around her, as well as the tangata whenua who live off the land. She quivers, lashed by the storm assaulting the Hokianga Harbour, and vows her revenge on those who would interfere with nature, murder innocent creatures and think they could replace the Creator of the universe. She's witnessed the unholy acts of contrivance within the sacred Maori burial caves nearby and she wants to alert the tangata whenua to the dangers surrounding them. There needs to be a symbol they will understand, as in the old days, a reminder to them that they too are the guardians of the land and must act on their inner wisdom and intuitive knowledge.

She waits until the winds are lashing the edge of the roof and then makes her ultimate sacrifice. She rips off her wing with her beak and flings it toward the ground. It crashes down onto the rows of shoes lining the entrance to the whare nui and buries them alive. The thunderous sound sends the participants of the GE-free hui rushing to the doorway to witness an unusual sight. The wing of the great bird protecting their marae has been slashed off by the wind. But the cut is so clean, it almost looks as if a knife edge has been run between her body and her wing. Piripi and Waka bend down to lift their sacred white heron, their kotuku, from the dirty shoes and onto higher ground – the carving table which stands nearby. The onlookers are stunned by this act of defiance, this act of war on their marae.

"It's a sign of defiance against the US war on Afghanistan," utters one old kuia. "I told you it would come to this."

"No. It's related to the struggle for the land, the fight to keep Aotearoa GE-free," adds Koa. "Or else it would not have happened when we were discussing the issues."

"That's all bullshit," chips in Hemi. "My dad told me this stuff is all superstitious rubbish. It's simply a bloody big wind, enough to rip the mast off a boat. You people need to get real."

Moana nudges him to keep quiet. "How dare you talk to your elders like this, Hemi. You're not with Tony now. You need to be respectful of your heritage."

"It's all mumbo-jumbo," exclaims Hemi. "Dad says it's Stone Age crap. He heard it all on radio. Some professor of literature, a poet, Snarl Steddy or something, said on radio that it's all crap and that our race would be better off learning how to read and write than paying attention to this medieval magic. Even I can tell a storm when I see one." Moana tries to hush him up. She notices how like Tony he looks when he is angry or defiant.

"The boy's got a point. It is pretty rough weather," adds a Kawakawa man. "Maybe we'd better get back and batten down the hatches."

"Not before we've voted on our stance." Irihapeti urges everyone back into the whare nui to continue the meeting, though she is shocked at the destruction to their sacred kotuku guardian. "Piripi and Waka will have the wing fixed in no time."

"Ka pae. We will," asserts Piripi, but he knows it will be a major job. The bird was carved out of one piece of kauri from the Waipoua Forest that was granted to them when the road was widened and some dead trees were harvested. The wood was cleaned and blessed by the elders, and they may need to start from scratch with another piece to maintain the sacred energy. However, he wants to avoid this. He hopes to repair the wing and retain the wairua of the bird he came to love so much in the process of the carving. She spoke to him then and has spoken to him since. Even now, she urges him this is a sacrifice for the good of all, and they must be willing to do the same when the time comes.

"Has everyone read the flier from Greenpeace: Genetically Engineered Trees in New Zealand?" asks Irihapeti. There are nods from the masses. "Are there any questions?"

One woman stands at the back of the whare nui. "Yes. If International Paper and our own RichTree Resources have joined forces, and they plan to invest US$60 million into researching and developing GE trees over the next five years, then won't this make them a danger to our native forests and our natural sovereign rights?"

"It sure will," replies Irihapeti. "They are now the largest GE tree research programme in the entire world.

237

This is a huge threat to our natural resources and we need to take the initiative on this."

"Aren't those RichTree Resources fellas backed by International Seed Corporation?" pipes up a voice from the crowd.

Koa replies. "Sure are. International Seed Corporation gave them money initially, then withdrew, throwing their resources into their own seed projects. But they still hope that the GE experiments will make the trees Roundup-resistant since they will make more sales in the long run."

"Sneaky buggers!" replies the woman.

As the korero continues, it becomes clear to all that New Zealand, despite declaring itself clean and green, has been involved in several GE tests and field trials already. Independent research backs up the Greenpeace material and by the end of the hui, they vote to lobby Carter Holt Harvey to abandon the GE tree trials currently being conducted and to scrap any further plans for developing GE trees in Aotearoa. They also draft a letter to RichTree Resources requesting that they withdraw from their GE research and commit to responsible forest management as described by the Forest Stewardship Council formed in 1993. Copies of letters and replies will be sent to all major newspapers, *Mana* magazine and Greenstone Pictures who are planning a documentary on the issue as it affects tangata whenua. A vote is taken which is 100 per cent against any GE experiments. This will also be communicated in all further correspondence and details sent to the GE-Free Coalition.

As the hui disbands, tangata whenua gather around the fallen wing of the sacred kotuku, offering their suggestions on its repair and condolences for the accident. Many say it is a sign from above that all is not right, that they must act now against these travesties against Papatuanuku and Tane Mahuta. The one-winged kotuku smiles down on them from the top of their whare nui, pleased that her sacrifice has not been in vain.

"Tataramoa." Mere gestures to the pointed leaves and delicate white flowers of this vine which grows wild all over Aotearoa.

"How did such a striking plant get the name 'bush lawyer'?" asks Kuini, delighted to be back home and in the forest again after she and Cowrie left the hikoi to make its way to Wellington.

"The elders told me that because the vine will latch on and cling to any person or animal nearby, it was dubbed the bush lawyer." The wahine chuckle. Very apt.

"So what's it used for medicinally?"

"You boil up the bark until it turns into liquid and then drink it to ease constipation. A Rawene tohunga also said that an infusion of the root bark helps cure diarrhoea and many other stomach complaints – but I have not tried that one out yet."

I might give it a go on Tony, thinks Maata. It could cure his underwear problem. I'll slip some into the next infusion of tea I make for him. She carefully strips off some bark in the way that Mere has taught them, just enough for her needs and not so much that the plant will be harmed. Like using some of the plant for grafting and sustaining the species but not robbing it of its spirit or life force. Maata is still so shocked by her encounter

240

with Mike and his killing of the fantail that she has not yet shared this with any of the others. She does not want to blow her cover so early. However, if she can find a quiet moment, she might tell Cowrie. Her aunty always knows what to do in such circumstances. But she's still lying in bed recovering from her scrape with nature, needing plenty of rest right now and very peeved that she had to miss out on the rongoa trip today.

"And you all know what this is." Mere points to a tree with heart-shaped leaves and tall thin cones that spike the air as if mimicking lights on a Christmas tree.

"Kawakawa" comes the chorus, for this is the tree after which the Northland township of Kawakawa was named. "It's also known as the pepper tree, and a decoction of the leaves is often used as a treatment for boils and for kidney complaints."

"Isn't it an aphrodisiac, like the Fijian kava plant?" asks Koa.

"Yes, the tohunga often used it for this purpose, but it's not as strong as the Pacific Island versions of the plant."

"It makes a wonderful tea," adds Irihapeti.

"And if you take off a leaf and chew it, it tastes just like pepper. You can use it to season your food. I often put it in casseroles and anything cooked slowly so the taste really infuses into the dish." Moana chews on a leaf of kawakawa, delighting that she can cook anything she likes and go back to her favourite foods now she is cooking communally on the marae and does not have to please the pie-and-chips tastebuds of Tony. Still, she misses some parts of him, especially his humour

241

when times are tough. She wonders how he is getting on. She'll ask Maata sometime, since she's heard from Mere that Maata is doing his housework for him. Glad someone is and that it's not me right now. Maata will be safe with him. She's too young for his needs, thank Papatuanuku.

"And this precious plant will be your saviour every time." Mere holds up the branch of a rather scrubby tree with bright yellow flowers.

"That's gumdigger's soap!" exclaims Kuini.

"Ka pae. Also known as kumarahou. You'll see it growing on the outskirts of the bush and along the roadsides all over Tai Tokerau, showering the landscape with its golden flowers. This is like liquid gold, the kauri gum of our ancestors, for it heals just about any complaint you can imagine – colds, asthma, bronchitis, aching limbs, influenza and is even great for the kidneys."

"How do you use it?" asks Maata.

"Just boil up the leaves and let them soak for a while. Then drink the liquid and you'll be right as rain the next day, I promise you."

They each take small samples of the leaves to make a concoction on their return. "Maybe this will heal Cowrie?" asks Kuini.

"It will help as a tonic, but I can find even better for her particular complaints," replies Mere, moving the group deeper into the bush.

"What about mahoe? That helps for rheumatism, doesn't it?" suggests Irihapeti.

"Ka pae." Mere points to a large stand of whitey-woods bursting with bright purple berries. Their trunks are covered in a white fungus that looks like paint carefully applied for artistic effect. "We'll collect some leaves, put them into the hot tub tonight, and bathe Cowrie in it. Once it has infused into the hot water after about an hour, she will feel the benefit. It can help cure rheumatism and eases all aches and pains of the joints."

"I'd like to prepare the bath and look after her," offers Maata, thinking this could be a good chance to talk to Cowrie in private about what has happened and ask her advice.

"Ka pae, Maata." Mere is pleased she is looking after her whanau so well. She has calmed down a bit after the sea incident and seems to be really maturing.

They come to a clearing where there is a field of kikuyu grass, and Kuini tells them how the women of Mohala created their organic garden by placing cardboard over the grass and carefully building up compost and mulch from there until they had raised beds boasting the most luscious vegetables. In among the kikuyu are sow thistles poking their heads up bravely. Mere bends and breaks off a few leaves. "Puha or puwha, depending on which iwi you come from. Most of your grandparents ate this daily, boiled it up with pork or mutton bones and ate it like spinach. It is rich in nutrients and is used for all stomach ailments, for healing boils, and also for women giving birth. It was helpful in expelling the placenta and this was a sacred act since the placenta, as most of you know, has to be carefully wrapped and later buried and a tree planted over it to ensure the healthy growth of the child and its spiritual development."

"But that puha tastes bitter. The white gooey stuff is yuck!" Maata screws up her face at the memory of it.

"The milky sap from the puha is best used for boils and not eaten raw. But once the leaves are simmered, you'd never know it wasn't spinach."

"Yeah – and not only with pork." Kuini grins. "Remember that old song we all used to sing? Puha and Pakeha, puha and Pakeha, the finest food you could ever wish for, puha and Pakeha." She sings it to the famous old Chesdale Cheese ad that used to grace their screens and has now become a cult symbol for packaged Pakeha food. It was a tangata whenua spin on the tired old jokes about Maori eating Pakeha and being cannibals. They reclaimed the joke by saying the puha tasted best with Pakeha – a few boiled Europeans – and sang it to the Pakeha idol of colonialism, the television that made this ad so famous in the first place. Kuini smiles at the memory. A wonderful piece of kitsch Aotearoan history which had a point to it also.

"Didn't Captain Cook get his crew to collect heaps of puha to be boiled up and served to those stricken with scurvy?" asks Maata. "I recall something like this from my school studies."

"You may be right there, Maata. He had a botanist on board the *Endeavour* who collected all kinds of traditional herbs and kai and noted how they were used by early Maori."

"Pity we didn't have copyright over our medicines then, eh?"

"We still do not have this finalised in legal form, but it is on the way. I don't think anybody minds if people use these medicines for their own healing or for that of their whanau. But when it comes to making huge amounts of money and multinationals wanting to use traditional medicines, then we need to protect our heritage from being exploited," volunteers Irihapeti, who is deeply concerned about this issue. Rose Pere had raised her awareness about the value of medicinal Maori herbs at a hui years ago.

"Ka pae, Iri. We need to protect the spiritual values of these plants and make sure they are not purchased by the corporations and that we lose them forever. This has happened to some indigenous groups. We must watch out for this, while also wanting to share our knowledge with those who will respect it."

"Like the land, eh?" asks Maata.

"Yes, my love, just like the land," replies Mere, her hand on Maata's shoulder. There is a swoosh of wings and a kukupa lands on a branch of the large tree towering above them with its dark green shiny leaves glistening in the sunlight. The olive-feathered, creamy-chested wood pigeon leans over to feast on the scarlet berries. "The kukupa is known as the kereru by some tribes, mostly in the South Island, and the puriri was called the New Zealand oak by the early European settlers because it reminded them of the old English oak they had left behind. Its leaves were boiled in water to relieve ulcers, back pain and even sprains. Maata, you might like to add a few puriri leaves to the hot tub tonight. A kuia from Kaitaia also told me that she cured her husband's kidney ailment by getting him to drink puriri leaf tea every day for a year. So it's a very useful old oak."

245

As she finishes speaking, the kukupa dangles its tail downwards and drops a long stream of creamy liquid onto Kuini's head and the ground nearby. "Now, that's very useful. Depending on what she's eaten today, we might return here to find baby puriri trees and maybe some small nikau palms. She loves the bright nikau berries as well." Mere turns toward Kuini, who is getting out a handkerchief to clean her hair. "Kuini, if you don't wash your hair, you might sprout a beautiful nikau over the next few months." The wahine laugh as Kuini replies that she'd rather see the plants growing in the soil, thank you very much! The kukupa flaps its wings, as if agreeing with her, and jumps down to another branch to reach for some more of the luscious berries to gorge on. She's in no mood to be dieting today.

Days and weeks go by, as the hikoi wends it way toward Wellington like a snake following its prey by scent, gathering information and tips along the way. They get emails from small townships all over Te Ika a Maui, and learn about the organic growers and their struggles to keep Aotearoa GE-free. Maata has alerted Cowrie to the suspected experiments on the Pratt farm, and a group of eco-activists at Te Kotuku marae vow to discover more. Meantime, Waka and Piripi work hard to restore their sacred carved kotuku to her former state. Piripi is visited by her in his dreams and she guides them along the way, offering suggestions for the future preservation of Papatuanuku and her rich heritage.

Finally the day of reckoning comes, and the hikoi presents it petition against GE to members of parliament on the steps of the Beehive where they meet. It is a colourful gathering and they watch it live on the net as Sue Bradford, a Green member of parliament from their Northland region, greets the marchers with her speech of welcome.

Sue Bradford
Welcoming the GE-free Hikoi
Parliament – Wednesday, 31 October 2001: 3:15 pm

First, I welcome this opportunity to acknowledge and
tautoko the hikoi that has arrived at Parliament this
afternoon, having walked and travelled all the way from
the far north. The hikoi started off early in October to
make its protest against field trials and the possible
commercial release of genetically modified organisms into
the natural environment of this country. I met with the
people from the hikoi last night, and today, and recognise
their courage and determination in taking that long journey.
I know it has not been easy for them, and as someone
who has survived a hikoi myself, the March Against
Unemployment that went from Te Hapua to Poneke in
1988, I am well aware of the difficulties of the long march
and the tensions that arise, but to a good purpose.

It was very fitting that the hikoi started in Northland, an
area of this country that is absolutely passionate about its
natural environment. We have some of the most beautiful
beaches, islands, seas, rivers and forests of this country.
We are passionate, not just that we have all this, but that
we want to keep it that way. The beauty of the far north
is a microcosm of Aotearoa and there is no place for
genetic engineering in our home.

Just recently we had the case of the genetically modified
tamarillo field trials carried out by HortResearch in
Kerikeri. There is a proposal at the moment that
chloropicrin may be applied under plastic to stop problems
arising from the fact that genetically modified crops have
been grown at Kerikeri. We do not know what will come
from this, but we are now assured that HortResearch will
do everything that they can do to mitigate the risk from
those crops. We do not want to see any more field trials
in the north or anywhere else in this country.

Many indigenous people in this country, as in other parts of the world, are deeply uncomfortable with the prospect of genetically engineered contamination of the natural world. I commend those members of the Government's Maori caucus who have had the courage to at least try to change the direction that their leaders have, unfortunately, taken. There is a tremendous groundswell around the country that has been growing over the past few years against the mixing of plant and animal genes with human DNA. It is not only Maori who find that the mixing of human and animal whakapapa is "bizarre and offensive".

Transgenic experimentation goes against some of the most basic instincts that have been our legacy for endless generations of life on earth. I believe that to deliberately contaminate our whakapapa is spiritually, ethically, culturally, and biologically abhorrent to the majority of people in this country, whatever background we come from. We want to keep the whole of Aotearoa "GE-free". The people in the district that I come from, would like to see Rodney become "GE-free" as soon as possible. We have a choice in this country about which way to go. To become a genetically engineered biotech wonderland is not economically or scientifically the best way forward. The "GE-free" register is growing daily. Many people are signing up and saying that the only buffer zones they want in Aotearoa are the Tasman Sea and the Pacific Ocean.

For Maori and tauiwi alike, deep concerns are being ignored by this week's Government decision. I would like to make it very clear that the package that the Government announced yesterday in response to the Royal Commission report is not Green Party policy. We have not in any way signed up to it. As far as I am aware, we remain the only party in this Parliament committed to keeping genetically modified organisms out of the water, the air, and the earth of Aotearoa.

This is just the beginning of the struggle. We are sorry that it will have to continue and that a lot more work will have to be done before we get the country we want. I tautoko all those who are taking part in this struggle. The debate about genetically modified organisms is not about different world views, but about the one environment that we all share.

The crowd cheers, and flags and banners proclaiming "GE-free Aotearoa", "Keep Frankenfish Out", "Stop GE in our Forests NOW!" fly in the air above the heads of the marchers. The black, red and white Tino Rangatiratanga Maori sovereignty flag waves in the wind, and several members of the hikoi, from Del Wihongi to Titiwhai Harawira, speak passionately on behalf of tangata whenua being united against a GE future.

"Ka pae. We need to do something about this locally now." Cowrie talks to the members of TEA – Te Kotuku Eco Action – who gather around the computer screen to see the hikoi live. "So far, we've found out that there's a GE experiment going on at Pratt's farm. It involves inserting the DNA from pine trees into kauri seeds to increase their growth, along with an added dose of growth fertiliser marketed by – you guessed it – International Seed Corporation. The intention is to have instant kauri forests and to produce large species like Tane Mahuta within a few years instead of centuries. But as you know, Tane Mahuta is God of all forests in Aotearoa and this must be seen as an assault on our culture and spirituality as well as our natural heritage under the protection of Te Tiriti o Waitangi. The Crown cannot sign a treaty with us for land and grant us protection of our natural resources and then let these eco-vandal scientists have free rein."

"Too right! Let's break in and rip up the plants!" Moana is furious at Tony for allowing this to happen on their farm.

"Tai hoa, Moana. If we do that, then we may release the seeds into the surrounding forest by mistake. We need to really plan this move carefully." Irihapeti is always wary when it comes to working with plants and making sure they do it properly.

"Yes. And I suspect from what Maata has managed to find out that, as gruesome as this experiment may be, it's probably a cover for something even worse. She and Waka followed one of the scientists down to the Maori burial caves. They got as far as the entrance and saw that it is lit up inside and wired for security and there is video surveillance. They hid in the bushes and waited. On following nights, men went in and out on schedule and it may be that they are doing some kind of cloning there."

"Oh, no. Not in the caves. They are sacred to my whanau and all our ancestors," groans Moana, shocked to hear this news for the first time. "That he could defile Tane Mahuta is one thing, but to desecrate our sacred burial caves and use them for unholy experiments is unforgivable. There is a tapu on the caves. Anybody who defiles them will be held accountable by sources higher than us."

The group nods in assent. They all know stories of things that have happened to people who have defied ancient taboo and reaped the results of their acts. Some have been poisoned, others withered away from unidentifiable and incurable diseases. Some have fallen from cliffs or been swallowed up by the sea.

"I need to warn Tony that he could be harmed also. After all, he is the father of my children." Moana pleads with the group to let her talk to him, but they feel it is too early, that they should discover what is really happening inside the caves before acting in ignorance, then make a considered plan about the best way to handle this.

"How can we find out, though, if there is so much surveillance up there? There's no way we will get any closer than Maata and Waka have, and that's because they already have clearance and an excuse to be on the land." Koa voices her concerns while putting on the kettle for a cuppa.

"Just a minute. Didn't there used to be a rear entrance to those caves? I recall going up there as a kid and finding a tunnel that led into the smaller caves beyond the main ones."

"Ka pae, Cowrie. You're right. My kuia took me into the tunnel when we were kids and there is one leading right up behind the main cave. Let's go and check it out. I know the way to it, and we could use the old track, cut across the back paddocks and enter the tunnel at dusk. That way, they'd never catch us, and we could monitor their activities without being seen." Moana is pleased to be of use to them because they have all looked after her and her tamariki so well since they returned home to Te Kotuku. She has grown to love these eco-activists whom

252

she'd have given a wide berth when she was still with Tony. They are just like all the other wahine – only perhaps a bit braver. And they do not care what anyone else thinks. Even when some of the older ones feel threatened or say they do not follow politically correct protocol. They live with passion and they believe in their heritage and the causes they embrace. What's more, they are willing to do something about it. That's enough for Moana to embrace them as sisters.

"Right. Let's form a core group to go to the caves and suss out what's happening. Who's up for it?" Cowrie counts the hands. "Looks like Moana, Kuini and I. That's enough to get help if we get stranded. I think you should stay out of it and keep your nose to the ground around Tony, Maata. You've done brilliant work in befriending that spade-wielding murderer, Mike – and, since you've gained his trust, you will be invaluable to our operation later. We may need you for evidence." Maata is disappointed that she will not be in on the main action, but pleased her efforts have been rewarded with praise.

They continue discussing the breach of their wairua regarding the interference with the seeds of the kauri tree and what legal redress might be available as well as political action. It is decided that Mere will get on the net and find out what she can about the legal issues involved and co-ordinate with Iri on this. Irihapeti will make sure all goes well back at base camp, Te Kotuku nursery, in case the others get stranded or captured at Pratt's farm. Koa will relay the news to the Wild Greens as a support group, if they cannot get into the barn enclosure and destroy the plantation successfully and safely when the time comes for this action.

Korero continues on the vital importance of GE-free groups working as necessary within their own areas of concern as well as in the wider frame of Aotearoa. This takes them late into the night, and several brews of kawakawa tea are needed to send the wahine to sleep after their activist energies have been excited.

As Cowrie lies in bed that night, she recalls a story told her by Monoloa, a student from the Marquesa Islands she met while protesting. She remembers the gist of her words.

We of the Tuamotu talk of Atea, God of Space, and Tane, God of Men. Originally, they lived in divided realms layered within the wide open space of the sky. After their tribes quarrelled, Tane fled for safety to earth. But he vowed revenge. With the help of Ru, the turtle, and Ru, the humpback whale, they waged a war of potent chants and warrior action against Atea. Finally, he was defeated when Tane stole flames and set fire to the heavens above them, causing lightning to rain down on Atea, killing him. But Atea's mana did not die. It lived on in the islands and was handed down through ancestry.

But why has this come to her now? Maybe it's telling her they should set the barn alight? Or maybe attach a fuse to the wires leading into the cave? No, this cannot be so. Then they could broadcast the contaminated seeds. The Koori tribes of Australia set the plants and trees alight in order to spread seed, not to contain or destroy it. No, fire and lightning cannot be the answer here. She drifts off to sleep, forked lightning spiking her dreams, fusing her spirit, urging her on as Pele rages over the mountains of her ancestral mindscape, the fiery volcanic activity sparking the edges of her consciousness, urging it to flow toward the waiting waters at the foot of Kiluaea, to sizzle and be consumed by their oceanic embrace.

Cowrie wakes with a thud as a bird hits the window of her bedroom and slumps down the wall. She gets up to see if she can help and leans over to notice it has landed on a rock in the garden, its neck twisted and broken. A tui, whose white-throated cry will never be heard in these forests again. One sacrifice too many for an earth laden with too many deaths and devastation by human will, altering the balance of nature, the pattern of survival. Even building a cottage in their territory is an invasion of their land. We have all caught this disease of colonisation, she thinks. But now we have to learn how to deal with it. And live together peacefully. As tempting as it is to want utu – to call for revenge on Pratt and his eco-vandals – we must not be as stubborn and brutal as George Bush and his Conscripted Murderers in Afghanistan. I'd love to see the Taliban nailed to the cross for their treatment of women, but not more innocent Afghan men and woman and their tamariki murdered in the process. Enough is enough. Cowrie worries she is losing her spirit, her will to fight these issues. She slinks off to bed and enters a dreamless sleep.

It is a full moon and Hina guides the wahine across the fields towards the tunnel leading to the caves. Moana is in front and they manage to walk the overgrown clay track without using torches. But once they enter into the tunnel, they need their caving caps, borrowed from Tipo's boys. The caps are fitted with lights, and the one Cowrie is wearing has a video camera. The rock slopes downward and they come to what looks like a solid wall. Edging up to it, there is a vertical drop of about twenty feet.

"Shit! I never banked on this. Dunno if my turtle body will fit into that hole. Whad'ya reckon?"

"I've come prepared for this." Moana drops her backpack and pulls out abseiling ropes. "Got these from our shed when Tony was at the pub. He used to take us out climbing in the good old days just after we first met. Comes in handy now, eh?" She grins at them.

"Great work, Moana. You're a beaut." Kuini winks at her. "Okay, let's strap it around Cowrie and she can clamber down first and help us when we arrive."

"Dunno if I'm up to that," mumbles Cowrie, still tired from her disturbed sleep the night before.

"Sure you are, Turtle. Here, lean on me and then edge down. I'll tie you up to this rock and ease you down gently. Trust me." Kuini helps Moana secure the ropes as Cowrie teeters on the edge, hardly daring to look into the wet cave below. Bit by bit, she eases herself down, her hand tight on the clasp below her body, just taking out as much rope as she can handle for each stage of the drop. Just as she is about to land, a twig scrapes the side of her face that is nearly touching the cave wall. She brushes it away, but it clings harder to her face, as if gripping onto her for dear life. Suddenly she realises it is no twig, but a giant cave weta, so large that it covers the entire side of her face and its barbed legs are hanging onto her lips and the edge of her nose and her eyebrows. She wants to scream but knows the scientists could be on the other side of the wahine right now. She has no idea how far away they might be. She cannot blow their cover now they have come this far.

Cowrie is terrified of wetas and this might be her one moment of bravery in a lifetime. She grits her teeth and winces, praying the weta will dive off once she reaches the rock floor of the cave safely. But it digs its sharp legs into her face even more strongly. She can see its jaws out of the corner of her eye. Jaws, she knows, that are capable of biting through manuka trees, let alone soft facial flesh. The weta is moving, doing gentle push-ups as they slide down the rope together. Its body is shivering. It's then that Cowrie realises the creature is as frightened as she is. That they are bound together on this strange journey into Hades, the descent to the bowels of the earth and beyond. For the first moment in her life, she feels strangely connected to this creature. It is actually as frightened as she is, and she hopes she will bear it safely to the rocks below. As the weta grips onto her face, Cowrie grits her teeth again and lets out another length of rope. This time her feet bounce off the wall of the tunnel and touch hard rock. She carefully balances herself on the ledge, just as in the sea cave, and remembers to stay calm. As she steadies herself, the weta leaps from her face gratefully and into a dry rock crevice. It slinks into the rear in the dark.

Her tug on the rope alerts the others that she is safely down and they pull the rope back up for Kuini's descent. Cowrie hopes another weta is not waiting for her, but is touched by this moment of connexion she had never expected might happen in her lifetime. She has always had a terror of these creatures, said to be so strong they would survive a nuclear holocaust, along with some fellow cockroaches. Cowrie vowed she would not want to be a survivor at that rate. Now she may reconsider. Then again, a few million weta might be a different proposition. Within minutes, Kuini has joined her at the foot of the drop, and then Moana. Cowrie does not have time to share her experience before they are crawling on their bellies through the next passage in the tunnel, about as wide as a sea turtle within the curve of a wave.

By the time they reach the far cave, they can hear voices. They remain still, listening to the sounds and trying to locate their source on the other side of the rock wall. Kuini spies a slit in the rock near the top, just over a ledge. They climb up and peer into the room. The sight that meets their eyes defies belief. The large cave they remembered as kids has been turned into a laboratory.

It's as light as a McDonald's restaurant and about as gaudy. But apart from that, it looks like a regular science lab. So why go to all the trouble to place it out here, hidden from everyone? Well, nearly everyone. The two women had dreaded to see hideous malformations, kunekune pigs wandering about with duck heads or fish flailing in shallow water, not able to hold up the weight of their own heads. But the scene was nothing like that. It was so prosaic, so hygienic, so normal – nothing but test tubes and lab reports, files and containers of frozen embryos.

Kuini fixes her binoculars on a filing cabinet and reads the label Frozen Embryo Files, and her breath stops a moment. She notes: "Frozen Embryos. Pigs. Sheep. Lambs. Humans: Male; Female. Eggs: Human: Female." She whispers to the others. "What the hell are they doing with human embryos? I thought that was illegal?" Suddenly, an alarm rings through the cave. The sensors have been alerted to a foreign presence. The lights go out automatically and they are left in pitch-black darkness.

The wahine switch off their head lanterns, so that they do not shine into the cave and give away their presence. They remain, frozen, on the rock ledge, as immobile as the frozen human embryos waiting their turn to change the course of civilisation, sitting inno-cently within an ancient cave in Aotearoa, a cave still inhabited by the spirits of their ancestors. The ancestors do not approve of their fate, and they will not shrink from taking their revenge, as surely as Tane stole flames and set fire to the heavens and threw lightning at Atea to kill him. They will avenge Tane just as he sought utu on Atea. And like him, they will win, perhaps destroying everything in their path along the way, like revenge on the Taliban is doing. Women have always been caught in between the warring actions of men seeking utu throughout the ages. And now, in these dark times of terror.

"The lights have gone out. It's totally black in the cave, but I can hear their voices." Irihapeti watches the computer screen where the digital video pictures are being relayed back from the camera inserted into Cowrie's cap.

"Whad'ya reckon's happened?" replies Koa, edging up to the screen to see for herself.

"Dunno. Can't be a power failure or we wouldn't be able to see them. Maybe they switched off the lights because they heard voices? I heard Kuini whisper something about human embryos."

"You've gotta be joking. D'you really think those fellas are playing about with human cells?"

"Yeah – like as not they'll cover their tracks with that spin about stem cell research to help modern medicine, but we know they are all after the same thing – to clone the first super human – and then they are on their way to infinite riches, for sure."

"But that couldn't possibly be happening here in little old Aotearoa, could it?"

"Sure," Iri answers. "Why not? We're already leading the world in genetic engineering in the development of forestry gene research. We were the first country to give women the vote. The first to be nuclear-free. Why not be the first to clone a human being?"

"Because there are ethics involved in giving women the vote and becoming nuclear-free. It's different."

"Sure is, but where's the ethics in the genetic forestry research – and where's the ethics in cloning human beings? Once you begin down that path, where do you stop? That's precisely why we should not start in the first place."

"I agree with you there, but others argue that we'd still be in the Stone Age if we thought that way."

"Who says we wouldn't have been better off there?"

"Well, you'd miss some of your modern comforts, my love, that's for sure. Like your hot tub at night and your *Marae* programme on Sunday television!"

"The hot tub is lit by fire, and if telly never arrived, we'd probably be sitting discussing the same issues on the marae that the *Marae* programme is doing on the telly."

"You're incorrigible, Iri! But yeah – we need to get real about this now or it will be too late. Don't worry – I was just being devil's advocate for a while." Koa rubs her shoulders, still watching the empty screen in case one of their friends might suddenly appear magically from the blackness.

"So long as we can hear their voices, then I don't think we need to get too worried at this stage. They will think to speak directly into the camera once they remember it's there and alert us if anything is wrong."

"Yeah, I s'pose so. D'ya think we should tell Mere and Maata though?"

"No way. Not after the last time. We'll handle this

until we know there is a true emergency, then alert them. Otherwise we'll have half the community of Te Kotuku, plus the cops and medics and tohunga, out there before we even get a chance to find out what is truly happening." Iri tries the focus on her computer to see if she can zero in on the scene and pick up any more light or detail. 120, 140, 160, 180, 200 per cent . . . no luck . . . it's just more of the same. She changes the screen and scrolls through the emails.

"Hey, Koa. Check this out. A response to the so-called war on terrorism by Arundhati Roy, remember, *God of Small Things* and *The Cost of Living*?"

"Great. What's her take?"

Iri scrolls through the words and hooks onto the last few paragraphs. "She sees Osama bin Laden as a kind of dark twin of Bush and draws analogies between the actions of Bush and Bin Laden. Brilliant stuff." She reads on.

At the end, Koa replies. "I see us faced with the same kind of dilemma with GE. We might not just be murdering embryos by cutting out their stem cells – and far be it from me to play into the hands of the right-to-lifers – but we may be committing a larger mass murder by altering the blueprint of life as we know it. We may be committing ourselves to endless cycles of reproductive disasters just as we are enduring endless cycles of revenge and warfare at the hands of madmen like Bush and bin Laden. It's not just a matter of win or lose, of revenge or not, but it's ultimately a question of how we want to live our lives now and in the future. And in asking these questions, making these decisions, we are carrying all our ancestors before us and our descendants after us along for the ride. We are changing the nature of life as we know it and have known it, not just for this decade, but forever."

Iri watches the caterpillar chewing away the ends of her basil leaves. "And you, old fella, you're doomed to be obliterated too. There'll be no right-to-lifers holding placards for you."

Koa massages Iri's shoulders, feeling the tension and strain within her body. Suddenly, the screen lights up again. She sees the tip of Kuini's nose as Cowrie motions towards her, and then the camera points into the cave again. It is lit up like a candy factory and everything seems to be back in motion. If they can only get Cowrie to face in toward the filing cabinet again and see if they can read the labels, then they'd be able to zoom in and have the evidence they need. But a big man stands between her and the files, his back to them. After a while, he turns around and she recognises the face. "Oh, God, no. Let it not be true." Koa stares at the screen in disbelief as the knife of betrayal rips through her heart.

"Mere, come and look at this. It's so true of Cowrie, you will be blown away." Maata has a set of cards laid out in a shell pattern and the daily meditation card is placed face up to the skies.

"I like the illustration very much. But what is it about, Maata?"

"It's a new kind of Tarot deck that offers inner guidance. Waka got it for me at Rawene Wholefoods, y'know, where the books are at the back of the store looking out to the sea."

"Ah, yes. I have seen them there. How sweet of Waka to do that. He must be really fond of you, eh?"

Maata pretends she does not hear the question and focuses back on the cards. "This is the Turtle Card. And I pulled it today by chance. I asked the deck about future directions for me, for us, for the planet, and this is what came up."

"You could ask your own ancestors for such advice and get guidance as well, Maata."

"I know – but this is connected to us. It comes from American Indian teachings."

"Via some Pakeha fellas, no doubt."

"Maybe – but it relates to Waka and me more than some of the old fellas rabbiting on here."

Mere sighs. So this is what it has come to. Well, maybe the young get their information from different sources, but it still might be the ancient wisdom. Who am I to dictate to them?

Mere listens politely as Maata reads to the end of the text. "There is some wisdom in there, Maata. You may need protection working at Flyworks and for Mr Pratt. Take note of what they say. And also their warning for us to maintain our sacred connexion to the earth. Papatuanuku. That's vital always, but especially at this time."

"I think I'd like to be a turtle, like Cowrie," says Maata, looking out to the sea rolling gently in beyond the herbs and dunes.

"You have to earn that right, Maata. Or you'll be, what do these fellas call it, a 'space cadet'. We've got too many of those wandering about the earth already, like Bush and bin Laden. We need to be truly grounded. Both feet firmly on the earth."

"Or maybe one foot on the earth and one in the sea, like Turtle Woman, eh?"

"Laukiamanuikahiki? Ka pae. We could do with her protection right now. I hope you pulling this card is not a sign that Cowrie is in danger. I don't think I could ever go through that again."

"No, she's protected, Mere. It says so here. And you told me before to have faith in this."

"So I did, Maata." Mere sighs and returns to her email, her head full of turtles and sea creatures. First up is a message from Greenpeace. Mere reads it then prints the message for Maata. She takes it to her.

"Here, Young Turtle. You can do something constructive for your sister Humpbacks and Minkes."

"Thanks. Mere." Maata takes the sheet of paper and reads:

The so-called "scientific" whaling fleet is again making preparations to head to the waters around Antarctica to conduct its annual lethal hunt. Greenpeace around the world will be taking part in a global day of action at Japan's embassies and consulates to call on the Prime Minister of Japan to stop the fleet from departing. In New Zealand we met with a representative in Auckland this morning. You can see photos on our website now.

We need your help to give this message a strong voice from people all around the world. Please add your voice to this call by visiting: http://www.greenpeace.org.nz/action

In 2002 the International Whaling Commission will hold its annual meeting in Shimonoseki – the home of the whaling fleet. Greenpeace will be campaigning in many ways to ensure that this meeting is a victory for whales *not* whalers. An international Global Whales Action Team has been set up to allow you to get ongoing updates on the campaign and receive further action alerts as we need your help on the campaign.

You can subscribe to the Global Action Team or send a whales e-card to a friend now at:
http://www.greenpeace.org.nz/action

Thanks,
Malcolm Wren
Greenpeace Aotearoa / New Zealand

P.S. There's also been some significant developments in the GE campaign so we'll be sending you out an update on that shortly.

"That's great – I can email out cards to all those on our GE network and also my friends."

"Go for it. I've nearly finished on the net today and you can use it while I wander over to the nursery for an update on progress from Iri and Koa." Mere returns to the screen and Maata to the whaling sheet. She begins writing down the names of all her friends on the net whom she can send e-cards to and recalls she has the addresses of parliamentarians from the GE-Free Coalition site. She will send them cards as well. She'll sign them all Eco-Turtle. That can be her code from now on. She can't wait to tell Cowrie she's now formed a new clan of turtles.

By the time Mere arrives at the nursery, Koa is huddled in Iri's arms and both look as if they have been crying. Mere thinks the worst. "How are they? Any news?" She reminds herself to stay calm this time.

"Yeah, and it's not good," replies Iri, her eyes diverted to Koa as if a sign of warning.

"Why?" asks Mere.

"There's been a terrible act of betrayal."

This sounds serious, thinks Mere, working hard not to panic. "How come?"

"Do you feel up to explaining, Koa?"

Koa nods her head quietly. "You'd better take a seat, Mere. Use my old armchair."

Mere walks slowly to the chair, knowing she must this time brace herself for the worst. Iri and Koa are seldom so bleak and serious. Something terrible must have happened in the cave.

Koa begins slowly telling a story that does not seem to have anything to do with their dilemma. Mere knows better than to interrupt, but she feels a dread gripping her throat. Why are they diverting her attention now, at a time like this?

"I first met Bruce when we were working in the botanical gardens. He was an angel and it was he who alerted me to the dangers of the toxins we were using then. I had been quite ill from pesticide poisoning but had no real idea how dangerous these chemicals are. He set me on the path to reading Meriel Watts' *The Poisoning of New Zealand* and . . ."

Mere finds it hard to concentrate as Koa continues, the tension rising to her neck and causing her head to spin.

". . . the results of the herbicide tests showed that the Roundup had caused the haemorrhage in my right eye and it also affected Bruce badly too. That's why I cannot believe he could be such a traitor. We were lovers a while, and then he moved to Auckland to work for a large firm. I was so rapt for him. He always said he'd save the airfare and fly me up to join him. But I never heard from him again after that, never saw him until . . ." Koa's voice trails off.

Mere realises she is in pain and needs to keep talking, but wonders how this relates to the expedition to the caves. She figures only patience will provide her answer.

"Until today, on the video. He's working for the enemy. He's a part of the team cloning human embryos. I cannot believe I have made love to a person capable of being such a monster." She bursts into tears and Iri holds her closely.

"What team? What embryos? What are you talking about, Koa?" Mere cannot hold back any longer.

Irihapeti begins telling her about what they have seen so far on screen and the revelation from Kuini in her whispering to Cowrie and Moana. That they have no visual proof as yet.

271

"But what about the wahine? Are they safe?"

"We think so. They arrived at the main cave, although Cowrie was attacked by a weta on the way. We saw it in the corner of the screen as she abseiled down the rock. It took a while to figure out what those huge barbs taking up the entire side of the screen were, and once I realised, I gulped. I knew she'd freak out."

"So what happened?"

"She remained quite calm, though it was clear she was utterly relieved once the weta jumped off her at the end of the journey."

"You mean it stayed on all the way down? I don't believe you!" Mere tries to make light of this to cheer up Koa, but it does not work. By now, she knows they must be okay, at least.

"Yep. Our turtle slunk into her protective shell and made it back to shore, yet again," jokes Iri. "And I bet we'll never hear the end of it when she returns, either!" She picks up on Mere's attempt to be light-hearted to divert Koa's attention away from the pain she feels.

"For sure! So where are they now?" asks Mere.

"Still in the cave."

"Are they safe?"

"As far as we know. The lights went out for a while and we could just hear a few hushed whispers. They came on again and we got a good look inside the cave – but then this big Bruce fella took up the screen and hid the file names from us. The next thing, he turned around and Koa got a squizzy at his mug. She's been in shock ever since."

Mere considers the words a while and then breaks

the welcome silence. "Koa. I want you to listen carefully to what I have to say." Koa looks up as she speaks. She has a deep respect for Mere and needs her words at this moment. "*Uenuku-kopako kai awe whare*: Uenuku-Kopako eats the soot from his own house." If this man is a betrayer, he will reap the rewards of his betrayal, he will eat the soot from his house, live to swallow poisoned food on his land. But this does not mean the light cannot shine within him. Maui was a Light-Bearer. You will find many kinds of light-bearers throughout your lifetime. Some will seem to be true, others false. Sometimes the false ones turn around and commit acts of truth. Sometimes the true ones turn their backs and commit acts of betrayal. Maui himself changes shape to spy on his parents. You could say Cowrie and Kuini and Moana are committing acts of spying right now too. It does not automatically make them or their cause wrong. The true test comes in whether they cut off from their own conscience or stay tuned to it. The true test is in their chosen life path. It is possible to change from acts of betrayal to acts of truth."

Koa nods, still listening hard.

"Remember Sahara's mother, Elizabeth Green?"

"Koa was not at Te Kotuku during the Moruroa peace protests," Iri reminds her.

"Okay. Then I'll tell you. She was a good mother to her kids, but then found herself struggling to cope financially. She'd been an anti-nuclear activist but ended up translating for the French Secret Service, and eventually being offered a job as an administrator in their spying unit. The crunch came for her over the French nuclear

273

tests at Moruroa when her daughter, Sahara, whom she'd not seen in years, was videoed during the protest action at Moruroa. Elizabeth realised she could never live with herself if she committed her daughter to prison for standing up for what she believed in, just as she'd taught her to."

"So what did she do?"

"She handed in her resignation, edited the videos that were supposed to dob the protesters in so that their actions but not their faces were shown, refused to edit out the pathetic attempts of the French agents to capture them, and sent the videos to the media. Once they were shown, the French had blown their cool and everyone knew the Greenpeace story was valid. Through her actions, and those of others, the truth got out."

"Wow. That's inspiring."

"Yes – and what you need to remember is that this Bruce could change also. He does not have to take the big money and follow this path of destruction, not unless he has already lost his soul to International Seed Corporation." Mere hopes her message is getting through.

Koa looks up at Mere. "You mean I could do something to change his mind, stop the experiments?"

"Maybe so. You're in a stronger position to do this than any of us. What do you think your chances are?"

"I'd need to meet him on neutral territory. I guess I could find out stuff even if I cannot get him to change his mind and join our side, eh?"

"No harm in trying, Koa. It'd be apt redemption for his betrayal and a way you could also get him to redeem

274

those corporate acts of betrayal in lying globally that these poisons were harmless, just as they are trying to convince us that GE is harmless."

Koa feels a surge of energy race through her body, and filter through to every cell inside her. She has not felt this alive since she was first poisoned. Finally, a chance to redeem this terrible attempt to kill her spirit and body. She jumps up and hugs Mere. Iri is stunned at her transformation and inwardly thanks Mere also. For the first time in ages, Koa's eyes are alight, her soul on fire. Iri can see the joy springing up within her, like a new sprout responding to fresh air and clean water, shooting its head above the earth joyously. Koa is Joy. Joy is Koa. Just with a suggestion, with hope, with a scent of truth in the air and a chance to redeem such evil.

"How's Cowrie and the others? Have they got into the cave yet?" Maata's eyes eagerly wait Mere's response.

"Yes. They have reached the cave safely and can see into it from a ledge near the top of the tunnel behind. Iri told me this morning that they got word from Cowrie that they will stay on as they have enough supplies for a week."

"But why do that? Why not come home and sleep in a comfortable bed and go back the next day?"

Mere sighs. "Well, for one thing, our Turtle had a giant cave weta settle on her face on the way in, so I doubt she'd risk that again."

"But won't there be other wetas in the cave?"

"Surely. But let's hope she is so focused on their spying that she will not be thinking about those kinds of dangers."

"Wish I was there. I'd turn my new turtleshell toward the wetas and the scientists and defy them."

Mere smiles. Such faith and hope. Such innocence still. Koa was probably like this before she was poisoned. She sees some of the innocence and beauty of Maata in Koa and often wonders what she was like as a child before the toxins invaded her skin, her psyche. She's a strong survivor, though. Mere has seen many who have not survived so well after such an experience. The feelings of betrayal last forever. It's not just one act, but a lifetime of being told lies that mounts up and sends some people off the rails. Their physical health declines and then their mental health. It's such a travesty. All the more reason to give Koa the chance to act now – for her own survival, and for the survival of the planet as we know it.

"Have you sent out those emails on whaling to your friends yet, Maata?"

"Yes. And I also wrote letters about it to Helen Clark and Marian Hobbs and Sandra Lee. They are the key ones, eh, as Prime Minister, Minister of Bìo-Security and Minister for the Environment?"

"Ka pae, Maata."

"You'd reckon, with all these feminist politicians in power, that we'd be sweet by now, eh?"

"What do you mean by sweet, Maata?" Mere has trouble with some of this modern language the kids use.

"You know. Sweet. Strong, happy, abundant, full of joy. Sweet."

"Yes. You'd think that for sure. But they are trying their best, I'm convinced of that."

"I'm not. Sandra Lee is tangata whenua. If she can go against those bloody goldmines being expanded and the earth ruined in the South Island, then she can go against GE as strongly. Her party said it was against GE then changed its mind. When I am old enough to vote, buggered if they will get my vote. I'm for the Greens. They are the only ones who have not changed their minds after the election. Besides, I like Nandor Tanzios.

277

Especially his dreadlocks. And he wears suits made from marijuana to parliament. That's choice!" Maata gives the thumbs up sign for Nandor and his suits, or his dreadlocks – Mere is not quite sure which gets the most attention for Maata.

"I think the material is hemp. It's a derivative of marijuana – and from a similar plant – but you can't smoke it."

"Who cares? He's still cool." Maata smiles.

"How are Waka and Piripi progressing with Te Kotuku? Does she have her wing back yet?"

"Nearly. I saw her yesterday in the carving studio. Her wing is being attached so it can move with the wind instead of just being solid. Waka says it makes her more like a real bird and she will not have to resist a strong storm again. Her wing can flow with the current, as if she is really flying."

"What a magnificent idea. I like it. I bet she will too." Mere imagines how graceful the sacred white heron will look when back in her rightful place, presiding over and protecting her marae again. "And how's your wee piwakawaka progressing? Do you think she'll survive?"

"Yes. I'm feeding her by hand with ground-up worms which Iri gives me from the compost. She's still weak, but getting stronger."

"Nothing that a bit of tender loving cannot heal, Maata. Is Waka helping you too?"

"Yeah. And guess what? Waka's gonna grow dreadlocks like Nandor. He's started already."

"Will you love him more then?" asks Mere.

"Don't be silly. He's the same person as before. Just looks more cute."

Thank goodness she has her priorities in place, thinks Mere. Let's hope that Koa does half as well when she has to confront Bruce again. The worst thing would be if her old defences gave way and she came under his charms once more. That would be disastrous for them all, and especially for Irihapeti. She knew it was a risk when she suggested the idea, but one they needed to take. She sends a karakia of protection for Koa, embracing her in the sacred wings of Te Kotuku, knowing that, like the wounded bird, she is capable of repairing her wings again, of flying as she once did, if she can complete her mission.

"We need to turn off the camera, Cowrie." Kuini reaches for the switch.

"Why?"

"I'll tell you later." Kuini clicks the switch up and huddles back into the ledge.

"Bloody hell, it's getting cramped in here. How long do we have to stay?" whispers Cowrie.

"Longer than you think, Turtle. Moana went back to get more supplies and warmer clothes for us and found the end of the tunnel blocked with rocks."

"D'ya reckon they are onto us?"

"Yep."

"Then why don't we alert Iri and Koa? They can send for help from the outside."

"Because then they will panic. Moana reckons she can remove the stones, one by one, and get out. She's back there having a crack at it now. If she can't, then we'll make a decision on what to do.

"But won't Iri and the others freak out if they don't hear us?"

"Yep. That's why we are turning the camera back on for a moment but not talking about it. Okay?"

Cowrie is not sure she likes this plan, but does not want to blow the operation either. "Okay."

Kuini reaches up and switches on the tiny camera. She whispers into the microphone. "I know you cannot answer us, Iri. But we just want you to know we are okay. We need some more sleep so we are going to switch off for a while, and we'll tune you back in when there's something to report. We're thinking of you all. And of the kai moana we are missing. Cowrie's getting sick of eating roasted wetas." She grins.

"Don't even mention the word," whispers Cowrie, as Kuini reaches up to switch off the camera.

Irihapeti returns from planting the new pohutukawa seedlings at the end of the dunes. She glances at the screen. It's black again. Damn, she thinks and tries to fiddle with the keyboard. Nothing happens. It could be a blackout, or they could be in danger. "Hey, Koa. Come and have a squizzy here." Koa emerges from the spinach patch and walks toward the nursery office. "It's blanked out on us again. Hope the battery is okay. I gave them several spares. They should be still on line."

"That's it, then. I can't wait any longer." Koa rips off her work apron and her leather gloves and dials a number on her cellphone. It rings three times. "Is that Tony Pratt? It's Koa here from Te Kotuku marae. Maata cannot clean today but has asked if I can come instead of her . . . Yes . . . yes. I am a good worker and she has told me what to do. What's that? Yes, I'll be sure to bring up some more kawakawa tea. It's addictive isn't it? . . . Sure. I'll keep out of the way of the FarmCorp scientists. Don't you worry. In fact, one of them is a close friend of mine and I would like to see him if that's possible . . . Who? Bruce. He's very tall and has a pony-tail. You know the one? They have afternoon tea at 3 pm? Well, that's fine. I'll be up at noon and I can make tea for them at 3 pm . . . Thanks. That's no trouble at all." She pushes the end button with glee.

Irihapeti is amazed Koa could be so calm and smooth. She has not seen this side of her. "You ain't seen nuthin' yet!" exclaims Koa. "Okay. I'm off. Got some preparation to do and cleaning stuff to buy. See ya back here tonight."

"Don't you want me to let Maata know first?"

"All sorted, honey. She's sick at home with Mere today. Spoke to her earlier. I offered to do her work for her and it was when I was mulching the spinach that the idea of using this to our advantage really started to grow."

"You be careful, Joyous One."

"I will. I hold you close to my heart." Koa puts her hand on her chest.

"Thanks Koa. Me too." Iri blows her a kiss and insists that she call on her cellphone if she is in any danger at all. Koa promises to do so and leaves, sending Iri a kiss from her open palm. Iri catches it mid-air and folds her fingers carefully around the kiss, as if to preserve it and protect it forever.

Moana returns to the ledge defeated. "I can't remove the stones. They're too heavy. I think we should get help from Iri now."

"Let me go back with you and try," Kuini offers. "Cowrie, you stay here and monitor what's happening. Get a close-up zoom on those filing cabinets if possible, so we have proof of the existence of human embryos in their research. We won't get far without that."

Cowrie stretches her limbs as the others crawl back down the tunnel and up the abseiling rope to make their way to the entrance of the cave. Trying to get stones away from there will be difficult, but Kuini is very strong and they have a better chance together. Cowrie switches on the camera, presses her face hard up against the slit in the rock and watches as the scientists go about their work. There is very little speech. They seem totally preoccupied by their tasks. The fella with the pony-tail breaks the monotony by dropping a specimen phial, and this infuriates the shorter one.

"For Christ's sake, Bruce. You'd drop your bloody head if it wasn't screwed on! Lucky that wasn't Liquid Gold. That would've cost you your job."

As if I'd care, thinks Bruce. I'm only really hanging on for the money. The excitement ended some time ago when they did their first stem cell experiment. Once he knew it could work, he feared what might come of it and drew back from the idea of completing the task. Then Steve offered him more money and the promise of huge riches once they cracked the final code, and by that time his marriage was on the rocks and he desperately needed the money to support his ex-wife and their son and daughter. It's worth it for them, he kept telling himself. That's the only reason he's stayed on to work in this damp cave on areas of science that he knows from his religious upbringing and his ethical conscience are wrong. And for Karl. "Sorry Steve. It won't happen again."

"It bloody better not," grumbles Steve.

Cowrie notices there is tension between the men. The taller one with the pony-tail seems to not have his heart in his work. Steve, on the other hand, is like a religious zealot. He works at least sixteen hours a day and seems completely driven. When things do not go right, he gets extremely anxious, as if his life is on the line with this work. Pony-Tail, on the other hand, acts as if he disapproves of the work. He grimaces behind the back of his boss and often drops or breaks things. It's almost as if he is trying to undermine the work and yet, when he concentrates hard, his hand is steady and the boss seems very pleased with him. There's a kind of push-pull, love-hate relationship between the men. She gathers that Pony-Tail has most of the knowledge and that Stevie-Boy needs him and could not complete this work without him. Pony-Tail knows this and sometimes deliberately makes Stevie-Boy work hard for his support.

Cowrie's left leg is still giving her strife after the surfing accident and she moves it into a more comfortable position, dislodging a stone which bumps against the rock wall as it heads for the floor of the tunnel. She glances back into the cave to see if there is any reaction. Steve looks up immediately, his head listening like a doe in a field of hunters. "Did you hear that, Bruce?"

"Hear what?"

"A falling stone. The boys went around the perimeter of the cave after we heard those noises yesterday and found the entrance to a tunnel. It got quite narrow then there was a drop of about twenty feet. They found an abseiling rope there and got worried that maybe climbers were still using the tunnel. Then they noticed it had 'Pratt' in marker ink on the plastic and realised it must've been used by Tony's boys. They left it dangling in case we need to use the tunnel at any stage. Then they blocked the entrance so nobody else could use it and in case any animals wander in from the neighbouring farm. The last thing we need is some redneck farmer marching up to Pratt and demanding to know why his sheep are missing and snooping about."

"D'ya reckon there's some animal in there?"

"Well if any kids had got trapped, they'd have called out by now. And we haven't heard any bleating. I reckon it's just a few rats or stoats that are using it. Still, they won't be getting out now. So we can count on stoat stew if we get trapped here." Stevie-Boy laughs.

"It'll taste better than that possum stew that Pratt laid on us last night," replies Bruce. "I thought you were getting us caterers for this part of the operation. Really looking after us."

"I would if there was such a thing in this Godforsaken place. But, you wait, Bruce, m'boy. You will soon have caterers begging to serve you. You'll be lazing about some idyllic Mediterranean sea port, with a beautiful woman lying beside you."

Ugh, thinks Bruce. He's got no idea I love men. The last woman I had took off with my two kids, and then I realised when Karl came back into my life that we'd always been in love, ever since school. He hates me being away doing this work, but he likes the idea of us retiring in comfort once this job is over. "Sounds delicious," says Bruce, thinking of a tanned version of Lockwood Smith rubbing his shoulders and massaging his abs.

And so the soap opera continues. Cowrie had half-expected to see weird animals with twinned heads and three tails, but this gene-splicing human embryo trip is really incredibly long and boring and the blokes doing it even more tiresome. It's like watching paint dry, she thinks, yawning and wondering if it might be a good time to alert Iri to their predicament and at least get out of here. Then Bruce moves away from his table, putting the filing cabinet into full view again. Cowrie aims the camera in its direction. She is sure that Iri will be able to see the labels and zoom in on them.

An hour later, Kuini and Moana return. "No luck, Turtle. We can't move the stones. It feels like they got a dozer and ran a dump full of rocks into the entrance. There's one spot where we could see light coming through but we could not budge the rocks," Kuini whispers.

"Let's alert Iri then. I think I've got a good shot of the files now."

"Great. That's about all we can do at this stage."

It's then that they hear a slow moaning, as if an animal is in pain. They press up against the slit in the rock to see what is happening. The moaning increases. "Bruce, go and see what Danny is doing." Bruce goes off into one of the side caves and returns a few moments later, his face white. At the end of the rope he is holding is a creature like they have never seen before. It resembles a kunekune pig but has red blotches all over its body and sores leaking pus. It struggles to walk at all, as if its body is too large for its legs, which are very thin and wobbly. Steve grabs the rope off Bruce and tries to pull the creature towards him. It crumbles under the weight of its body and slinks to the cave floor. It's then that they recognise the sound it makes.

"Baaaaa . . . baaaaaa . . . baaaaaa." It is a sheep in pig's clothing, some kind of aberrant experiment gone awry. The animal writhes in pain, as if in its last throes of life. "Well, that's the end of LambPork Ltd. You'd better tell MagicMilk to courier up the rest of the funds so we can do more trials on their WonderPig," advises Steve. "Take all the usual tests and then administer a lethal injection. Put the poor bastard out of its misery before anyone finds out it ever lived." Bruce looks at the slobbering LambPig and fights back the tears. He'll never get used to this kind of work. He'd far rather be back grafting trees, despite the toxic risks in botanical gardens.

Cowrie, Kuini and Moana are glued to the slit in the rock, barely believing what they see. It seems that these men are experimenting in all areas, taking as much GE funding as they can and trying to see what eventuates.

288

All they need is one hit to get the jackpot, and they will never have to rely on research funds again. Genetic gambling. They have turned a sacred Maori burial cave into a brightly lit modern casino. But they are not gambling with man-made money – bits of paper with pictures of the Queen on them. They are gambling with our genes – the very make-up of our lives, the DNA that separates species and makes us each unique. They have the power to destroy this uniqueness forever. They have the power to ruin lives in the process. The groaning LambPig is dragged from the room and back into the smaller cave. The wahine avert their eyes. They hope it has been saved on film by Iri.

They wait until the men leave for their afternoon tea break, then try to contact the nursery. "Iri. Are you there? We hope you got all that on tape. Hideous. We're locked in the tunnel. They've jammed up the end with rocks. Get some help. Say that you think some climbers may have got into the tunnel by mistake and need rescuing and that you'll keep it quiet and respect their secrecy. Thanks. We'll wait here until you come. Make it soon. The air is getting stale and we are very cramped. Kia ora." They switch off the camera to save the batteries.

Koa finishes her work and begins making a batch of date scones for Tony and the boys. Tony sits at the kitchen table, his hairy arms and back protruding out of his white, stained singlet. "You'd better whip that off too and I'll put it in the wash."

Tony looks down at his chest. "Yeah. Had bacon and eggs for brekky. Bloody eggs broke getting to my mouth. It's these wretched shop eggs. No grunt to them. Not like the barn eggs we had as a kid."

Koa hands him a fresh shirt as he passes her his singlet. "Why don't you get some roosters and hens, then? We have a good supply at Te Kotuku and they eat organic grains. Their eggs are delicious."

"Don't think I'll be around here much longer. Thinking of a trip abroad once these FarmCorp fellas have finished their work."

Koa takes the plunge. "So you don't think you and Moana will get back together again?"

Tony hesitates a moment. "Seems that way. Thought I was in there for the scrum but then I heard she got herself another fella. Pipi or something. Well, she can have all the pipis and cockles and whatever she likes from down there. I've got bigger fish to fry." Tony acts brave but he looks as if he could crumble if a feather was waved in front of his nose now. Koa has seen Moana with Piripi and they get along well, but she does not think it's much more than friendship – yet. Still, she's much safer with him than with Tony. "I reckon FarmCorp will want to buy up the farm after all this work and money they are putting into it – and then I'll be sweet," he adds, grinning, hoping this will get back to Moana. Serves her right for deserting him.

"But won't you miss the kids?" asks Koa.

"Sure. But wherever I live, they can come and visit me for a holiday. The money from the farm will more than provide for that." And a lot else, thinks Tony, with luck.

Koa mixes dough, adds milk and dates, then places blobs of it onto the greased oven tray. "Been ages since I tasted good date scones. Moana was too busy with the kids' homework to make any treats. Not like the good old days when we first got together. She'd do anything to please me then." Yes, too much, thinks Koa, placing the scones in the oven.

"How many men are working here?"

"Why do ya ask?" Tony is suddenly suspicious of her.

"So I know how many scones to butter."

He grins. "Usually about eight come up for arvo tea. The others have their thermoses and stuff down at the nursery."

"So what are they doing down there?" asks Koa, hoping it sounds casual.

Tony looks at her closely. No harm in letting her know how important he is. They'll never know. "Secret experiments. Sticking genes from pine trees into kauris. Makes them grow like bloody triffids, evidently. That Bruce fella knows all about it. He's the boss man at the nursery. Howd'ya first meet him?"

"We worked together at the botanical gardens."

"I see. Boyfriend was he?"

"Yeah. For a while."

"You like your chances with him now, eh?" There's a glint in Tony's eye. He fancies himself as a bit of a matchmaker. After all, it was he who linked up half the local farmers with their missuses. He knows the district like the back of his hand – and all the farmers' daughters, mothers and sisters.

Koa notices his interest. "Maybe. I would quite like to talk to him alone if he comes up. Is there a place we could go to be discreet?"

Tony chuckles. "I knew it. Could tell in your voice on the phone. They don't call me Tricky Tony for nuthin', ya know. Take him into the front room. It's always quiet there. I don't s'pose you'll be needing the bedroom this time, eh?" He grins, showing a tooth missing at the front.

Koa squirms but acts calm on the outside. "No. I'd just like to talk with him and catch up without the others teasing him."

"No worries. You just rely on me for that. I'll make sure he's tipped off and I'll give you the wink. Then you can just lead him up the garden path. Mind you, if it all works out, I expect an invitation to the wedding." He sticks his tongue between the gap in his teeth, trying to dislodge a piece of bacon stuck there from his breakfast.

Koa grimaces without him seeing. "I think you're putting the cart before the horse a bit here, Tony."

Tony dislodges the bacon and flicks it out onto the table. It lands on the clean plate Koa has placed in the middle, ready for the scones. "Oops." Tony picks up the plate and wipes it with the back of his hairy, grubby arm and sticks it back onto the table. "There ya are. Good as gold. I'm off to have a shave and I'll bring the boys up."

"Thanks, Tony." Koa waits until he has left the kitchen and then puts the plate in the sink and gets out another one for the scones. Ugh. I'm so glad Moana got out of here, she thinks. And took the boys. He's not an evil man, just rather stupid. And I'll bet that's why the GE boys chose this farm. A place where they could be boss and have a lease they can leave if it does not work out. And poor Tony has no idea they will dump him like a can of diseased worms also.

By the time the boys arrive, Koa has baked and buttered two dozen date scones and placed some hibiscus flowers on the table floating in a bowl. Water for the tea is bubbling on the stove and the kawakawa brew sits next to it. She's put in a strong mix, hoping it will make Bruce and the boys drowsy and off their guard, just enough to let out a few secrets. As they enter the door, she recognises Bruce immediately. He's much bigger than when she knew him, that much she realised from the video. But still those same green eyes, albeit dimmer than before. Something of that old sparkle is missing. She'll find out what it is before the end of the day. Bruce recognises her immediately. "Koa, what on earth are you doing here?"

The others sit down to their scones and Bruce and Koa catch up on their old days at the botanical gardens.

293

After a while, Tony comes over. "Hey, haven't you got work to do in the front room, Koa? All that ironing. Take Bruce in there and stick him in the rocker while you finish the work. I wanna make sure I've got some decent clothes for the TAB dinner at the pub tonight. Ya never know, I might pick myself up a fancy lady." He laughs.

Koa grimaces. "Come on through, Bruce. You don't mind if I iron while we catch up, do you?"

"I'd love it." He glances over at Steve. "I'll be a bit late back, boss. Just catching up with an old mate."

"Just be careful what you say," warns Steve.

"That's all right. I have no interest in your work, just in finding out about Bruce since we last met. Strictly personal," she adds.

I'll bet, thinks Steve, as he watches them exit the kitchen.

Once they are ensconced in the front room and Bruce is settled in his chair, Koa pretends to iron while she carefully asks questions. She finds out all about his life and relationship with his wife, but he barely mentions his work. Finally, she gets him onto it and discovers that he misses the botanical job; he was brought in to do the kauri experiment and then the project diversified. When she asks more, he closes up.

It's not until she mentions Irihapeti and talks of their love that he opens up and talks about his passion for Karl, and says that is the reason why he is risking all to complete this job now, and for his kids. Koa sees they have something in common that the others do not and asks more questions, all the while feeding him more of the kawakawa tea and manuka honey which he loves so much. Gradually, his guard relaxes and he leans close and whispers into Koa's ear.

"You know this GE stuff everyone is up in arms about? Well, that's why we are here. It's not really Farm Corp, but a research group related to MagicMilk and International Seed Corporation. We're in with the Big Boys now and it sure pays well, with more to come if we pull it off."

"Pull off what?" Koa whispers back.

Bruce takes a deep breath and tells her they are experimenting with human embryos, that he knows in his heart and soul it is wrong, but that he just wants to finish the work and then escape with Karl. They intend living in Rarotonga where Karl once taught. When Koa questions him further, she finds out that the research money will already provide for a handsome retirement fund and asks why he wants more if he abhors the work so much. She asks what all their work against toxic poisoning was all about, and whether he really wants to sell his soul to the devil so easily. By the time the kawa-kawa tea has done its work and Koa hers, Bruce is nearly in tears. These feelings have been eating at him for a long time, but he has pushed them down. Now he is wracked with anxiety and guilt over his abandonment of his once strong principles.

"And what will Karl think of all this when you tell him you were a part of cloning a human being? He sounds like a man with ethics from all you have said. Do you really think he'll stay with you then?" She sees him crumble. "I wouldn't." By this time, Bruce is weak and weepy. He's been close to this state for weeks but meeting Koa again has stirred up all those old emotions and nostalgia for their work together, their closeness in struggling against their own toxic poisoning.

Koa shakes her head. "I can't believe that after all our shared pain and hard work in fighting against DDT and Roundup that you'd end up working for the company that produces the stuff. What on earth has happened to you, Bruce? You're not the same loving person I once knew."

Bruce takes her hand and begs her forgiveness. He's always regretted abandoning Koa for the big money offered to him in Auckland, and now he knows he could lose Karl the same way. And perhaps his kids once they find out. Karl knows he earns big research funds, but he has no idea about the true nature of the business he is in now.

Koa straightens up. "The only way I can or will forgive you, Bruce, is if you have the courage to leave the work. And also to tell the truth publicly about how this industry is obtaining funds for unethical research. Speak the truth, as other scientists have. You'll be remembered, just as the Physicians and Scientists against Nuclear War and those against GE are now." She tells him about the brave paper they'd read on line by Peter Wills, the Auckland University physics professor. "He had the guts to speak out publicly and bugger the research funds. You need to do that too, Bruce. Then Karl and your kids can be rightly proud of you. And so will I."

Bruce listens to Koa, his head in his hands. She knows he is a good man underneath, that he will follow his heart unless he has changed beyond belief. Finally, he raises his head. "You know, Koa, I lost one of my closest friends in the September 11th twin towers disaster. Alan Bevan. He was an environmental lawyer. One of the best. He was on the plane flying toward the White House that went down in Pennsylvania due to the actions of a few brave men. I knew my mate was one of those men. That he'd never have stood by and let that happen. I know in my heart that he sacrificed his life to save those of so many others. I sat glued to the television, didn't go to work for days afterwards. I felt like such a shit, to have copped out on my ideals, to have compromised like we said we never would. I nearly gave up my job at that point. I could barely function. It was like some kind of mid-life crisis. Then Steve got the MagicMilk grant and offered me more money than I could ever believe existed, just to come here and work, let alone the wealth we'd make if any one of these experiments hit the jackpot. I reasoned it would only be one more year before I could retire, and Karl and I could finally live our dreams. It seemed worth it at the time." He nearly chokes with anguish. Koa offers him more kawakawa tea.

"What about now, Bruce? You owe it to your friend Alan, to Karl, to your kids, your family, to me, to the planet. The plants we once nurtured. This earth we so love. Remember those days when we stayed up all night just to see the rare tropical orchids flowering, and the care we took to make sure nobody else working there would ever be subjected to toxic poisoning again. Remember the day your first bromeliad flowered and we could not believe the exquisite colours of the purple and red blooms. You said it was like watching a mother

297

give birth to her young. You wanted so much to have kids – and now you have them, you are working to leave them the inheritance of a poisoned world, and one forever altered by genetic mutation which cannot be reversed. They may never have a choice of organic food as we have. They may be controlled by genetic forces that we can only imagine in our worst nightmares. We can never better the beauty of nature. It's our inheritance. Do you really want to ruin that for your kids?"

Bruce remains quiet for a long time. "If I leave, will you help me get the word out? Do you have networks where we can really have some influence? I don't want to sacrifice all the hard work and research for nothing. I want to make a difference, like Alan did on that flight. I want to reach a wide range of people if I speak out, and I need to know I have some protection too."

Koa smiles. She takes Bruce in her arms. He feels soft and warm, just like the old days. "Just you say the word, Bruce. Come down to Te Kotuku marae tonight and we'll show you our network. Iri has access to a huge range of eco-activist groups on the net. We'll get the word out there, let it blossom like wildflowers, and then sit back and wait for the mainstream media to pick it up. We could leak it anonymously, and you could save your reputation. So long as you give us all the details. Can you get us copies of the files?"

"Yes. I have copies. It's top secret, but I am in charge of them." Bruce hugs Koa warmly, so relieved that he has been finally able to unburden his heavy soul.

Tony walks past the room and nudges open the door. He notices them hugging. Bloody perfect. You haven't lost your touch, Tony. Next thing you know, they'll be breeding like maggots. He grins and closes the door, very pleased with himself. He walks back into the kitchen and finishes off the remainder of the date scones while listening to talkback radio, totally unaware there is a quiet revolution taking place in his front room.

Iri stares at the screen in disbelief. She cringes as she watches the poor animal trying to move but falling under the weight of its own bloated body. It is neither a pig nor a lamb, but a strange and weird mixture of both. It cries like a lost lamb in pain but grunts like a pig in labour. She can hardly believe her eyes. After days of watching a boring laboratory where nothing much seems to happen, it's as if Orson Welles has suddenly taken over the direction and she is watching something from a bad Hollywood movie. Mind you, they all thought the same when their eyes were glued to the telly as shots kept being repeated of the planes flying into the twin towers, one from the right into the first tower, then one from the left into the next tower, forcing it to crumble like a Sylvester Stallone action adventure. For her, this is as calculated and as chilling. She fears for her friends now that she realises what danger they may be in. What if they get caught trying to escape from the tunnel?

Irihapeti pauses the video while pouring out more manuka tea and stirring in rewarewa honey. The phone rings. It's an order for more organic spinach, bean and sweet pea seeds. Iri notes it down in the book. "We'd also love more of those purple and cream potatoes – and the urenika. They are beautiful," the voice says.

"Thanks so much for providing us with healthy seeds. Our kids are even getting interested in gardening now. They love it when your courier parcels arrive and can't wait to get planting. Can you send us the catalogue of your heritage organic fruit trees? We are thinking of starting our own orchard now." Iri listens intently, noting the requests, but her mind is still on the video. After the call, she returns to the computer and keys in "play".

She listens as Kuini tells her that they are trapped in the tunnel, that they need help. Iri jumps to her feet. Koa may be in danger too. They are all up at Pratt's farm and Koa will have no idea that the tunnel has been blocked. She needs to get help fast. She runs out to the carving studio to alert Piripi and Waka.

Night falls and they are still trapped in the tunnel. By now, Moana, Kuini and Cowrie have crawled back to the entrance and are waiting for Iri, Piripi and any others from the marae to rescue them. They hope that their message has been received. They have no way of knowing, other than their faith in Irihapeti.

They tell stories to keep their spirits up and to allay their anxiety. They discuss how strange it is that their sacred kotuku lost her wing in a storm that was not half as strong as the many they'd endured since Cyclone Bola hit the coast with devastation few years back. Moana thinks it is a sign that she is displeased with the current events – the war of revenge being waged by the United States, what they call their war against terrorism; the sacrificing of this inspired land of Aotearoa – land of the awakening dawn – to genetic manipulation when the tangata whenua of the land are united against this desecration. They face an era like the colonial ripping away of their native land but in such a way that they can never be returned again and healed. Kuini says it is like the French taking away Moruroa and Faungata'ufa and then expecting the Maohi people to return and eat from contaminated islands and oceans. They recall the day Te Kotuku was raised onto the top of their wharenui and

302

blessings and karakia were spoken and chanted for the protection of the marae.

"You know, it's just hit me that we always see Te Kotuku as a protective influence. But what if she were to invoke her Pacific Island powers and take her own form of revenge?"

"Whad'ya mean, Cowrie?"

"When we were protesting at Moruroa, one of the Tahitian wahine told me about their reef heron, also called kotuku, who had powers to take revenge on others when necessary."

"In what way?"

"Well, there was this fella called Rata who was son of an ariki nui of Tahiti Tokerau. Rata was born in the season of maroro tu – when all the flying fish come leaping near the reef and the herons swing by for a feast. On the night of his birth, Tahiti Tokerau wanted kai moana for her dinner so there would be plenty of milk for her baby. They rowed out over the reef with torches and all the maroro flew like wildfire into the flames and the tangata whenua caught heaps of fish that night."

"So where does the heron come into it?"

"Wait, Kuini. Have patience."

"Okay." Kuini is enjoying the storytelling, despite their circumstances.

"While they were fishing, a vast darkness swallowed up the stars hanging above them. It was the gigantic wingspan of Matuku tangotango, the demon bird, chief of all the devil birds of Puna's land called Hiti marama. Nobody knew the bird was coming. This Heron-of-Darkness, swallower of the stars and people, swooped

303

down and grabbed Rata's parents and flew away with them to Puna's, where he landed and divided up his catch."

"Some bird, eh?"

"Sure was. Puna got Rata's mother and planted her in the ground, her head below the earth, and used her feet to hook her food baskets. Then Matuku bit off the head of Rata's father and swallowed it whole, casting out his body for the Fish Gods to eat. Pahua nui, the monster clam who lies in wait for the canoes, ate some. So did Totoviri, the Giant Swordfish who eats the hands of paddlers. All the monsters in the sea cave got some to eat."

"Lucky your sea cave adventure was here in Aotearoa and not in Tahiti, eh, Cowrie?"

"Maybe," grimaces Cowrie, not yet quite over it.

"So what happened to Rata?"

"His grandmother, Kui Kura, looked after him, cut his birth cord from his mother and fattened him up and raised him as her own."

"Another Mere, eh?"

"Yeah. That takes courage too."

"Sure does."

"Anyway, I heard heaps more stories in Tahiti about this kotuku, Matuku tangotango, and lately I've been wondering if our own kotuku might invoke some of his powers to protect our land. D'ya reckon it can work this way, Moana?"

"I wouldn't put anything past our Pacific Gods. When they get furious, they will avenge as sure as Bush and bin Laden are doing now," Moana replies.

"But didn't we all agree that utu is not the answer, that

we must seek remedies beyond that cycle?" Kuini asks.

"Yes, but there are times when the Gods feel violated. And that's when they are capable of all kinds of acts. It's our job as humans to try to evolve to a state where we no longer need to act in this way – but clearly we are not there yet. Current events are showing us this very strongly."

"But isn't it also true that there are often times of darkness and terror before we can evolve to a higher plane of existence? Maybe we are enduring this right now? Perhaps this is the lesson we should be taking from these events?" Cowrie offers.

"I'd like to think so," replies Kuini. "But it depends on our responses. The good thing is that there are huge numbers of people globally thinking more clearly now. Most do not want war and revenge in this way and most do not want a future of genetic manipulation to hand down to their children. That much we do know."

"Well, I'd like the Heron-of-Darkness to swallow up these scientists right now. Cause a flood to fill these caves and destroy all their experiments."

"Be careful what you wish for, Cowrie. We could all drown if that happens," Moana warns.

Just at this moment there's a scratching noise at the other side of the entrance, and a male voice. But it is not that of Piripi. Cowrie thinks she recognises one of the voices of the men in the cave. They all do. They look at each other in stunned silence. They have not made a contingency plan in case the men get to them first. They may well need the help of the Dark Heron, Matuku tangotango, in the cruel hours ahead.

Irihapeti cannot find Piripi. Waka says he went into Rawene to teach a carving course and will not be back until late. Iri knows she will have to be patient as they need the van and his strength. All she can do is go back to her computer screen and wait, hoping the wahine will contact her again, that they will be okay. But should she tell Mere and Maata? She agonises over this for a while, drinking far too much kawakawa tea to calm her nerves. She checks the net and writes emails against GE to politicians and pressure groups in an attempt to do something positive while she waits.

There is a tension in the air as she wonders what Koa is up to and if she is safe, whether they will get to the tunnel before the others find the women. Finally, she bites her pride and calls Tony Pratt's cellphone to see if Koa is still there. She's far too late returning home, and Irihapeti smells the stench of something wrong. "Yeah, Tony here. Just a minute. Someone's banging on the door. Hang on a tick." She hears his footsteps pounding the hard wooden floor of the old kauri villa as he saunters over to the door. "Gidday, Bruce. What the shit are you doing here at this time of night? Yeah . . . yeah . . . shit a brick. Just a minute, I'll get the tractor and gear . . ." He yells into the cellphone. "You still there? Yeah

306

– there's been some kind of accident up here in the caves. Bloody freak flood by the sounds of it. I'd better go." He hangs up. Dead silence.

Irihapeti is frozen to the ground. She cannot move. Her head is filled with wild scenarios, of Koa finding the wahine, of being trapped inside the tunnel with them. No – they are blocked in. They will be drowned alive. There's no time to save them now. All because she delayed and waited for Piripi to return home. She'll be responsible for their deaths. She tucks the phone into her jacket and races out the nursery door, not thinking to leave a note for the others, as she had insisted they do next time an emergency happens. She jumps onto her motorbike and thrusts it into gear with a kick of the pedal. In a cloud of clay, Irihapeti zooms down the rough track and over the rugged farmland on her way to the Pratt farmstead, her heart in her throat.

On the way, images crowd her head. Memories of wonderful feasts with Cowrie and Kuini, of sharing the rongoa hui with Moana, of how brilliant her life has been since she and Koa fell in love, and how the organic nursery and seed-saving programme really took off after her arrival. Koa has been a saviour and soulmate to her, an angel who flew in from the sky and shared her vision of a healthy planet and what they could do to help others to enjoy this. Her work with the tamariki on the marae has been so empowering, getting them involved in all aspects of the organic growing and the saving of seeds. Educating them to live in a better world. And now all this is at stake because they dared to challenge the status quo, demand a better future for their kids.

And because Iri did not act fast enough. She spurs her feet into the side of Artemis, her bike, as if she is a horse and will be swifter for the encouragement. The stars are covered by clouds and Hina hides inside her grey cloak, as if darkened by the giant wingspan of a matuku moana flying through the heavens above.

Irihapeti arrives at the farmhouse to find it abandoned. She grabs a torch that she sees behind the kitchen door and makes her way toward the Maori burial caves. She remembers going there as a kid and is sure she can find her way. She must. Eventually she arrives. The waters have receded as fast as they came. There is a scene of utter devastation before her. The bodies of men float face down in the water and animals lie dead, stuck in the mud as they tried to escape. Some of the men are trying to administer resuscitation and others are being loaded onto a Flyworks helicopter. She looks for the bodies of her friends. She scans the bush for some sign of them. But nothing.

Between gasps, Tony Pratt tells her that a freak flood gushed through the caves and destroyed everything. All their files and their experiments are ruined. That according to one of the men, it was like an earthquake. One minute they were leaving the cave in the moonlight, the next thing the moon was obliterated from sight. They heard what sounded like the swoosh of a giant wingspan, as if an airplane was bearing down on them, then a thundering behind. Images of the giant birds crashing into the twin towers filled their fears, tugged at their hearts. Water started rolling down from the hills above, like a storm deluge or a tidal wave. Some of them scrambled to safety and the rest drowned in the flood, which was unlike any deluge he'd ever seen. "It came out of nowhere with a whoosh of wings and just destroyed everything in moments. It disappeared back into the earth as forcefully as it appeared, leaving this bloody great mess behind."

It is clear now that the only survivors are those in the copter, and that her dearest friends have died, fighting for a better world – as Cowrie always vowed they'd do, if and when the time came. Bruce is nowhere to be seen. She cannot even ask him if he finally met up with Koa. She is sure Koa went down to the tunnel to make sure Kuini and the others were okay. That'd be so like Koa. And she's died, just like them, because she wanted to leave behind a stronger, cleaner earth. The only small redemption Iri can find is that Koa would have wanted to go this way, fighting those who poisoned her, poisoned our planet. Iri crawls through debris over the caves to the tunnel behind. The water has thrown the rocks in the entrance out like pebbles in its path. But still no sign of the wahine. She carefully enters the tunnel. The water is still up to her knees. She calls out their names. No replies.

She makes her way to the point where the tunnel drops down and sees the rope dangling over. It has been ripped by the force of rocks crammed against it and has broken in two. There is no way they could have escaped. They could never get up a vertical drop of about twenty feet without a rope. Iri drops down onto her knees and utters a karanga of grief, letting it pour around her, wind its way into the depths of the caves. She thinks she hears another karanga in reply. She listens. But she knows it cannot be so. Her mind is playing tricks on her. It's just an echo. They cannot possibly have escaped this devastation. She weeps and weeps, on her knees, the water still up to her waist, in the pit of the tunnel.

Ko roimata, ko hupe nga kaiutu i nga patu a tenei tangata nui, a Aitua. Only tears can avenge this great personal calamity.

Roimata
Roimata
Roimata.

The tangata whenua do not see their kotuku flying back to her post in the dark of the night. They have no idea she has been on a mission of mercy, has called upon the powers of Matuku tangotango to help her on her journey. She lands safely back on the marae and folds her wings into her belly.

The next morning, they wake to the news of the tragedy. Iri is back at Mere's cottage. They'd stayed up all night in mourning and are planning the tangi now. Mere switches on the television to see if the news has spread to the media yet. The United States is still bombing Afghanistan. They've hit civilian homes and even killed some of their own forces when a bomb landed on the wrong buildings. Swollen, tear-stained faces beg them to stop their destruction. The Taliban are retreating, but they know this will never be the end. It will just be a new beginning. An unholy jihad is gathering force in these acts of revenge. Some kids have set fire to their school gym and received over a year in jail for it. A training ground for their future criminal careers. Great, thinks Mere. Physicians and Scientists against Genetic Engineering are speaking out against the government's decision and warning of the dangers to come. Then a lady comes on, flying about the room as if her cleaning

311

liquid has enabled her to suddenly do all her housework in one minute and left her free to drink chardonnay with her yuppie mates for the rest of the day. "As if," says Maata. "Rich chicks like that have cleaning slaves." She still has no idea of the fate of the others. She has been asleep most of the night, and Mere is waiting for the right time to tell her the news. By now, Mere and Iri are in the kitchen, hugging each other for comfort.

Maata suddenly calls out from the lounge. "Haere mai, haere mai. Cowrie and Kuini are on the telly." They cannot believe their ears. They rush into the lounge and there is Bruce, the fella with the pony-tail, a microphone thrust to his mouth, talking about the "unfortunate experiment" up in the Hokianga. The media are all over him. Behind stand Cowrie, Kuini and Moana, grinning. Then the scene cuts to pictures of the kunekune creature falling under its own weight, sores pussing out of its body. "Gross. Yuck!" says Maata, still unaware the others had been in any danger and relishing their apparent victory. Finally, Cowrie comes on screen and describes how Bruce and Koa (quick shot to Koa) rescued them minutes before the flood, how they heard the thunder of the water and ran for safety to the house. There they grabbed the van, with Bruce's files and documents safely inside his locked bag, and tore off to Rawene, calling the media by cellphone on the way. Behind them, Rawene Wholefoods rises out of the water like a vision and a lone matuku moana perches triumphantly on the mooring poles.

When asked what could have caused the flood, Cowrie says she has no idea, but that the genetic engineering experiments were taking place inside ancient Maori burial caves and that their ancestors would have been furious; that all the tangata whenua knew there was a tapu on the caves and so the scientists were foolish to ever think they could get away with playing God inside such a holy place. One of the Pakeha reporters behind her sniggers, and at the same time the matuku moana flies over and drops her breakfast onto him in a great creamy dollop. The reporter jumps back and the cameraman smiles. He'd had this coming for a while. Maata laughs. "Did ya see that sea heron. Ha! She showed the fella." Cowrie explains to the camera that they'd had no time to alert relatives that they were safe because they had to get the news to the media immediately and she sends their love to Te Kotuku marae.

Irihapeti looks at Mere and laughs with relief. They no longer have to organise a tangi, and their loved ones will return soon. Mind you, they will still have to answer for not calling on the cellphone when they knew they were safe. But for now, Iri and Mere are so relieved that they just embrace each other and dance around the room. Maata joins them, thinking they are just happy that the others got on the breakfast news.

Outside, as the morning sun beams warmth onto the marae, Te Kotuku flaps her wings in the breeze, pleased to be drying them after such a wet night out. *Ta paki o Ruhia. Looks like fine weather ahead.* She opens her beak and yawns, then settles back to admire her beautiful marae. Organic trees and plants feast off the replenished soils and wave their arms in the sea breeze. The mamaku stretch their ferny wings toward the

313

horizon and send out baby black fronds to celebrate the birth of a new day. Kukupa feast off the bright scarlet puriri berries. White-throated, paua-coated tui sing of voyages to come, and waiata that go back as far as their ancestors who navigated by cowrie shell charts and stars to find their way across the sparkling Pacific Ocean to these peaceful shores of Aotearoa. Te Kotuku relaxes with pride.

Ta paki o Ruhia.

GLOSSARY

ae	yes
aki aki	red-billed seagull
ariki nui	chiefs
aroha	love
arohanui	much love
atea	space
babaco	fruit
bro	brother
cuzzy	cousin
e hoa	eh, friend
feijoa	green fruit of the guava family, originally from South America
gumboot tea	everyday black tea
haere mai	welcome
hangi	underground oven for steaming food
hapu	sub-tribe
hikoi	march
Hine Raukatauri	Maori Goddess of Music
hoki	fish
hongi	greeting by pressing forehead and nose together
huatau	beauty
ika	fish
iwi	tribe
ka pae	it's good
kahawai	fish
kahikatea	white pine
kai	food
kai moana	seafood

Kai-kea (Hawai'ian)	name of a goddess; literally, light sea
Kai-uli (Hawai'ian)	name of a goddess; literally, dark sea
kanuka	large manuka or tea-tree
karakia	prayer
karanga	call
kauri	tree
Kawakawa	name of a town and also of a plant
kereru	native wood pigeon
kete	woven flax basket
kia kaha	stay strong
kia ora	greeting; also affirmation – that's fine
kiokio	edible fern; tall cabbage tree
koata	joy
koauau	traditional bone flute
kohanga reo	early childhood school for total immersion in Maori language; literally, language nest
kokako	bird
korero	talk, speech
koru	fern
kotuku	white heron; Te Kotuku, name of marae
kowhai	tree with yellow, bell-shaped flowers
kuia	wise women of the tribe, older women
kukupa	North Island term for kereru or wood pigeon
kumara	a root similar to a yam
kumarahou	plant
kunekune	native pig
kura kaupapa	secondary Maori schools.
Laukiamanuikahiki (Hawai'ian)	Turtle Woman
lavalava	cloth worn around body
lei	flower garland
mahalo	thanks

mahoe	tree
mako	shark
mamaku	black tree fern
mana	pride
manuka	tea tree
Manukau	harbour and town near Auckland
marae	meeting place
matuku moana	sea heron
Maui	Maori God
maumau	fish
mohala (Hawai'ian)	gently unfolding creativity
mokopuna	grandchildren
morepork	owl
Muriranga-whenua	mythical woman who lent her jawbone to Maui
Nga Puhi	Northland tribe
nikau	palm tree
pa	site of village
pakauroharoha	feather fern
Pakeha	white person
Papatuanuku	Earth
paua	bright blue and green shellfish
Pele (Hawai'ian)	Goddess of the Volcano
pingao	grass growing in sand dunes
piwakawaka	fantail bird
pohutukawa	native tree that blossoms red in summer
Poneke	Wellington
ponga	tree fern
powhiri	greeting
puha, puwha	edible weed
pumoana	shell used for musical instrument
puriri	large native tree

putorino	flute
raupo	plant used for weaving
rengarenga	lily
rewana	Maori bread
rewarewa	native tree
rimu	native tree of the pine family
rongoa	medicine
rongoa hui, *rongoa Maori hui*	meeting over Maori medicinal plants
spoots	shellfish found in Orkney
tai hoa	wait up
Tainui waka	waka or canoe belonging to Tainui tribe
takapu	gannet
Tamaki Makaurau	Auckland
tamariki	children
Tane	Maori God
Tane Mahuta	God of the Kauri Forest
Tangaroa	God of the Sea
tangata whenua	people of the land, used for Maori in Aotearoa
tangi	funeral
taniwha	mythical beast; water monster
taonga	sacred gift, treasure
tapu	sacred
taro	edible root, like potato or kumara
tataramoa	brambles known as "bush lawyer"
tauiwi	foreigner
tautoko	support
Te Puna Kokiri	Ministry of Maori Affairs
te whenua	the land
tena koe	greeting
tena koutou katoa	greeting to all people (more than two)

tino rangatiratanga	Maori sovereignty
toetoe	long grass like pampas grass
toheroa	large prized shellfish
tohunga	medicine person or wise person of the tribe
torea	oyster-catcher bird
totara	large native tree.
tuatua	shellfish resembling pipi
tui	parson bird with white feathers at throat
urenika	Maori potatoes
utu	revenge
wahine	women
wahine toa	strong women
waiata	song
wairua	soul
waka	canoe
wakame	edible seaweed
weka	flightless bird that sounds like a kiwi at night
wenewene	gourd; also used of convulvulus
weta	large insect like a giant barbed cricket
whakapapa	ancestry
whanau	family
whare	hut or house
whare nui	large house or long house

Other books from Spinifex Press

Cowrie

Cathie Dunsford

Cath Dunsford's first novel (of a series I hope) is a gentle determined, insightful and womanful book.

– Keri Hulme

Cowrie is tightly woven, textured with colors, tastes and smells . . . and definitely worth the read, so go bug your local bookstore. – *Fat Girl Magazine*

ISBN 1-875559-28-2

The Journey Home: Te Haerenga Kainga

Cathie Dunsford

This is lesbian fantasy dripping with luscious erotic imagery. – *NZ Herald*

ISBN 1-875559-54-X

Manawa Toa: Heart Warrior

Cathie Dunsford

Cowrie boards a ship bound for Moruroa Atoll during the French nuclear tests. As international attention increases, the stakes rise sharply. She is joined by Sahara, a young peace activist from England, and Marie-Louise a French nuclear physicist. But can they be trusted? Can anyone be trusted?

The novel is suffused with Maori culture, women's culture, and a passion for the beauty of Aotearoa, the land and the sea.

> – Sue Pierce, *Lesbian Review of Books*

ISBN 1-875559-69-8

Song of the Selkies

Cathie Dunsford

A tale of seals and women and the Orkney Islands.

Cowrie and Sasha must turn detective to discover the truth behind Morrigan and the song of the Selkies.

ISBN 1-876756-09-8

Car Maintenance, Explosives and Love and other contemporary lesbian writings

Susan Hawthorne, Cathie Dunsford and Susan Sayer (eds)

An anthology which explores the mechanics of daily life, the explosiveness of relationships, and the geography of love.

ISBN 1-875559-62-0

All That False Instruction

Kerryn Higgs

Passionate, funny and heartbreaking, this remarkable novel traces a young woman's turbulent coming of age. Originally published under pseudonym of Elizabeth Riley.

An explosive mix of raw sanity and wicked humour – a bombshell of a book.   – Robert Dessaix

. . . a feminist classic.
          – Debra Adelaide, *Sydney Morning Herald*

ISBN 1-876756-11-X

Figments of a Murder
Gillian Hanscombe

Babes is about lust. Babes is about power. But what else is she up to? Set in London *Figments of a Murder* is passionate and satirical, probing images of self, sex, stardom and sisterhood.

A rich and robust satire of feminist politics combined with a murder mystery. May scandalise the sisters, but some wonderful writing.
 – Anne Coombes, *The Australian Year's Best Books*

ISBN 1-875559-43-4

Fedora Walks
Merrilee Moss

Fedora walks a tightrope, balancing the satirical and the silly, but never falls down in its loving subversion of gay Melbourne and the crime genre. – *The Age*

ISBN 1-876756-04-7

Still Murder

Finola Moorhead

Why has Senior Detective Constable Margot Gorman been assigned to watch over a raving woman in an asylum? And what is she raving about? Does it have anything to do with the dead body discovered in the park?

I delighted in Moorhead's intricate and lucid manoeuvres through the genre. *Still Murder* is an elaborate jigsaw of rival perspectives and rival documentations, and yet unfolds with deceptive ease.

– Helen Daniel, *Australian Book Review*

ISBN 1-876756-33-0

Darkness More Visible

Finola Moorhead

Wry, sardonic, cool and spirited, its themes of subversion and survival are exciting and marvellous . . . a contemporary classic.

– Debra Adelaide, *The Sydney Morning Herald*

ISBN 1-875559-60-4

The Bloodwood Clan
Beryl Fletcher

The Bloodwood Clan deftly mixes elements of thriller, social commentary and feminist psychology. I'll be disappointed if it's not included in next year's Montana shortlist. – Iain Sharp, *Sunday Star Times*

ISBN 1-875559-80-9

Love Upon the Chopping Board
Marou Izumo and Claire Maree

Autobiography, duobiography, love story, cross cultural reflections, lesbian history – *Love Upon the Chopping Board* is all these things and more.

ISBN 1-875559-82-5

If you would like to know more about Spinifex Press, write for a free catalogue or visit our home page.

SPINIFEX PRESS

PO Box 212,
North Melbourne,
Victoria 3051, Australia
http://www.spinifexpress.com.au